The *Kraken's* *Mirror*

❧

MAUREEN O. BETITA

✿

Decadent Publishing
www.decadentpublishing.com

The Kraken's Mirror
Copyright 2011 by Maureen O. Betita
ISBN: 978-1-936394-76-0
Cover design by Dara England and Razzle Dazzle Design

Published by Decadent Publishing Company
Look for us online at:
www.decadentpublishing.com

Printed in the United States of America

To René
Sail into adventure
w/ the Kraken!

Maureen O.
Betita

~DEDICATION~

To the crew of the RomanceWritersRevenge.com.
You know why!

℘

Prologue

Silvestri could feel Mick at his back, watching. The card game progressed with little attempt at fair play. He kept with it, biding his time as he lost again and again. The curse stepped in when he won his next hand and the next, no matter how they cheated. The dealer glared at him and raised objection to the last hand.

At the same moment, the fire in the hearth flared from a simple bit of warmth to raging hell. It roared into the room. The smell of burning hair rose to Silvestri's nostrils, then the charring flesh. Mick's hand gripped his shoulder to haul him away from the table, already crackling as the fire spread merrily amidst the screaming and shouting.

He climbed to his feet, showing no panic, leaving Mick to gather the coins. With a sigh, he looked around the small tavern, filling with smoke and death. A great crack sounded above him, and he turned to sweep Mick under his arm. A beam slammed into the space Mick vacated.

Fucking curse. No discrimination.

"That was more than good luck," Mick said, as they hurried away from the burning building. Nothing more was said until they were back on the water. Mick took the oars, stepping casually to the bow. The candle lantern at the stern cast a shadow, hiding his face. So like Mick to keep to the shadows when uncomfortable.

The stink still lingered in his nose. Burning flesh wasn't something a man forgot easily. The lingering impressions from the bar were hard to shake.

"All the idiot did was cheat," Mick softly murmured.

Silvestri shifted on the stern bench, trying to see some light shine on Mick's face. Was he smiling? Or grimacing? Impossible to tell. "I told you it was getting worse. I thought it was just my imagination. I hoped your impression would confirm that," he said.

Mick chuckled. "He wasn't even a good cheat. But why the whole tavern? Because of one card shark? Your curse overreacted. Been doing that for how long?" The oars made barely a ripple as they struck the water. Mick knew how to approach a ship without detection.

Silvestri stopped his rowing. "I started keeping track ten years ago, when some idiot tried to start a fight with me and ended up with a broken neck. When Glacious first set this curse on me, the fool would have suffered a simple fall in the muck of the streets. I'd have laughed!"

Mick appeared to be listening, letting the cutter drift. Hard to tell with the younger man. For the last eight years, Mick danced close enough to reap the benefits of Silvestri's notorious good luck curse, but skated away before it managed to steal his luck. Mick beat the curse with this waltz.

Too bad Silvestri couldn't dance away from it.

Damn. He'd been an idiot when he was fifteen. But that magical bitch was incredibly beautiful. At that age, he hadn't looked beyond that allure and into her heart. "You know the story, Mick. Most don't have a clue."

"Aye. You told me. How she magicked you off your ship and offered you all the good luck in the world. Set you back aboard, none the wiser. All you need do was come back at your birthday and visit with her. You still do that?" Mick's tone was low. Voices carried far on the water.

"Can't help it. She anchored a deep compulsion in me."

"I imagine it's a cold celebration. Are you going to sail with my father? He needs someone to keep an eye on him." Mick's voice lightened his worry. Silvestri snorted, noting he made no mention of the real reason Daniel wanted him along. With the bearer of the good luck curse on board, the ship was guaranteed a safe voyage.

"What's keeping *you* from going with him?" Silvestri raised an eyebrow.

"I met a new woman, and it's at that delicate place. Don't want to just disappear for months," Mick answered, looking away.

A woman? Well, about time. That's why he required Silvestri. Fine. He'd do it. Daniel was an idiot who needed a bit of a keeper. Must be one hell of a woman. Shaking his head, he banished the fleeting thought of never having a woman to call his. Glacious and this fucking curse would tear apart any woman he looked twice at.

They bumped up against the Immortal. Mick reached for the net at the side and paused. "What is that?"

Silvestri followed Mick's glance to see a small Kraken caught in the net. He reached down carefully. "Help me."

"Help you what? I ate already, before your luck saw the inn burn to the ground. What do you want with that?"

"You want some good luck of your own? Glacious hates the Kraken, all of them. She has a collection of frozen ones at her palace. I figure if she hates them, aiding them helps me." He cupped the little monster in his hand and lifted it gingerly.

Mick snorted, but bent and lifted the net, holding it steady as Silvestri carefully unwound the tangle of line that caught the beast. He flinched away as Silvestri carried the squirming bit of slime to the other side of the cutter and lowered it back into the water.

Silvestri straightened and held Mick from climbing to the nets. "Mick, promise me. If you find Kraken in trouble, you help them out. Tobias, the magic man in Barbados, told me to never eat them. They remember—you do them a good turn, they'll do you one. You want good luck? This costs less than making a black bargain with that ice-ridden bitch."

Mick stared at him, cleared his throat, and then answered. His words were measured, slow, and steady. "I give you my word. Savvy? I won't eat them, won't catch them…as long as I don't have to touch one, I'll be kindness itself to them." He turned and set a foot in the net, muttering to himself, "Now, if they'll not eat me, we'll be fine."

Silvestri knew he was being patronized, but he didn't care, as long as Mick gave his word.

Silvestri snickered, looked at his slimed hand, and wiped it on Mick's boot as it rose past him.

He secured the cutter to the haul line and paused before boarding. Glancing down into the water, he considered the balance he carried. Fifty-five years old. Forty years of reaping the benefits and drawbacks, of her curse. Release—all he wanted was release.

Revenge wouldn't be bad either.

Chapter One

She handed the old woman a five-dollar bill and reached into the dark, fabric-lined barrel. Her arm went in past her elbow and she fished around, trying to figure out what her fingers touched, what her money would surprise her with. One finger stroked an interesting texture and with an *oof*, she pushed her arm in another few inches to snag the prize.

"Ye find yerself somethin' sweet, lady?" The old woman grinned at her.

Emily held up her catch. A mirror? No, it held a photo.

"That be a nice piece a' swag! Who be next ta plunge inta the depths a 'Davy Jones' bag and see what the sea might release inta their grasp?" The woman hawked her wares to the busy crowd behind Emily.

Easing away from the pressing throng, Emily moved to an empty table near the food court to examine her find. It was round, like a hand mirror with a handle, but instead of glass, a photo of a man gazing into the distance filled the frame.

"A Hollywood pirate." Emily smiled. That seemed appropriate, here at the Northern California Pirate Festival. Older than most buccaneers, she found him interesting. Leaning against a railing with one leg raised, he reminded her of the *Captain Morgan* rum advertisement. His legs were encased in dark breeches and sported gleaming, black boots with the cuff rolled down at the knee. A good-sized sword fell at his side, and two pistols were tucked securely into a sash across his chest. Typical swashbuckler, though, definitely longer in the tooth than most movie rogues.

She stroked a finger over the weathered skin and creases at his temple. His hair flew free, fading blond to silver against a blue-tinged sky. There was no clear view of his eyes, but she bet they were sharp and full of experience. A shiver traveled up her spine at the thought. Probably extremely experienced.

She turned the frame over to examine the intricate pattern she'd felt there. It was fascinating, a bright white, like bleached bone. Carved or molded, she wasn't sure which, into a nest of tentacles. After a moment, she figured it out. A great ocean monster wrapped about the frame. On the front, suckers lined the circlet. The backside was bumpy, yet it seemed like a real sea creature, slick and smooth. Touching it reminded her of stroking a starfish at the aquarium.

Long tentacles wound down the handle, ending in a loop where a leather strip would easily attach. She turned the dainty once more to notice that at the top were two shiny, black eyes, with a knob between them she assumed was a forehead of sorts.

With a grin, she stroked the head. "You're a Kraken, aren't you? Caught a pirate in your maw, you clever thing!"

She dug into her leather sack for a slender strap. Usually, she carried a few—never knew when she might find something to use one on. She secured the frame to her belt, quite pleased at her little five-dollar trinket.

Wandering the fair, her hand continually dropped to fondle her pet Kraken, as she thought of it. It was so strange to be here by herself. Last year, Tom was here with her. Laughing, holding her hand, examining the wares, trying to figure out how things were made. Since he was an engineer, such things interested him. Her husband squatted and conversed with the tradesmen, asking questions and taking notes, always intending to undertake these projects. He'd planned to carve a chair, assemble a faux cannon, and stitch a leather pouch. Tom figured there were years ahead of him to do it all. Damn, she missed him.

This weekend she paid tribute to her late husband and how much they'd loved attending events such as this one. She wasn't sure she'd ever be up for another, now that he was gone. She'd raise a glass to his memory. He'd been gone eleven months. A stupid accident, a drunk driver, and her world turned into a lonely place. It took him, the dog and the cat. He'd made a trip to the kennel after a cruise vacation and been nearly home. She'd heard the crash, the sirens racing down the road....

The trucking company settled a small fortune on her, since the driver lived long enough to reveal the company knew he was a drunk when they put him on the road.

She'd received the settlement check a week ago. Not that it made up for anything.

A man nudged her. "You done looking at the books, ma'am?"

Ma'am. She was now a ma'am. Growing old was the pits.

"Yeah, sorry." She moved back, without buying anything. Brought a ton of money and found nothing she wanted to spend it on. Maybe she'd go look at the long, leather bodices.

The merry chatter of the crowd surrounded her as she wandered. The squawk of three parrots riding the perches fastened to a handcart made her smile. She'd seen that show— they were amazing birds. And the old salt who trained them did a great job at engaging the audience. Even now a trail of youngsters followed along, eyes on the bright plumage. She bet they thought to snag a feather.

That would be a tricky thing to accomplish, seeing those bills and the sharp eyes of the birds. As if they knew what was going on around them.

Maybe they did. She was a believing sort of woman, well aware there was more to the world than she would ever understand.

She dodged the Scottish pirate on stilts, his furred legs going all the way to the teeny, tiny shoes he balanced on. This time she kept her head down, not wanting to stir the stiltwalker's ire. She'd giggled at his legs the first time she'd passed him, and he'd stalked after her, asking her, "What was so funny?" A good bit of show, but she wasn't one for drawing that sort of attention to herself. He did an excellent job, staying in fierce character on his ridiculous stilts, wearing his kilt and all.

When she reached the booth she sought, none of the fancy bodices appealed to her. Maybe she was getting too old to imagine herself wearing copious amounts of leather? She didn't even try one of them on. It was hard to get one of the young salesclerks to meet her eyes, let alone answer questions about size. She wasn't young, tall or slender—hence she didn't count. The festival was proving a depressing situation. True, the young and perfectly thin salesclerks always ignored her, but today it compounded her blues.

She promised herself to stay for the concert, due to start in several hours. Shifting her small, black backpack to one shoulder, she wandered over to the bone pin stand. At least no one thought it odd if she covered her bag with witty sayings. Oh, she liked this one. *Don't Worry, It's Not My Blood.*

Good one.

What the hell—she liked her plain leather bodice, and it went well with the dark blue, checked shirt, black breeches and *Teva* sandals. At fifty-three years of age, she was invisible to most of the young people working the booths. Someone ought to clue them in on whose wallets were fat and whose were thin.

Sigh.

It was time to eat and drink. She reached down to touch her new frame and held it up to once more admire the pirate's picture. There was something compelling about....

"Fuck!"

A mother with two kids in tow glared at her for cursing.

She ignored the outrage. The photo was gone! She'd been right initially; a mirror reflected her face back at her. She saw no signs of glue. She'd assumed it was secured, but it wasn't. She scanned the ground at her feet. Her heart beating with disappointment, she retraced her steps from the last few hours, scanning the ground as she went, but finding nothing.

By the time she gave up, she was thoroughly hungry. And

angry. The photo was gone. She knew it was stupid to be disappointed about losing a picture. Now she owned a lovely mirror. Still, a sense of loss ate at her. She needed chocolate. And liquor. Maybe something salty and greasy.

She bought a passable rum punch—not great, but acceptable. Years spent as a bartender developed her drink palate to a particular degree. She purchased a plate that included a corndog and a handful of fries. Ice cream would be next...and maybe another punch.

Sitting at a table, she ate, one eye on the mirror set in front of her. It upset her to lose the image. Losing it shouldn't bother her so much. It was just a picture. A nice souvenir should be enough.

This trip wasn't working out at all as she'd hoped. Coming to the pirate fair alone probably hadn't been a good idea. But it was the first stop on the way to her new life. House sold, possessions stored, new mini RV parked in the overnight lot, waiting for her next adventure. Once the event was over, she'd head for the open road.

She pulled out her cell phone to check the time and looked at the posted schedule for the concert stage. Two more hours, and she'd already seen everything that interested her: the merchants, the small shows, the food booths. But she wanted to hear the Sea Dogs. She and Tom once joined in a small pirate cruise out of Sausalito, and the same group entertained them for several hours. It was a good memory. Resigned to amusing herself, since her appetite for shopping never materialized, she pulled out her new book.

The romance novel she'd begun the night before simply didn't hold her attention—another young, thin virgin trying to escape her fate. She was tired of the same plot and wanted something different. Closing the book, she left the table and stood in line for another snack.

She strolled over to the harbor walk and settled down behind a wall of hay bales to enjoy her ice cream and punch, finding some protection from the breeze blowing off the water. San Francisco wasn't the tropics, no matter how the festival liked to portray itself.

The ice cream tasted good, a rich mix of chocolate and peanut butter. The butterfat coated her tongue. Next, she pulled out a small bottle of rum she'd smuggled into the fair and spiced up the beverage. She crossed her legs, dug into her backpack, found a small booklet she'd picked up on women pirates and settled down to read, sipping her improved drink.

Falling asleep wasn't part of the plan. Between the rum and the long drive to San Francisco the day before, exhaustion overcame her. The few drops left from her cup spilled onto her new mirror, still secured to her belt. She'd clean it up later, she sleepily thought. Was that a bit of fog creeping in? Pulling her breeches down to cover her lower legs, she let the drowsiness win.

She crossed over between one breath and the next.

❧

One last thrust brought him some satisfaction. He collapsed, gasping, on the soft, white breasts of the working girl.

"You feeling better, Captain?" She giggled.

He hated women who stifled their laughter and seemed to consider a high-pitched titter an appropriate response. He patted her shoulder, deciding not to attempt conversation with her. She'd served her purpose. Her services took the edge off his hunger, though not by much. He rolled off her and tossed her a small bag of coins, dismissing her. His eyes drooped and sleep beckoned.

But the moment his eyes closed, the stranger's visage glowed on his eyelids. There she was again, still lodged in his brain. The same place she'd been for the last eight hours—ever since he woke up that morning. Her face—eyes bright, though weary—hinting at some loss. Nice shade of brown, like her short hair. Shorter than he'd ever seen most women wear their hair. Hell, most men for that! A wild mix of brown and grays. She wouldn't giggle.

He liked her lips. Hell, he loved them. The thought of that soft mouth against his set him on fire. A slight tilt at the left side betrayed some humor. He wondered what she sounded like when she laughed.

When he opened his eyes, his cock swelled once more. It was no use. Sleep wasn't on his agenda, and the whore was gone, happy with her payment. He slid a hand down and stroked his prick. Damn, who was she, and how the hell was he going to get her out of his head?

Chapter Two

Emily started when someone ran into her leg. The sound of a dropped bottle brought out the scold in her. Great, some drunk kicking her...awake. She'd fallen asleep?

"What?" A man's shadow loomed above her.

"Do you mind?" Emily rolled her eyes and rubbed at her calf.

He squatted, sweeping a large hat aside to study her. She met his eyes and glanced at the container rolling away from her thigh. She reached for it. "Yours, I assume?"

"Yes, thank you." He took it from her, shook it, and tossed it aside. "Empty, anyway."

"Don't leave it, you twit! Haven't you ever heard of recycling?" She struggled to her feet, taking his offered hand. He was a gentleman, at least, and took her weight without complaint. She could appreciate that, even if he didn't seem to care about the environment. She stalked to where the bottle now rested against a wooden wall. Picking it up, she looked around for a trashcan, preferably one that separated recyclable materials.

He stood next to her. "Pardon me, Lady. What are you looking for?"

"A trashcan," she replied. Gazing about, she whistled. "They did a nice job over here. I didn't notice when I sat to…uh…relax. What time is it? I didn't miss the band, did I?"

"Your pardon, the band? What band?"

"The musicians! For the stage? Damn, I don't believe I fell asleep. Shit." She shook her head, tucked the empty bottle under her arm, and bent to collect her bag.

"Musicians? You're looking for musicians! I can help you with that. Here, let me have the bottle, since it's valuable to you. I'll take it back to Sam—he can reuse it if he wants." He held out his arm. "Allow me to escort you. The best music is found at the Barmy Cock. I am Captain Michael March, at your service. I do hope you are uninjured."

"Yeah, I'm fine." She shivered. "I should have known it would get chilly once the sun set."

"Please!" He gallantly slid out of a soft captain's coat and placed it over her shoulders. She was dealing with a real player who took the role of gallant seriously. With a grin, Emily kept in character. "Call me Lady Pawes, Captain March."

"Oh, Michael, please. Or even Mick. Lady Pawes? You like to take your time?" He smiled at her. They were close to the same height. He had her beat, but not by much. The faint light gave the impression of black hair, long and held back in a ponytail. A short beard and stylish mustache completed his pirate persona. He set his hat back atop his head before offering her his arm.

"Oh, no, not that sort of pause." She halted abruptly when they turned onto a street. A real street—not the grassy lanes she'd traveled earlier that day. "They transform the fair for the evening?"

He tilted his head at her with the question. "I'm not certain what you're asking."

She wasn't supposed to notice changes to the grounds? She sighed, probably not. If she was going to participate, she needed to just accept that these pirates took their roles quite seriously. He led her to a lit doorway—a riotous sound spilled out to greet them.

"But here we are! This is the Barmy Cock. The crew is meeting me here later, but please be my guest until they join us." He led her through a ragged set of doors into an actual room, not a temporary fabric booth. They brought their own tavern! What a grand bit of theatrics. A long bar took up one side, and Emily was tickled to see the number of bottles and brands on display. Her type of tavern!

Three hours later, she found herself standing behind that lovely length of wood, next to a giant of a man. Sammy worked serving drinks, but once she'd advised him on how to mix what she liked to call a rum sunset—since it ran counter to a tequila sunrise—he invited her to join him.

Mick's crew joined the growing crowd. Emily felt right at home as Sam handed her the bottles she couldn't reach, and she mixed, blended, laughed and totally reveled in playing pirate bartender. Somehow, the reality of Mick's officers consisting of only women didn't surprise her. She didn't blink to discover that he was *a* captain, but not *the* captain of this particular band of sailors. He was the type to let a woman make assumptions regarding his importance.

Mick's motley group gathered at one side of the bar, attempting to convince her to drink with them. When the band started playing, Sam lifted her over the bar and insisted she join the rest in enjoying the music. "None are gonna want anything fancy while there's dancing. Go, enjoy the music!"

But dancing was thirsty work, and by the time the band played their closing number, Emily was thoroughly soused. She bent down to pick up her pack and fell. Sliding over to rest her head on the legs of a barstool, she decided to sleep. Screw it—she'd stay until morning.

She vaguely heard the argument going on above her. *Sweet that they were concerned about her.* The trip out to their ship telescoped to nothing more than being helped to a hammock.

Chapter Three

*A*fter waking from a troubled sleep the next morning, he walked deep into town. The unknown woman haunted his night. His time on the island was limited by his curse, but he enjoyed walking on solid ground, no matter the duration. The residents greeted him cordially enough, but he knew that warmth would turn to chill if he overstayed his welcome. By noon, thirst drove him into a tavern he seldom visited. The Barmy Cock was too bright and cheerful for him normally, though he always made sure a bottle of rum from an exotic port arrived for their shelves after every voyage. A sort of toll, since Sam ran the bartender's union.

The residents, the tavern keepers, the whores and shopkeepers all knew him. He was a famous man. "Hey, Captain Alan, come try the new drink!" Sam beckoned him to the bar and held out a tall glass filled with a dark-orange tinted fluid.

He scowled at it before he took it and held it up to the light. "Seems a bit…colorful."

"Aye, but she knew how to use the rum you sent last visit. She called it a rum sunset, and it's tasty." Sam beamed at him.

With a grimace, the captain took a sip. Another. He tilted his head at it, trying to figure out what he tasted.

"Good, ain't it?" Sam snickered. "A bunch of the boys tried

fancy drinks the entire evening."

"You hire a new bartender?" He held out the glass. "Another."

"No, she came in with Mick and got a little bossy. I thought to quiet her up, put her behind the bar...."

"Put Sam to shame, she did." Sally, Sam's wife, slid up next to him. "Short thing, but feisty. Held her own with them."

"Did Captain Jezebel see her with Mick? If she did, that's the last of the wench. The woman does not tolerate doxies. Pity—this is good."

"He introduced her to the whole gang. Tink took a real liking to her. When Mick's captain gave her the eye, the new woman literally laughed at the idea of dallying with Mick. Jezebel let her be, once that were clear." Sam took the empty away and brought out a plain bottle with a shot glass.

He smiled to himself. Yes, they knew him well. "I didn't see the Cursed Quill this morning. They leave last night?"

"You know Jezzie. She's not going to take a chance on Mick doing something stupid and risk your curse striking. She likely saw the Immortal and left early. I think they took Pawes with them," Sally said.

"New crew member? Pawes?"

"That was the name she claimed. I think she was shanghaied. They carried her out of here, clean passed out." Sam shook his head. "Pity, I would have hired her. I made sure she got her share of the tips, though."

"You're an honorable man. Jezebel wouldn't steal anyone. Now, I...I would chain her to the bar if she walked into a place I owned. But I have a reputation to uphold." He filled the shot glass and downed it in one gulp.

"She weren't shanghaied. She had nowhere to stay. Sure, they'll see her somewhere safe." Sally smacked her husband's arm. "I may ask the union to keep an eye out for her, and make sure if word comes of her needing a job, we get first chance at hiring her."

"No place to stay? She new?" He glanced around the bar. "What does this girl look like?" he asked almost absently, making conversation. A girl who mixed concoctions like that might be interesting to meet.

"She weren't a girl. A woman. Short, nicely rounded. Really short hair, sorta spiky...interesting face." Sam polished up the bar, but the captain froze, his shot glass poised at his lips.

"A mature woman?"

"I'd call her that," Sally replied. "I liked her hair. It would certainly be easy to tend to. Most practical. What do you think? Would this work on me?" She held out a large napkin. "I did this sketch from memory."

He carefully set the shot glass down, untouched, and took the napkin. He pretended to study the haircut as if sizing Sally up for one like it. But, he was staring at a drawing of the woman who'd been haunting his thoughts. She'd been here the night before, while he'd been wasting time on some sweet-faced whore.

He set the napkin down as if it burned him. "You ought to do one of yourself with the hairstyle, Sally. I can't see it from this."

"You're right!" She grinned at him and set about badgering Sam for another of their precious linen napkins to draw on.

Neither noticed him carefully fold the other drawing and tuck it into his coat. He left a few minutes later. He wondered where they had sailed to...and what it would take to find them.

ക

Emily woke up with her head pounding. "Fuck...."

"Well, that is what it sounded like. Good dreams?" A familiar sounding voice interrupted her moaning. Perhaps from the night before? Some blonde beanpole with a totally inappropriate name.

"What?" She raised her heavy head and eyed the top of a blonde head to her right. When she twisted, the hammock swayed, making her belly swirl unhappily. Tink sat on the floor, going through the contents of her pack. Yes, Tink, that was her name. "Hey! Oh, shit!" Emily put a hand over her mouth.

"Yeah, don't throw up on me. Behind you, on that stool,

there's a hangover remedy. Shut up and drink it. Trust me, it will help."

Slowly, Emily turned her head the other way to see the stool. And a mug of something still steaming sat upon it. Her hand trembled as she reached for the remedy. She knew from past experience that moving slowly was the best way to avoid nausea. She tried to sit up and floundered, but a steady hand from Tink gripped the netting of the hammock and held it still insuring the drink didn't spill.

She'd slept in a hammock?

Inhaling gently, Emily closed her eyes. "It smells good."

"It is good, and it will do the trick. Mama Lu's cures work. Drink it, Pawes."

Pawes? Oh, yeah. She'd given her bartender name. Tom used to call her Crewperson Pawes when they played at pirate, a reference to the ring of paw prints on her right bicep applied when she was eighteen, in memory of Magic, her dog. When she met Tom Pawes, it fit twice—seemed like fate.

She never yet found a hangover cure worth much, but she'd try anything once. It was years since she'd drunk enough to earn one. Halfway through the remedy, she realized the headache was fading. When she drained the last drops, her stomach settled. She set the empty mug back down on the stool. "I'm impressed—and get out of my stuff."

"Trying to find some clue to where you live." She held up a driver's license. "Emily, or Pawes if you like, you're a long way from home. You found a portal, didn't you?"

"A what?" Emily slowly maneuvered herself to one side of the hammock and sat up.

Tink tossed the card back in the pack and handed the bag to Emily. "How else did you get to Tortuga?"

"Tortuga? Listen, I went to the pirate festival yesterday. Today is…where am I?" Emily looked around the low-ceilinged room. "And why is this room moving?"

"Well, because we're at sea. I didn't intend to steal you away. Once we were back on the ship last night, I had command—Jezz and Mick being busy in their cabin. She sure liked your rum sunsets. Put her in a real sweet mood. I spied

Silvestri's ship and knew the best course was to get out before Mick fucked up."

Emily stared at the woman who was still sitting cross-legged on the floor. Slender to the point of too thin and very tall, from what she recalled of the night before. With a talent for cursing. Why they called her Tink was beyond comprehension.

Turning her head, Emily gazed at a small square of bright light. She slid off the hammock and slowly approached it. What it framed made her heart stutter. The sea, not the murky, deep blue of the Pacific, but the clear, turquoise blue of the Caribbean. She'd been there and recognized the hue. She reached out a hand, hoping to find a window or a screen, but instead she felt the spray of the sea on her fingertips.

She fell back on her butt, accepting that she was on a ship. Moaning, she turned to Tink. "What the fuck! What sort of nasty trick is this? How the hell did you get me here? And why? I'm not worth that much!"

"Yeah, but you make some mean drinks." Tink uncoiled from the floor—no, the deck. She stooped to avoid the rafters at her head, gazing over at Emily. "Listen, you found a portal. I don't know where or how…I'd guess at this festival you mentioned. Don't get your panties in a knot about it. Portals are actually fairly common back in Tortuga. We'll find it for you and get you back, if that is what you really want to do. Most people who find a portal arrive where they actually have reason to be."

"I have reason to be in San Francisco today!" Emily refused to believe what this strange woman said.

"Well, instead you're aboard the Cursed Quill, sailing the Caribbean, and it's 1697. But be cool—it's not like you think. Come, let me show you the head."

By the time her tour of the Cursed Quill was done, Emily was convinced she'd lost it. They possessed a shower and a modern kitchen, along with a clever flush toilet that Tink said composted. A good-looking sailor walked by her with an *iPod* strapped to his arm. Yet, there was no doubt they were in the Caribbean, and to all outward appearances, the ship was a period sloop.

Tom also dreamed of sailing and spent long hours building models. She knew ships from years of his talking about them. No real pirate ship would have this many modern conveniences, unless it were one of those tourist excursion ships. That had to be it.

But after crawling over the lower decks and finding no engine of any sort, she gave up. Either she was indeed insane, or a group of pirate enthusiasts took the game too far, and she was the captive of a group of completely mad re-enactors. She started searching for hidden cameras. Was it a reality show? *Shanghaied by Pirates?*

Three days later, she stopped looking for any other explanation. She dined with the women she'd met at the festival bar, meals she knew no period ship would serve. Mick tried to describe the situation to her and only confused her further.

It was Captain Jezebel who finally explained it in a fashion she almost believed.

"The best I can figure…Tortuga, this Tortuga, fell through a sort of time tunnel. It's the center of this universe. And everything that is lost or thrown away finds its way here. Like the island of lost toys in the Christmas movie…?"

Emily nodded. "Okay. People and *iPods* and refrigerators?"

Jezebel shrugged. "Inventions that got lost or never happened. Hey, I'm not a scientist. I suffered misery in my own world, then fell here thirty years ago and made myself at home. Most of the crew can tell a similar story."

"Not me, I wasn't…too miserable." Emily sighed. "Hell."

"Yeah, hell. Think about it. We'll get you back to Tortuga, and you can look for the portal you fell through and decide to stay or go back. You want to stay? We'll find work for you. We make out pretty good, raiding the occasional Spanish ship. The Spanish here carry a lot of booty and very few weapons. The French merchants beg to be robbed. I swear they line up for it—easy pickings." Jezebel held out the bottle they'd been sharing. "Or stay on Tortuga and work as a bartender. You're good at that. But there's real benefit to being part of this crew, as you'll find out."

The captain looked away, and Emily figured there were still secrets not being shared. Fine, she'd wait. Or not. When she got home, she'd have a wild story to tell, about the hallucination she suffered at the pirate festival.

Her ass hurt and she shifted, looking for a more comfortable position before replying. "I still think I'm totally bonkers, but when I was younger, I read some fantasy where things like this happened. So, I'm going to wait and see. If I'm crazy, I'll embrace it and enjoy the pleasant aspects." She claimed the bottle and took a swig. "I'm sure I'll meet the unpleasant, eventually."

Jezebel laughed and returned to the wheelhouse, leaving her to sit on the steps and watch the beautiful men as they hauled lines, tightened knots and polished bits of brass to a high shine.

Tink sauntered over and sat next to her. "Still convinced you're insane?"

"Partly," Emily replied.

"Partly? You're in good company!" Tink snickered. "We're not going straight into Tortuga. Silvestri should be gone, but until we're certain he's out for the duration, we'll be careful."

"This Captain Silvestri? Mick scowls and snarls when I ask...."

"Mick ain't reasonable about him. You see, Silvestri's cursed, and it isn't safe to fixate on him. Mick danced around that curse for nearly ten years, staying close enough to benefit from it. The curse finally turned on him and Mick got away with his life, but it were close. Mama Lu warned Jezzie that it's still waiting to land on Mick, but he thinks differently. He wants the Immortal."

"Okay, what curse? And Immortal what?" Emily figured another pirate story wouldn't be amiss. She didn't believe much of what she heard, anyway. Especially the stories about Tortuga. The place must be huge to include everything the crew hinted at. A swamp? A forest full of wolves? *A castle on a hill?*

"The Immortal is a ship. And years ago, it belonged to Mick's father. He sailed off one day, and when the ship returned, Silvestri captained it. At first, Mick accepted that his father had returned to England, but then he changed his mind. He won't say why. Now, the curse—Silvestri is cursed with good luck."

"Uh huh." Emily turned to look at the quartermaster, Tink's job on board the ship. It seemed to be something like a union leader, far as she could tell. "And how is good luck a curse?"

"It's a curse if it comes at the cost of every bit of good luck belonging to those around you. Think about it! He isn't welcome to stay anywhere for long. Can't get close to anyone. Mick managed by dancing close, then darting away—like some insane game of tag. Silvestri knew what Mick was doing and didn't discourage it. Probably the closest thing the man knew to a friend in decades!" Tink polished her dagger, using a scrap of fabric looped around her belt.

Emily considered the information. "He knows what his good luck costs others?"

"Oh, he knows." Tink admired the shine of the blade. "It's not a bad curse, for a pirate, I mean. Most of our good luck comes at another's bad. But his knows no boundaries—friend or foe pays. His crew seems to be immune, but they are a coldhearted bunch and not much company for the captain."

Her heart sank. "Oh, what a misery."

"He doesn't look wretched, so don't go feeling all sorry for him! The only one who seems close to him is Mama Lu. The curse is probably too frightened of her to attempt taking payment."

"Mama Lu is the potion woman? Why would a curse find her frightening?" Emily lifted the bottle at her side and took another swallow. She was drinking too much, but it numbed her confusion—and fear.

"Oh, you'll see when you meet her," Tink said mysteriously, then shot to her feet, yelled something at one of the men in the sails and took off, climbing easily to the first cross brace.

Emily envied Tink—her own knots weren't tight enough to be trusted anywhere on the ship. Helping out by washing dishes each night was not a terribly glamorous way to spend the rest of her life—if she didn't find a portal home.

She pulled her leather pack close and peered into it. She kept checking her cell phone, some perverse part of her still thinking it might work. Rolling her eyes, she tossed the device back into the bag. Damn, the stickiness of sweat and salt spray coated her body, although she took a clean cloth and wiped herself down every day. They boasted a shower, but were stingy with it. She couldn't blame them. The sponge bathing helped, but her scalp was driving her crazy. Janey, the bosun, promised her a showering slot if she signed on with them.

Tink said she ought to rent some time in the bathhouse back in Tortuga. "The cash Sam gave you for helping out at the bar is a fair cut. If you need to, you can get new clothes, a bath, and a few things to make your cabin more comfy. If you stay, of course." The woman laughed at her.

They all appeared to find hilarity in her reactions. But it wasn't mean spirited. Emily supposed they'd heard attempts to rationalize what was going on many times, from others who fell into this freaking looking glass world...looking glass?

She reached into her bag and withdrew the mirror. Examining it carefully, she wondered if it were somehow responsible for her being here. Not that she fit through this glass. It was too small, and she was too big, and there was no bottle to drink from. Yup, no *drink this* potion that she remembered.

"Fuck, I'm going bonkers." She pulled out her scarf and wrapped the mirror.

"Hey, that's a nice bit of swag." Mick bent over to examine her find. "May I?"

She handed it to him. "Got it at the fair I was visiting."

He held it up and stroked the tentacles that formed the handle while admiring himself in the glass. He turned it around. "I like this. Looks like him!"

"Uh...like who?"

"Well, the Kraken! The elder Kraken, of course. They only turn this fine white as they age. The youngsters are still green and a bit slimy...." His voice trailed off at her expression. He tilted his head at her. "Don't believe me, do you?"

"Okay, I figured it was a Kraken. I've heard of the Kraken...but to hear him...her...it referred to so causally is a bit startling."

Mick handed her mirror back, stepped to the railing and leaned on it, looking out at the water. "Well, you're right. I'm not sure if the Kraken is a he. Since there are young, seems likely it's a she."

"Maybe it's a hermaphrodite." Emily snickered at Mick's startled expression. She noticed it was possible to tell who stepped through a portal and who was born here by how they reacted to certain words. "Or maybe the younger is a clone. Some technology to clone may have fallen here." She chuckled when Mick tried to look like he understood her. She pushed to her feet. "Never mind, Mick, I'm being silly. You ever meet this Kraken? Is it fierce and hungry all the time, or is it a friendly beast?"

"Depends on whether it had eaten recently. I met a youngster, after it consumed a full meal of sperm whale and it was kind enough to haul my cutter to a nearby island for me. The trick is never assume one way or the other. I was told if you do good to them, they'll return the favor. That young one could have made me desert, but took me to safety instead, so perhaps that is true." He eyed her speculatively and set a hand near hers on the rail. He wasn't flirting, she knew that. He was a touchy-feely sort of man.

"You would be welcome to stay."

"Yeah, I know. Everyone says so. I have to see if I can get back, Mick. I'm not done with my life there." She pulled her hand away, spun her wedding ring on her finger and his eyes darted to the movement. Emily stopped immediately. Mick was likeable, but her past heartache wasn't his business.

He wisely said nothing. She moved up next to him at the rail to gaze out at the sea and thought about Krakens.

Chapter Four

Tink led her over the crest to look down on Tortuga. "Good, I don't see the Immortal. I'll send Chester down to let Jezzie know she can bring the ship in. It will take till the late afternoon for her to anchor. It's a steep path to town, but at least it's downhill. Let's go."

Emily put a hand on her side, gasping for breath. She glared at the tall pirate.

"A bath?" Tink spread her arms wide, posing like she was presenting the prize on *Wheel of Fortune*, and Emily nodded. She was weary, but the thought of a soak in a tub of hot water gave her energy.

It took an hour to hike down to the city. And it was a city, no small village or settlement. Her eyes scanned where it wound around the steep hillsides, spreading in multiple directions away from the bay. Mist clung here and there, which confused her. Mist? In the tropics? But she didn't nag Tink about it. For all she knew, the haze was perfectly normal. And if it wasn't the case for her reality, was it natural for *this* reality?

Her head hurt.

But the bath made the walk worthwhile. Tink left her at the bathhouse, saying she'd be back in an hour or two and not to wander far if she finished early. Emily sank into the suds and swore she'd never get out. Every ache from the last few days faded away. She washed her hair three times, scrubbed her feet till they tingled, and lounged until the water grew cold.

Finally, she crawled out of the tub, not terribly eager to change back into her filthy clothes. One of the women noticed her reluctance and offered a skirt for a price. Emily took it, packing the filthy pair of breeches into a ball and using a sash to tie the ball to her belt.

"You have a shirt, maybe?"

"Sorry, luvy. But you can get one down the street. The Silk Emporium is bound to have something you'll like."

She probably overpaid for the skirt, but it was worth it. She couldn't figure out the coins Sam gave her, not for lack of trying. Mick tried to teach her the system, but once he'd shown her a huge coin that he said was worth the least amount of trade value than another of a different color, that he said was worth a lot more…she gave up. Math was not her strong point. Nor was memorization.

She just trusted no one would cheat her too badly. Hell, it was all play money, anyway, right?

She wandered down the road, looking for the Emporium. Tortuga during the day was pretty quiet. She didn't recognize anything. And this was not the site of the pirate festival. In fact, nothing struck her as familiar.

Once she'd found a new shirt in a lovely old-rose colored silk that caressed her breasts, even when snuggled up tight by her bustier, she kept searching.

She walked for hours, looking for either the Barmy Cock or the stack of hay bales she'd fallen asleep against. As the afternoon approached, she found herself missing Tink.

"Well, crap. I lost her. Didn't think I'd gone far. And now…." She peered up and down the street, muttering, "I've gotten myself lost."

She didn't like the energy of this area of town. She turned to see three men eyeing her, blocking the road. With a start, she spun about, searching to the left and right for a way to freedom. A narrow path was steeply cut to one side, but it seemed like a good place to lose them. She dashed, hearing the men behind her.

They shouted at her, promising not to hurt her.

Emily didn't believe them. She'd seen that expression once, on the face of a man who robbed the bar she'd worked. Her body wasn't in good shape, but it was downhill, and adrenaline worked to see her get far enough away that she was able to turn and hide in a small, green area. The three bullies tore past and on down the slope.

Still afraid, she sagged against the tree she'd found and tried to compose herself. Her breathing slowed and quiet sobs started. Drawing her knees to her chest, she bowed her head and cried for several minutes.

"What happened, girl?"

She started, ready to dash away when she saw an old woman standing in front of her.

"Oh. I was…chased. Three men were after me. I'm sorry. Am I trespassing?" Emily struggled to her feet.

"Not at all, this is my herb garden, but running from those brutes is reason enough to find shelter here. You come with me, and I'll give you some tea. It might calm you down. They might come back this way…." She turned and headed through a short gate, concealed by the greenery.

The idea of them coming back was enough to make her hurry after the old woman. The elder was extremely tall, with deep nut-brown skin, and long, gray hair braided down to her knees. This Caribbean must like tall women. Emily followed, eyeing the beads, ribbons and dangles in that braid. Must be hard to sleep on.

"You can call me Louisa, girl. And you?"

Sharp eyes met hers at the door, curious.

"They call me Emily Pawes," she replied. "Miss Louisa. Or…Mrs…uh, ma'am."

"Just Louisa. Now, you sit here." She pointed to a chair cleverly carved from a single log to include some back support. It was surprisingly comfortable. She sat while the old woman brewed tea, using what appeared to be some sort of propane tank and burner.

"Now, you don't appear settled, Emily. You fresh ta our Tortuga?" Louisa set the teapot down on the table, took a seat, and poured.

"I guess. Does everyone know about these portals and people coming from other times?" Emily asked.

"It be part of who we are, and what Tortuga is. We be an adaptable population. Sometimes people come through that don't belong here, and they figure it out fast and move back. You one a' those?"

"I don't know. I guess I'm trying to figure that out." Emily sighed and looked away. Those deep, green eyes nailed her like laser beams.

"Tell me where you been? How long you been here?"

She found it easy to talk to Louisa. The old woman chuckled at hearing about the bar and waking up on the Quill.

"That be a good ship to stumble aboard. Most be congenial here and tend ta be careful of strangers. Since it be hard to tell the wolves and sheep apart."

"The three men that chased me saw me as a sheep." Emily shivered. "I know that look."

"Ya gots to learn how to put on the wolf ta not be taken advantage of. So, is Michael still sailing with the Quill?" She maneuvered out of her chair, and Emily jumped to her feet to help out.

When Louisa took her and shoved her toward a mirror, Emily went, staring at her reflection with that old woman peering over her head.

"Now, you see how startled you look? You need to school yourself better and not be such an open book. Those wide eyes, looking around at everything, avoiding mine. You be sending out sheep signals. As bad as standing in the street and saying, 'bahhhh'." She smiled crookedly, removing some of the sting.

Emily narrowed her eyes and lifted one corner of her lips in a partial smile to show she understood.

"Ah! Now that ain't bad! You don't want ta necessarily lock eyes with those you meet, but focus above their knees. Don't slump; keep your shoulders back. Get a weapon and learn how to use it. Knife, pistol, staff—it doesn't matter as long as it's something you can find confidence in. That Tink knows knives. Michael knows pistols."

"Any weapons ever cross those portals?" She'd been wondering about that.

"Some sharp blades, but nothing fancier. I sometimes think there is a sort of protection. I hear of some nasty ways to kill from those who travel the portals. Pistols that can fire over and over again, and invisible blades. Nothing we want over here." Louisa ruffled her hair. "I like how short you keep this. Much easier ta care for then what I got."

Emily noticed that most women here wore long hair. She supposed it was the style of the day, but it appeared really impractical to her. "Thank you." She found it impossible to meet Louisa's gaze. Even as a reflection. "Why can't I find the portal I came through?" It didn't hurt to ask.

"I don't know, girl. Perhaps you don't want to. What are you searching for?"

"A portal."

"And what does your portal look like?"

"I don't know. You mean, they aren't all the same? Hell." Emily leaned back to stare at the ceiling.

Louisa laughed and returned to her chair. "No, girl. You don't know what yours looks like. You have a problem."

"Maybe I'm not supposed to go back." Emily sat again and closed her eyes. "I'm terribly confused."

Louisa took her hand and stroked the fingers. She turned it and gazed at the lines on the palm. "Confusion gonna be your friend for a while. But in the end, I think all that worry gonna be worth it."

Emily focused on the woman and tried to jerk her hand away, but Louisa held it firmly.

"Don't hurt ya to listen. Confusion is not a bad thing—it creates opportunity. And you be ripe for fresh chances. Take them, Emily." Louisa's stare bored into her. Her skin flushed hot, then cold, before the room blurred.

When Emily woke up, she was leaning against the tree in the green area and the daylight was quickly fading. Damn. Her pack sat at her side. Reaching in, she felt around; seemed everything was there. "Did I fall asleep, have a nice dream?"

Once on her feet, she noticed the note, pinned at eye level

on the tree trunk.

Go downhill, make a right at the big oak.

"Well, fuck it. I hope Tink is at the bottom of that hill." She stretched as she considered the advice Louisa gave her, about standing straight, going eye to eye, and maybe learning some weapon skills. She'd do what she needed to do. She didn't like being confused, but at least, it left room for hope. If Louisa was right, a chance for change was at hand. Couldn't get much more changed than this, she thought.

After Tom died, hope disappeared, and life turned into waiting for death, which didn't make for bright days.

Walking out of the park area, she quickly moved down the path. She hoped the oak would be easy to recognize…"Wow!"

The massive tree loomed in front of her was the biggest oak she'd ever seen. Even in the fading light, it was easy to recognize. Turning to the right, she observed the light of the setting sun glowing above the water. She'd made it back to the harbor.

But reaching Tink or the ship anchored out in the harbor was problematic. She saw no service available to take her out, and a young lad told her it was suppertime. "No one be available for an hour or more."

"Great. Well, do you know where the Barmy Cock is?" she asked.

"Up Broad Street."

"Thanks!" She turned and looked. Five streets branched out and headed up slope. "Uh, which one…?" But the boy was gone.

"Be logical, Emily. That is an exceptionally broad street. I'll stay straight, and if I don't find it, I'll turn around and come back." Talking to herself gave some small bit of courage.

Shoulders back and standing straight, she started up the hill. The dark fell a lot faster than she'd anticipated, and typically, she brought no shawl or coat. Tink suggested she look for one, but after the bath, the last thing she'd wanted was another layer of clothing. She'd been comfortable and didn't want to sweat.

Dumb.

She shivered and kept walking, hoping the exercise would warm her. Her head swept from side to side. People started spilling out into the streets, and she considered asking for directions again, rejecting the idea as it might be seen as a sign of weakness. She'd walk five more minutes, then turn back around.

Five minutes later, she heard some sweet music coming from a building at the top of the street. The tune sounded very familiar. Heart lifting, she wandered over to look into the window. It was dim in the room, but she still recognized the movement. They were waltzing. She smiled and set a hand at the sill, content to watch.

⁓

Silvestri left Tortuga determined to chase down the Cursed Quill and discover who this new arrival was and why he kept seeing her everywhere his eyes rested. Even with his lids closed, her face rose to his mind. One day out, he realized the most logical thing to do was lurk around Tortuga. They'd be back. They seldom roamed far from the port. The Immortal usually went much farther afield.

He ordered the ship on a slow circuit of the island, keeping far enough from shore to prevent his curse from lingering on the island. A surly crewman climbed aloft to keep a sharp look out for the Quill. When out of the wind shadow of the island, no one liked lookout. It was cold that high up the mast. When the ship was sighted, and he realized they were setting course for Tortuga harbor, Silvestri ordered anchor set at Filly Beach and walked into the city.

The dark enveloped the town completely as he began strolling down Broad Street. He hadn't slept for more than an hour at a time in the past two days—longer than that and his cock woke him up, driving him to locate her. It hammered at him to search out the woman he kept seeing in his dreams and take her to bed. When he walked the deck, her face appeared in the sails, her hair in the white spray off the bow. If his hand lingered on the wheel or the rail, his palm caressed her cheek. She haunted him.

Lifting his face to the sky, he inhaled. If she were here, he'd know it. A faint scent he associated with her, though he hadn't named it yet, made him turn to where Broad met South.

When he recognized her silhouette, peering in a window at the vampires waltzing, he moved up behind her. A deep breath filled his head with the fragrance of apples. Yes, that was the scent. He placed a hand on her right forearm, his left swept around her waist, and he bent to her ear. "It isn't safe to spy on them."

She started and her hand touched the window in reaction. A white face filled the window, inches from hers, and eyes of total blackness glared at her. A loud hiss sounded from behind the glass. The blast of magic hit him indirectly, since he was shielded by her body, but the force of pure anger struck her full on.

She fell into him. He steadied her and backed away into the shadows, away from the window. She trembled. "What...? I was only watching!"

"Yes, and they object to being spied on."

"Why?" Her voice carried nothing but confusion and hurt. A hand rose to her face. "My eyes! I can't see!"

"You've been blasted by a vampire. It will fade. But until it does, your eyes will be sensitive to light." He hadn't been fast enough to keep her safe. But this might work to his advantage. With a short bow she couldn't see, he apologized. "I'm sorry I wasn't quicker."

"Did you say vampires? Waltzing vampires?"

She rubbed at her right eye, and he snatched at her hand. "Don't touch them—it will make it worse."

Her body sagged, and she took a deep breath, hugging her torso. "My day can't get much worse."

"Oh, I'd never say that." Keeping hold of her hand, he kept her close. Together, they leaned on the wall, where they could hear the music, but no windows gave visual access to the full moon dance.

"Ah, yes. Vampires. This is their initiation dance, and the citizens know to leave them alone. You aren't a citizen. That is obvious."

"No, newly arrived. But...vampires? And no one hunts

them? Or worries about them?"

"No. They struck a bargain with Tortuga nearly a century ago. We leave them alone—they leave us alone. They are free to convert and initiate those who want to be turned."

"What does Tortuga get out of it?"

He watched as she eased away from him. He allowed it.

"Protection. No one attacks or invades. If they do, the vampires are free to feed, harvest.... It's only happened once. They are basically normal people, with an odd appetite."

"Who like to waltz and can cause blindness with a hiss?" The way she stood, arms wrapped tightly around her torso, provided a sweet view of her full bust. He took advantage, eyes wandering over those luscious mounds as he ignored the tone of her voice. She was offended at the idea of the extremely effective vampire defense? There would be time to learn.

Clearing his throat, he smiled. "Yes. The vampires like to waltz. And the only guest allowed is the initiate. They come to town when the moon is full—otherwise they remain in the castle."

"The castle on the hill? I heard of that." It sounded as if she held back a laugh, the pitch of her voice rising as if slightly hysterical. "I suppose there is a graveyard full of zombies and a forest inhabited by wolves?"

"No, the zombies stay in the swamp. Most of the werewolves choose to wander the forest. Why are you laughing?"

The enigmatic woman turned away from him, chuckling. "Oh, relishing the clichés. I'm...Pawes. Call me Pawes." She held out a hand, moving it side to side as if searching for him.

"Ah, women do like to take their time." He pressed a quick kiss on her knuckles and slowly released her.

He detected a slight hesitation before she nodded. "Yes. While men generally are in a hurry." She turned her face toward him. "And you?"

"Call me Alan, Miss Pawes."

"No, Pawes or Mrs. Pawes if you like, please." Drawing a deep breath, she tried to focus on him, then winced, closing her eyes tightly. "You were behind me. Why didn't it hit you?"

"Because I was behind you, but I twisted my face away in time. Let me escort you somewhere quiet and buy you a drink."

"Are your intentions honorable?" Her head tilted.

"Of course not, but not actually dishonorable. I promise to warn you if driven to some despicable bit of deviltry." He must have impressed her, because a smile danced across her face— that upward tilt of her lips to the left exactly as he remembered from his dreams. He wondered if the rest of the details were the same.

Setting her hand at the crook of his arm, he urged her forward. "I promise a good glass of wine, or tankard of rum— whatever you would like."

"I was looking for the Barmy Cock."

"Too bright for the condition of your eyes, but I can take you there later, if you wish." Plan in motion, they stepped from the walkway. Acting the concerned guide, he directed her carefully, warning her where the ground sloped or if there were steps. He held her arm the entire walk to the Raven. Once there, he led her to a dark booth at the back of the tavern. "Sit. I'll place the order. What would you like?"

"Wine? That would be nice." She sat back. He paused, watching her hands rise to her face, then slowly move back to lay flat on the table. Good, she remembered to be careful.

After a whispered consultation with the owner, he joined her. He set a tall-stemmed, delicate glass in front of her and guided her hand to it. Sitting down kitty-corner to her, he studied her face.

She winced when a serving girl walked by with a dimly lit lantern. He commented, "You are extraordinarily sensitive. Let me place a wrap around your eyes to protect them."

She nodded, and he carefully wound a narrow scarf around her short, wavy hair, enjoying the brush of it on his fingers. She sat back and he smiled, quite entranced.

This was going to be delightful.

Chapter Five

*E*mily knew the only sane thing to do would be to run for the hills. She should be...no, she probably was, wrapped tightly in a straightjacket and calmly pounding her head against a rubber wall somewhere.

Nope, not sitting in a tavern, blindfolded, with a man who admitted to dishonorable intentions.

Yet, that was where she found herself.

Her knee touched his leg. He sat quite close, this mysterious man. What did he look like? He smelled good, like a fresh breeze on the bow of the ship.

The wine wasn't bad, so she took another sip, trying to think of what to say.

"Thank you for the wine—it's nice. So, did you tell me your name? It was quite kind of you to help me, but you know, if you have things to do or plans for the evening, I don't want to keep you."

Nice? She'd barely touched the wine. The best she managed was *nice*? Why did she feel completely out of her element? Twenty years tending bar should have her prepared for anything and anyone! Her bartender self was certainly faster with conversation than to end up with *nice*. Damn, he made her uncomfortable.

Not actually unpleasant. But...something she hadn't

experienced in an awfully long time. She wasn't sure she liked it. She was fifty-three! A widow! He was probably some handsome young thing, being kind to an old lady. Period.

"Yes, it's a nice wine. Not a real fine wine, but better than pig swill. I'm Alan. And my evening plans are not disturbed. Not at all."

He spoke with a nice, no, an especially yummy, deep and distinctive voice. She cleared her throat. "Oh, well, what were you about to do when the need to rescue me from vampires...?" She stopped, thought a moment. "Why make me blind? If they aren't allowed to be out and about selecting people snacks, why bother?"

Picking up her free hand, he patted it lightly. She wasn't going to like what he was going to say, she knew.

"Dear Pawes, the vampires have leave to punish those who spy on them. If I hadn't been there, you would have wandered off, sought the dark to ease your eyes, and they would have found you after the waltz finished. It is an unspoken agreement. They won't enter any establishments to hunt; don't worry."

"Oh. Well, thank you again." She pushed her glass away. "I feel a little sick." She took a deep breath and blew it out. "Well, I told Jezzie that I figured the unpleasant aspects of this experience would eventually bite me good. Didn't think I'd face being actually bitten."

His rough fingertips patted her hand, once more, then stroked it. "As for my evening plans, seduction and debauchery were on my agenda, anyway."

That drew her attention away from the thoughts of being some vampire's snack. She grabbed for the wine and nearly knocked the glass over. Her savior must have moved quickly, since the next thing she knew, his warm hand touching hers made sure she gripped it securely. She took too big a swallow and nearly choked before managing a comeback.

"Well, don't let me keep you. I was at the Barmy Cock some nights ago, and there are plenty of sweet, young things to seduce there. I have the blindfold to protect my eyes, so why not see me there, and you can take your pick." She tried to slide off the bench, but found a wooden barrier to her right. Damn.

Oh, she liked the sound of his sudden chuckle. She liked it too much! She'd already scolded herself enough on the Quill, for staring at the young hunks who worked the lines. It didn't make a difference to her that the rest of the crew enjoyed dallying with the boys. They *were* boys, and she couldn't look at them without feeling like a dirty, old woman. Well, look at them *that* way!

This Alan, well, he probably thought she possessed wealth or felt sorry for her. She'd grown accustomed to the blunt way the crew spoke of their sexual exploits. Jezzie would tease Mick while at dinner with ideas regarding their sexual play. Tink came striding out of her cabin one morning, rubbing her backside while complaining about Archer's heavy hand the night before.

The idea of seduction and debauchery seemed a bit tame compared to what she'd heard and seen on the ship!

Alan turned her hand upside down and dallied with her palm, sliding his fingertips up and down the lines. She wanted to pull away, or maybe that wasn't what she wanted. Damn! Her breasts ached, her nipples rising tighter than she'd ever known them to. Her belly clenched. Shit.

Another chuckle set her pulse pounding. He probably knew it, too. His finger lingered at her pulse point. Damn.

She had to be sitting in a puddle.

"But why would I want to consider the sweet, young things, when what I want is here before me?"

She jerked her hand away, suddenly angry. "You like teasing an old woman? Don't try to bullshit me! You want my purse, fine! Here!" She struggled to haul the bag of coins Sam had given her free of her pack. Plopping it on the table, she pushed back, into the corner and tried to glare in his general direction. "Don't fuck around with me! I'm not stupid. I felt your muscles, your broad chest...you don't want me!"

She heard nothing. Had he left?

"You smell like apples. It's quite intoxicating." His voice came at her left side, close to her ears, and the hair at her jawline stirred when he exhaled. An arm settled across her shoulders. He nearly crooned, "I don't need your purse. You're not an old woman, and I have every intention of fucking you." His hand cupped the back of her head as he finished the statement.

Emily's emotions veered between the fear of being trapped and the excitement of being wanted. Oh, God! Really wanted? Her lips parted, not sure what she was going to say, and he kissed her.

He took advantage of her open mouth. His kiss began with intense pressure, but eased after she almost jerked away. Thank God, he didn't stop. Her mind shut down, focused on nothing but the sense of his mouth on hers. Chills danced up her spine and lingered where his fingers pushed through her hair. His tongue teased at her lips, and she opened to the request. Tentative at first, she moaned at his continued assault. Her heart hammered beneath her ribs and wanting rose, drowning the remnants of her self-control.

When he finally pulled away, she nearly fell onto his chest. Somehow, he'd pushed the table back and moved closer, the heat of his body radiating along her torso. His free hand rested at her waist, fingers curled toward her back.

"Uh...wow."

The deep tone of his throaty chuckle answered her. Then the hand at her waist slid down to her thighs, and with a real display of strength, he lifted her onto his lap. And kissed her again.

This time she paid better attention, and a bravado she didn't know lived inside empowered her to mimic him. When his tongue withdrew, she bravely ventured forth to explore his lips, then the hot cavern of his mouth beckoned, and again she replied. She felt him smile and couldn't help but push forward for more. She acted like a student—she dared to act like a woman who lived in one of the romantic adventure books she read. The character she'd always dreamed of being.

As his hands slid down her neck, his knuckles brushed at the plump tops of her breasts, causing her to be terribly aware of how tight her bodice was. Her breath caught when he tugged at the tie of the rose silk blouse. Opening it wide, he dipped a finger into the valley between.

Emily trembled and her legs fell open, one foot hitting the toe of his boot as it slid toward the floor. She heard him moan in approval, a contented tone drifting away that communicated so much. She wasn't sure what she wanted to do. She knew she needed to…to do something. Object? Plead?

He shifted again and lifted her, pulling her left leg to the other side of his lap and she was astride him. Her head fell back as he shifted her hips closer. The terrible firmness of his cock pressed against her. He took advantage of her position, his lips traveling down her neck, along her chin and back to an ear.

"Apples," he whispered.

"Perfume," she gasped. "Glad you like it."

"I love it." His hands covered her breasts over the molded leather. "I want this off."

"Uh huh." She whimpered, trying to get to the tie. Yes, that's what she should do. Why wouldn't her fingers work?

He didn't interfere when she finally managed to release the knot and yanked the tie back through the eyeholes. When the bustier gaped open fully, warm hands took hold of her trembling fingers and held them still. She stopped tugging her blouse from the waist of the skirt.

"Enough," he said.

Damn, she'd been about to strip in a public place. She needed to get away from this man. Suddenly his lips locked on her right nipple, sucking it through the silk, and a shriek escaped her.

She slapped a hand over her mouth and fell toward him. Get away? Oh, shit! More!

She molded well around his cock. He'd been stiff since he'd seen her outside the ballroom. He'd listened to her babble, relishing the innocence she exhibited and loving the freedom her fortuitous blinding gave him to examine her physical attributes. Why did she trust him? It baffled him, even made him be more honest than normal.

He hadn't counted on laughing so often. His plans were

much more direct. So much for that scheme. She charmed him effortlessly with her bit of temper. It struck him as a different sort of innocence. He swept in, meaning to overpower her. Instead, he smelled apples again, and the longing for more than fast bedding filled him.

He backed down. He'd take his time. Her lips were the same sweet bits he'd dreamed. Her level of inexperience surprised him. The majority of his encounters involved professional women; perhaps, her reaction was normal. He'd noticed the ring on her finger, but it didn't seem like a wedding ring.

When she initiated, shadowed his techniques, his cock grew terrifically stiff. He fought back a groan of his own. The room he'd reserved was above. For the first time that evening, he regretted the blindfold. He wanted to see her eyes. Since that wasn't possible, he wanted to see everything else. Lifting her to his lap, he continued the kissing primer.

He drifted to her breasts; she trembled. So soft, fleshy and hot! He wanted more. Her body shaped itself to him, shaking with desire. He knew women, and from this point on, he was in control. He felt her acknowledgement of this authority as she shifted to a new, delightful position.

When she'd cooperated, helping to free her breasts from the leather and even signaling a readiness to strip, he'd stopped her. Time to see her upstairs. He paused, eyes locked on the taut nipple straining against the silk shirt, and he took it.

Her reaction drove him further. He stood, her ass cupped in his hands, and set her on the table. He continued to torture her nipples, squeezing, pinching, sucking and biting. Her fingers gripped his hair tightly, until the danger of losing fistfuls threatened if he didn't ease off. He didn't believe she was even aware of how much she urged him on.

He slowly forced her fingers to release his head, setting her cooperative palms at her legs. "Pawes...."

"Uh huh." She sounded stuporous; he didn't want her so unaware. The advantage of lethargic cooperation paled behind the shine of a fully awake partner. He glanced at the wine glass—she'd taken little of it. Too little to be intoxicated.

"Look...blast. Pawes!"

"What?" She shook her head, and her arms rose to protect her breasts.

"Better." He grinned wickedly. "I like my partners to be more alert."

"Yeah, well, that's nice," she said. "Oh, hell, what am I doing? What were you...doing?" Her palms eased her breasts, cradling them. "Ouch," she said softly.

"You want me to stop?" He was curious. He'd no intention of stopping.

"Yes, no. I don't know!" She sighed. "I'm not used to feeling like this."

"You are not a virgin." He didn't actually ask, but stated. She was a mature woman, and no nun.

"No! I was married for over thirty years."

Her objection amused him. "Was?" He lightly touched her cheek. "He leave you? Divorce? Dead?"

"Dead," she whispered, bowing her head. "Only man I've ever known, Alan."

"Impressive." His hands seemed to have a mind of their own, rising to push hers aside and meddle with her breasts. He didn't betray how thoughtful her words made him. He'd be the second man to know her. "Good, not a virgin. I find inexperienced women quite annoying."

"Thought...thought men preferred virgins." She whimpered, but didn't try to block him access.

"More trouble than they're worth." He closely observed her tongue, darting out to lick her lips. He knew hunger and felt her tremble under his touch. "Damn, how long have you been widowed?"

"Almost a year." She reached up, searching for his face. She touched his chin and wandered with her fingers. "How old are you? What do you look like?"

"You tell me." He enjoyed this game. Her hands, small, shaking while they wandered the topography of his face, tested his patience. He contemplated sucking a finger into his mouth. She scratched at his beard, ran a thumb about the bristles. He kept it trimmed relatively short.

"Stiff...some gray hairs?"

He didn't say anything. She continued her journey. She lingered a bit on his lips before gliding her fingertips further. He kept cupping her breasts, but stopped fiddling with them. He was curious to see what she'd deduce.

She found the deep scar at his left cheek and tilted her head. "Hard battles? Or an angry virgin?" He chuckled. She actually snickered.

She continued along the bones of his face, lingering at the crow's feet to the side of each eye. She danced around the tangle of his brows, swept her fingers through his hair, down to his shoulders. She slid back up to the sides of his head, to his ear. Found the earring he wore.

"Gold?" she asked.

"Yes." He knew she couldn't tell metals with touch, so he'd give her that. "Your conclusions?"

Her arms dropped. Her head turned to the side. "Are we— can anyone see what you're doing?"

He thought of lying, but she didn't need the scare. "No, we're at the back, with one small entrance to the booth. Enough light for me to watch you, barely." He rubbed at her nipples, wondering why he comforted her. He fought to balance his desire to rut against wanting to know more of her than her body. "If the blouse stains, I will buy you another."

"How kind." She covered her tits. "I'm not...sure—"

He wouldn't allow her to finish. Sweeping down, he kissed her again, with fierce need, hauling her back to his body and pressing his stiff cock against her. She wrapped her arms around his neck.

Answer enough. He swept her into his arms and headed for the stairs.

"Sissie! Get her pack and purse and bring them up," he called to one of the serving girls.

He kicked the door open, spied the bed tucked up against a wall and strode to it. He lay Pawes down and sat on the edge. She turned toward him and set a hand on his thigh. He removed his coat and tossed it on a nearby chair. Sissie trotted in, dropped her pack and quickly backed out, shutting the door.

He unbuckled his belt and it followed the coat.

She sat up, reaching for him.

"How old are you, Alan? I'm not good at this. I can't tell from what I touch." She blew out a fast breath. "I don't want to have sex with a total stranger."

He bent to remove his boots. "What do you want to know? Other than my age."

"Are you younger than me?"

"No." One boot fell to the floor with a loud clunk. "I am somewhat grizzled, though still quite fit and spry. And I want you, Pawes." His second boot hit the floor.

She pulled her legs to her chest. "I'll be honest. I want you. I want you so much it frightens me. I don't know why I'm here or if I'll stay."

He laughed. "A sailor's dream woman!"

"You work on a ship? I thought so, from the lines on your face. And you smell of the sea."

"I captain a ship." He stepped off the bed and stripped away his breeches. Taking his cock in hand, he stroked it, eyeing her. "You're wearing too many clothes."

"*Oh.*" She removed her bodice, reached behind to touch the headboard, and folded the leather over it. Swallowing nervously, she pulled her blouse out from beneath an impressive, black belt and slowly shimmied out of it before setting it near the bodice.

His breath caught at the sight of her bare breasts. He fought to keep his hands still.

When she leaned back and went through some fancy back and forth to unbuckle her belt, he nearly leaped at her. He swallowed, holding himself steady

She sat back up and carefully removed the strip of leather. She kept a few items hanging from it. He took it from her. "Let me."

"Thanks."

He draped the belt, after making certain her dangles were safe, near her other pieces. No more waiting. He lay down next to her, though she still wore her skirt. He settled down against the wall, brushing against her to reach that place. She scooted closer to the edge. He pulled her back.

Reaching to her chin, he tilted her head to his. He took her mouth with the same explosive force he'd held back the first time. One hand seized her breast as she arched toward him. Her left hand gripped his hipbone, shaking.

He wanted her more than he'd wanted anything in his life. There was no reason for it, but it was the truth.

Chapter Six

She was out of her mind. She'd met him only a few hours ago. And now she sat on a bed, blindfolded—sure, to protect her eyes—but if she wasn't nuts, she'd wait until they were better to have her first fling since becoming a widow.

Her mind raced ahead of her body, thinking about what it would feel like, what he was like. At least he said he wasn't younger. Her drooping boobs, loose skin, belly wouldn't matter. Right?

What would this be like? Only the second man ever to touch her.

The fire between her legs screamed, overriding the remaining aspects of the situation. No self-consciousness, no worry there. It didn't care if he found her body repulsive, only that he found it. Quickly with his cock.

He slid over her, his hair touching her face. She fought back the urge to whimper. Guess he liked the wall. The kiss pushed her down into the soft mattress like a battering ram, and his hand at her breast started a combustion like she'd never known.

He was ruthless, manhandling her nipple, bruising her lips. She tried to peel his fingers off her breast; the grip was too much. He growled, snatched her hand away and held it above her head. His mouth took the place of his hand. That provided relief. Though relentless, he did seem to gain a modicum of control, sliding and pinching instead of biting and squeezing. He moved down her body with his lips, removing his grip from near the headboard.

"Don't move that," he demanded.

"Uh huh." Damn, she had no language skills! But she obeyed him. She was taking no chances on giving him a reason to stop.

He kissed her waist while his hand tugged at the knotted skirt tie. It gave easily, and he pushed the skirt down. Emily cried. She didn't know why, but felt the tears running from her eyes. He didn't appear to notice. She was glad of that, because they were beyond explanation. The blindfold caught most of the moisture.

He rose to his knees and tugged her skirt away. She lifted enough to make it easy. She could feel his cock at her thigh. It was so big. Oh, God! Would it hurt? Shit, she hadn't even used a vibrator in the past year.

He slid a finger through her pubic hair and down to her folds. He chuckled as she gasped.

"Nice."

His voice seemed more hoarse than before. She could feel his breath at her breast again. The right one, this time. He sucked the nipple into his mouth, his finger slid lower, took a slow turn around her aching tissues, and eased inside. She bucked and he bit, enough to relish, not damage.

The hardness of his cock, its length, the slickness at the tip, divided her focus. Her right arm was between the two of them; she forced it upward. Trying to take some initiative, she grazed the hair at his lower belly with her fingers.

He growled again. "No."

"Why not?"

He didn't answer, but went to his knees again, sliding his finger free. Oh! Fuck! Was he going to leave? Did she do something wrong? Didn't men like to be touched?

"Don't go!" she cried out.

"Go?" His hands urged her legs apart. "Open. Now."

She raised her knees, following his inclinations. She truly

didn't care at that point how this progressed. He wasn't leaving. He still wanted her. At least part of her. But what the fuck, she was only interested in one part of him.

He was suddenly gentle, moving atop her with care. Keeping his weight on one hand, kissing his way up her torso, he reached her face then paused. Alan stretched between them and slid one finger, than another, back into her, stroking her to incoherence. Not that it took much at that point.

"What?" She protested. "No, please, I want...."

His fingers left her then rose to paint her lips with the wetness he'd gathered. The smell of desire rose to her nostrils. He genuinely was intent on debauchery.

"Suck," he said.

She let him slip them into her mouth and she cleaned them off, out of her mind with what he was doing. He bent and delivered one last devastating kiss, then kept moving until the tip of his cock lingered at her slick folds. He stopped. She drew a breath to protest and he slid into her.

"Oh, my God!" she wailed. "Shit! Damn! Fuck! Fuck! Fu-u-u-u-uck!" Her hands gripped his hips, the hell with anything he'd said before. She dug nails into his ass while he kept to a slow pace, filling her, reaching and stretching her to an extent she'd never known before. So good!

He cradled her head in his hands. "Such a mouth."

"Fuck *me!*"

"I am." He pulled nearly free and went faster this time. "You harridan. More?"

"*Yes!*" She pounded at his shoulders.

He actually listened to her and thrust with more and more power, until she lost her mind.

◈

He doubted he'd ever forget that first time with her. And there would be more—he would drag her from the Quill with a sword, holding the rest at bay if necessary. Her cunny gripped him so tightly, so sweetly. And her mouth charmed him. Thirty years married and so hungry. Her fever nearly matched his.

Once he was certain of not hurting her, he let his control go.

He'd come close to doing damage to her breast; he must be more circumspect. She was anything but careful. Her nails dug into him. The pain added to the passion. She screeched obscenities, cursed him, and pled with him.

Her feet locked behind his knees, so that when he pushed, she rose with him. This drove him to an end. She hit the angle of her pleasure and fluttered around him, pouring out wetness as she rode him, sobbing in release. He bellowed as his cock delivered oblivion, collapsing atop her in a state of relaxation he hadn't known for days.

She wrapped her arms around his back, her legs slowly falling open.

"Damn." He heard her gasp. He lifted off her, giving her room to breathe.

Her sudden jerk to one side surprised him. She tried to bury her face at his shoulder. "Eyes!" she whimpered. "Burns!"

He quickly slid down to offer her more shelter. "It means they are nearly done looking for you. The spell is trying one last chance to flush you out. Relax."

The blindfold, fallen to one side, was barely visible. The light from the one candle, near the window, fell on the pillow. He quickly sheltered her eyes, shifting to provide shadow. "Close your eyes, tightly. Cover your face with your hand, while I snuff the wick."

Stepping from the bed, he walked to the window and took care of the offending flame. Outside, he noticed two figures across the road. They were destined to be disappointed. He wasn't. They'd leave now, and he could return to slaking his thirst. They would have to manage with initiates.

Turning again to the bed, he considered what he wanted next.

By the time a glint of dawn lightened the window, he relished the sound of her snores. His cock reclined, spent. But his time was up.

Once dressed, he slid the cover down from her shoulder to more clearly see the tattoo he'd caught a hint of in the faint light the night before. Above her left shoulder blade, he spied a circle of dog paws, dancing around a full moon. At her bicep was another ring of paws. He smiled. "Ah, the origin of the name...."

He wrote her a note and left it on the pillow.

Dear Mrs. Pawes,
Next rendezvous, aboard my ship. Last night was a pure delight. I look forward to our next bit of debauchery.
Alan

He removed a small pearl pin from his sash and secured it to her belt—a token of his appreciation.

He hauled his coat off a chair and her bag fell to the floor, spilling its contents. Going to one knee, he gathered up the items. A wallet of sorts displayed a placard. It bore her likeness. He smiled. "Ah, so it's Emily."

A small vial of liquid, hooked on a light chain, caught his eye. He unscrewed the lid and inhaled. The source of her apple scent. He liked it.

Lastly, a fabric-wrapped item. Curious, he freed it. The item fell into his palm; the carved Kraken coils made him start. He slid a finger down the handle, and his memories stirred. With a smile, he flipped it over to find a portrait of himself gazing back at him.

The shock threw him. He shot a glance at the woman, dead asleep on the rumpled bed. Confusion roared through him, anger. Did she cast on him? Was this a trick of Mick's? He surged to his feet, ready to confront her.

And stopped. No, he'd find Mama Lu. She'd know. Casting near Tortuga required her cooperation. And she would not do anything against him. Of that, he was certain. Fairly.

He swallowed, took a deep breath, and stooped to recover the scarf. He wrapped the frame, glancing down at it once more. Only to see his present face gazing back at him. He blinked, it blinked. A mirror. Now it was a mirror? Shaking his head, he finished wrapping it and returned it to her bag. Perhaps, it wasn't *her* magic—it *was* magic. Lu would know.

When he departed the tavern, he left instructions that Mrs. Pawes have every amenity available when she rose.

Chapter Seven

*E*mily woke slowly, her body aching, yet oddly at peace. She stretched, moaning. Her eyelids flickered, and the memory of the previous night's blindness caused her to open them wide, fearful it was still with her. A wall glowed inches away from her. She raised a hand and brushed at the plaster. Seeing the cracks, her worries eased.

"Alan?" She rolled over, expecting to see him in the room. It was empty.

Typical man. She guessed. She actually didn't have much experience with men, having married at twenty. But what she'd read led her to believe this wasn't unusual. And for men of this century? Who knew? She shrugged as she sat up.

She'd gotten what she wanted, she supposed. So why the acute sense of bereavement? One hand clasped the sheet to her chest, the other pushed her up to sit. Her fingers brushed against something out of place. A bit of paper?

She lifted the notepaper and read it. "Oh yeah? Your ship? Yeah, I'll skip on down to the harbor and ask for a Captain Alan of the ship something or another."

But the note lifted her heart some. It seemed stupid to care, but she did.

Good thing there was no e-mail or texting in this place, or she'd find herself stalking him. Searching Google. She imagined the personal ad.

Desperately seeking tall captain who rescued old woman from vampires the other night. Call me!

With a giggle, she set her feet on the floor. Standing, she moaned. Her body creaked, her back gave a loud pop, and her pussy pulsed. Wow. And she needed to pee.

She'd been surprised while she strolled around town the day before to see that the public privies were more than open cesspools. Instead, they featured a crude bit of what she'd term modern plumbing. She surveyed the room, noting a door at one corner.

"What the hell?" She checked it out and found a bathroom.

She returned, much relieved. Once dressed, she checked the room thoroughly, wondering if he left anything else. With a sigh, she deduced he didn't. After her bustier was secured, she pulled the belt from the headboard.

"What is...oh!" She unclipped the pearl pin from one of the buckles and smiled. Securing it on her blouse, she slipped into her sandals, picked up her pack and turned toward the door.

She paused, considering. What should she do? Her belly growled, making one decision for her. Breakfast first, followed by a visit to the Barmy Cock, where hopefully, she'd discover if the Quill was still in port. It appeared she'd be here for the duration. And should the ship be gone, perhaps Sam would take her on as a bartender.

Downstairs, a bright-eyed woman hailed her, insisting she sit down and have something to eat. "The Captain, he insisted we take good care of you, Misses."

"Well, thank you. I'm sorry I missed him this morning." Emily determined she would not be embarrassed. She was an adult, as was he.

"Ah, well those sailors often rise early. He was taking the ship out with morning tide. He knows not to linger too long in Tortuga." The apron-wearing matron smiled brightly. She chattered while setting a plate down in front of Emily that contained fried potatoes and sausages. Emily listened with one ear, her focus on the food.

She'd eaten poorly the day before—it was a pleasure to dig

in heartily.

"This is delicious, thank you." She took the drink offered, cleared her throat, and tried to think how to ask without asking directly.

"His ship? So, they're gone...?" She let the sentence hang. She was no good at this.

"Ah, the Immortal was here some days ago. It was unusual for him to return so soon. Misses? Are you all right?"

Emily pushed the plate away, a sudden dead weight on her chest. She'd slept with Captain Silvestri? Spent the entire night with him. The man Mick hated. Mick, who befriended her, watched out for her....

"Uh...no, I'm fine. I only realized... I was supposed to meet a friend at the Barmy Cock this morning. I should leave. Hopefully, I haven't missed her." She pushed back from the table. "Thank you—you've been quite kind. How much do I owe you?"

"Nothing, love. He took care of it." She reached out and tilted Emily's head to one side. "He said you were vampire blasted last night. I see no sign of it, so you shook it off right. The Cock is down Broad Street, on the right."

"Broad Street...it isn't the wide one, is it?" Emily asked, distracted by the shouting in her head. *Slut. Sleeping with the enemy. Fucking the enemy. Shit.*

Gloomy, she made her way to the familiar bar.

Sam at the Cock told her the Quill was still in port. "They were in here hoping to find you last night. Said they'd be back. Or, go on down. There'll be someone can see you out to the ship. You find a place to sleep last night?"

"Oh...yeah. Sam?" She looked up at the friendly man. Bartenders heard everything, knew everyone. But they generally didn't gossip. There was honor among those who worked the bar; they didn't blab about customers. Would he share with her?

"Yes, Misses Paw? What do you need?" He polished a glass.

"Don't you ever sleep?" she asked. It wasn't what she wanted to know, but it might make it easier to ask the second question. "I always slept till noon after a busy night."

"I ain't been to bed yet. I don't sleep until everything is cleaned up. Now, what do you really want to know?"

"Can't fool you!" She gazed at the glasses, lined up on the bar. "Why does Mick hate this Captain Silvestri so much? I know he blames him for losing his father? Is that right? I'm not asking you break confidence, but I'm new here and I don't want to stumble."

"Well, Mick's got his suspicions. When news came from England—I think it were a letter from his father's solicitors—he became determined against Silvestri. And declared he'd take back the Immortal. I don't know the particulars. I do know it's an empty hope. Silvestri ain't letting go of the Immortal. He doesn't seem to hold any enmity toward Mick. He goes out of his way to steer clear of the man." Sam set a glass down. "Why does it worry you?"

"I worry. Mick was good to me. And I don't want to do anything wrong. I don't know what Silvestri looks like, or the ship. I'm new here, and much is strange." Her eyes strayed to the large CD player and the speakers sitting on shelves high on the wall. "And yet, much isn't strange, but feels like it should be." She sighed. "I'm sorry. I didn't sleep well last night. I should head on down, in case they decide to leave. I don't want to miss them."

"Silvestri is a tall man—long, gray hair, some hint of the yellow it once was. Wears his beard short, and has blue eyes. He's a confident man, who dresses well. Silvestri is a working captain and that makes him strong. There's a crescent shaped scar on one cheek. Are you feeling well, you look like it's more than lack of sleep plaguing you?"

She swallowed her bile, sure now that she'd slept with Silvestri. Damn. "I'm okay. I should get going."

"Well, if they did raise anchor, you come back here. I can always use a relief bartender until you find your feet."

"Thank you! I appreciate the offer." She smiled crookedly, hurried out of the bar, and set her feet on the path down to the harbor. On the way, she glanced down to see the pin on her blouse. With a snarl, she pulled it off and made to toss it away, then stopped.

It hurt. And she didn't know if he knew who she was. Maybe it was a coincidence. Perhaps he wasn't trying to get back at Mick and it wasn't about using her.

She pulled her pack open and dropped the pin into it. It might be something Mick would recognize, and until she figured this out, she wasn't going to say anything. To anyone.

෴

Silvestri set sail for the backside of Tortuga. Mama Lu wasn't home, but her neighbors said she'd left the night before for the swamp shack where she mixed her potions. It would take some hours to get there.

He directed the ship's officers on where they were headed, entered his cabin, and fell into a deep sleep—the second in days.

He stayed down until the ship dropped anchor, late in the afternoon. Once roused, he went ashore by himself, tying the cutter up to a tattered pier and trading it in for a more shallow draft, narrow boat. Then he set out for Mama Lu's shack.

It took him two hours to make his way through the tangled roots of mangroves. By the time he reached her shack, he knew he'd be staying the night.

Mama Lu met him on the porch, sitting on a rocking chair and smoking a pipe. He inhaled deeply. It was good weed. She grinned and offered him a hit.

"Only the one, Mama. I need you sharp. I need me sharp. I brought a bottle. I need advice."

"Course ya do. And a bottle is always welcome." She took the pipe back and snuffed it. Saving it for later, he'd bet.

Ever since that morning, he'd found himself looking over his shoulder, expecting to see his benefactor gazing at him. More likely, lining up something nasty. He wasn't allowed to enjoy himself to the extent he had with the delicious Mrs. Pawes. He stood a moment, reflecting on his night.

"Tell me what troubles the legendary, lucky Captain Silvestri." Mama Lu interrupted the sweet memory of Emily licking his fingers clean. His smile disappeared. "Mama Lu, has anyone been casting against me? Is Captain March setting another absurd plan of vengeance in motion?" He'd meant to be less direct. Damn.

"Not wit' my help. No one casts on this island without me knowing it."

He considered a moment. "What about off this island?"

"Now you're asking a question worth knowing." She poured a drink from his bottle into an empty jar. After a sip, she grinned at him. "You meet the newcomer?"

"She's casting?" He didn't bother being impressed. Mama knew magic.

"Her? She don't believe in magic. Yet. But...magic is using her."

"I knew it!" He turned away, fist clenched. "Who?"

"More critical you ask what be using her. You tired of serving the northern witch, Alan? Ya ready to shed her benevolence and strike out on your own? That newcomer, she be the key to turn that lock," Mama Lu's voice softened. She set a hand on his shoulder.

Silvestri stared out into the dark swamp. A figure moved in the water. Two eyes, glazed and wet, stared up at him.

"You! Shhhh! Get 'way! There be nothing for you right now!" she shouted to the wading zombie.

"You feed them, so they'll keep coming back." With a sigh, he continued. "Be free of her curse? How?"

"Yes, I feed them. I grow the mold they like. But there's none ready to harvest right now. They're harmless and bring me what I need. Now, I don't know how this is gonna work. But the new lady, she be marked for you, brought for you. He's working for you, Alan."

He turned to look into her eyes. "He? Mick?"

She snorted. "That ain't likely! No, Captain. I remember, years ago, I told 'bout doing good ta the younger Kraken? The elder must have found out, and the tides turning. He's working for you. To pay you back and reclaim what Glacious steals from him."

He studied her, trying to put together what was clear to her, but still a mystery to him. A good turn?

Mama Lu laughed. "Such a small act of kindness. You don't

recall it? How often did you find young Kraken, tangled in a net? Climb down ta the waterline and...."

"...cut them free. Yes, I recall now. My crew thought I was mad, but said nothing." He did remember. He didn't believe in eating Kraken or killing them. But the elder Kraken wanting to pay him back? Was that possible? Kraken were hunters, not inclined to mercy. How was that woman, out of time and place, a part of this? "Wait, her mirror. The one that wasn't a mirror at first?" He lifted a hand and rubbed at his head.

"Yes, I think so. Alan, you've served Glacious for nearly fifty years. You done the time. The trick is to get away from her influence without surrendering the rest of your life."

He swallowed and took a seat, a spark of hope kindled in his heart.

"I need time to unearth it, Captain. Time to figure it up. And you need to take advantage of what the Kraken gives, without leading that ice bitch straight to her. Keep new sailor Pawes close, and see what you can divvy from her. He chose her and must have a reason for doing so."

"She sails with Mick and the Quill. She isn't my sailor, Mama Lu."

"He must be part a' the picture. And she be safer there than aboard the Immortal. It's going to be a fine dance, looking for a way to free you—might take some sacrifice. You gotta be ready, if you want to sail without that curse."

"You tell me what I need to do, I'll do it," he said.

"Aye. And you'll enjoy it, boy-o. She's a saucy one. I can smell her all over you. That must have been a rewarding night. You'll need more rewards like that. You seduce her, while I search for answers."

He smiled and raised an eyebrow. "You always make the nicest suggestions. I have an appointment with a galleon, fresh from Panama. After, I'll find the Quill and rendezvous with Mrs. Pawes."

"Not too often! But enough."

"Aye, enough." And maybe a little more.

And once he was free, a whole lot more.

Chapter Eight

She didn't share her nocturnal adventure with anyone on the Quill. She thought about it, but the idea of trying to put it into words...*Well, I was accidentally blinded by vampires and he...uh...saved me and we accidentally...sorta...well...*

Tink met her on deck, furious. "You were supposed to wait for me! You stupid bitch! I wasted hours looking for you."

"I hadn't gone far. The woman at the bathhouse directed me to a clothing store." Emily tried to cool off the angry woman. "I didn't mean to worry you."

"Worry, me? Oh, I wasn't worried." Tink stared at her a moment, then shrugged. The sailor was like that, always showing a blank face to the world. "What if you'd been hauled into an alleyway, robbed, raped, chained to a bed." Emily went white as Tink went on and on, listing the hair-raising dangers Tortuga harbored.

"I didn't know." Emily shook her head. "I met good people, and they kept me safe. Especially after it got dark. I didn't think I wanted to go wandering around after dark. Damn, those streets are confusing!" It wasn't *all* her fault. Fuck it!

"You have no idea what dangers lurk in Tortuga. We aren't the most popular ship! Lots don't like women with a command." Tink slid close to her and put an arm around her shoulders. "Pawes, Mick found you and brought you into the lighter climes of the city. There is a lot of darkness in those streets. And last night was the full moon."

"Yeah, someone told me about the vampire stuff." Resentment rose, and Emily pushed Tink's arm away. "If Mick hadn't found me, I'd be fine! I am an adult. I've been around a long time. I can take care of myself!"

She knew it was a lie, but Tink was such a know-it-all.

Tink gazed at her with disdain. "Sure, you can take care of yourself. You've got no fighting skills, and you're out of shape, with almost no muscle tone. You'd probably be run down like a rabbit by hungry hounds. Tell yourself you'd have been just ducky. I know better. And you owe Mick so much, stupid bitch!"

She stalked away, and Emily thought about her night with Silvestri. Even if she had the courage to speak up before, no way was she going in that direction now.

Nope, she kept quiet. Resigned to making the best of the strange situation she found herself in, she prepared for life in a fantastically confusing Caribbean.

She took Tink's word seriously and learned to load, shoot, and care for a pistol she got from Mick. He'd lent it to her to carry when they sailed into port to gather supplies, barter, and collect information. Tink taught her how to fight with a staff. Emily, being so short, found it wasn't the best choice for her. She took up knife throwing after one of the sailors offered to show her the techniques. And she practiced constantly.

She must be some sort of coward, preferring a weapon she could toss from a distance. She'd have a chance to run. But she was good at both throwing and running, so it was a win-win situation.

"Once you've thrown one knife, you need another ready. And you need to learn close fighting," Davis, her instructor, explained to her.

She hit targets quite skillfully, but in close quarters she shrank away and wasn't aggressive enough.

Tink proposed she needed to be scared more or pissed off. The quartermaster balanced on the rails one day and taunted

Emily during practice. The insults got nastier and nastier. Davis circled her, watching her reactions to the taunts. It made it difficult to battle the man.

And Emily grew more and more furious. She kept her eyes on Davis, something he'd taught her. When his eyes drifted to her bust at one of Tink's more pointed comments about being a washed up old lady with drooping boobs, Emily shrieked, "My eyes are up here!"

"Not as interesting," Davis replied.

She dove at him, and for the first time offered him some real challenge. Tink laughed while he disarmed her. For a moment, she panted, catching her breath. Tink snickered and set Emily off.

"*You bitch!*" She might be older, but she was fast. She rushed the quartermaster, and with a splash, they both tumbled over the rail and hit the water.

Once the ship came about and fished them out, Captain Jezzie called them into her cabin. "Tink, you made your point. No more taunting Pawes."

"Squirrelly bitch," Tink said, stripping out of her soaking clothes and kicking them aside to wrap herself in the towel Jezz handed her. "She needs to get laid."

Emily wrapped her arms around her soaked shirt and snarled.

"Pawes, you've been on the ship three weeks now and you pull your share. You work the lines, you mend the sails, help out in the galley." The captain tilted her head. "But Tink is right. You need to get laid."

"Oh, fuck off! What is with this crew? Nothing but overactive libidos! You all think a cock is the answer to everything!" Emily rolled her eyes, disgusted at the constant poking about why she wasn't dragging one of the hands off to her bunk.

"You want a woman? Fine. Hell, Tink tends to swing both ways."

Emily faked a gag and backed away. "Everything isn't about bed partners!"

"Well, it's often the answer on this ship. But fine, it's not about sex. You're mastering a few weapons. That will come in handy. What about a hobby? The tip money Sam shares with you when we're in Tortuga is good, but you're going to need more. A superior set of throwing knives isn't cheap." Jezzie sat at the table and poured herself a drink.

"A hobby? What, like basket weaving?" Emily shivered.

"Get out of those wet clothes. Use the blanket. No, not basket weaving. Unless you're good at it?" Jezzie raised an eyebrow.

"No. I can't weave worth shit. I took a class once, and I suck at it. I have no artistic talent to speak of." A sudden thought occurred to her. "Well, I did create some nice blank books once. I liked hand stitching the binding." She let her shirt plop to the deck with a splat and kicked off her shorts. Her skin was getting quite tanned, she noted.

Is skin cancer a problem here?

"Blank books? To write in? Those would be worth trade goods. What would you need?" The captain of the Quill seemed interested, so Emily sat down, made out a list, and also promised to stay out of trouble.

In the next two months, her fighting skills grew sharper. The close knife fighting got better, but not great. She did need to be angry, it seemed. When the ship visited different ports, she used her funds to purchase what she needed to bind paper into books, and within a month, she was making money.

That came in handy to make her cabin more like home.

And she looked at the deckhands. But no touching. Even when sexual frustration grew. Because the dreams drove her crazy.

Always him. His hands, his lips, his skin, whispers, curses and, the best of it, or worst of it, his cock.

She asked about him in ports, obliquely, only to be told he'd been there the week before, or was expected the week after. Not that she cared.

Three months, she thought. Twelve weeks since she found herself in this crazy world. She wandered a beach, somewhere in the Bahamas, considering that going insane wasn't too bad. This world didn't have the discomfort she was certain flourished in the real Caribbean. No bedbugs, no weevils in the food, no nasty ants or biting insects. Unless they were here, but left her alone?

She didn't know how it worked. They'd anchored for a few days, along a perfect white sand beach, with pale turquoise water. It was insanely divine. Part of the crew hunted for pigs. Some built a fire, some set up shelter, or gathered water. Jezzie granted her permission to hunt for plant dyes for the book covers. She wanted to try something new to make them more attractive.

At the last port, Mick had helped her find a pistol to purchase, which she carried, loaded and ready to fire. The new throwing knives were also strapped to her belt. And she carried water, bread, and some fruit.

"This isn't a big island, Pawes," Mick informed her. "You start walking along the beach one way, and when you reach the cliffs, turn inland and you'll end up back at this beach." He pointed her toward the north. "If you want to explore inland, keep the ocean to your right. There is fresh water."

"Do I need to worry about the pigs?" she asked, thinking of wild boar with fierce tusks.

"They stick to the thicker woods, to the south, where Tink hunts. Keep a sharp ear out and climb a tree if something sounds off. They'll wander away. You aren't tasty enough!" He grinned at his joke.

"Yeah, this tough hide of mine will protect me." She snorted and turned her attention to the north.

She carried a large basket with a stack of paper inside, intending to find leaves or flowers and see if they'd transfer color to the paper. There didn't seem to be any other way to find out. The dyers in town wouldn't share their secrets.

Damn, she was tired. Her dreams grew more and more intrusive over the past few weeks. At first, she'd dreamed about that night in Tortuga once a week. She'd take out the pin he'd left her and examine it, wondering what those dreams were all about. Some weeks, she was convinced he'd known who she was the whole time and the entire seduction was about using her to taunt Mick. Somehow.

She couldn't figure out how.

Other times, she about convinced herself that their meeting and wild night of sex were nothing more than an incredible coincidence.

Yeah, right.

What was it about this man? And why didn't the hunger she felt for him transfer to the men on the Quill? Several made it clear they'd enjoy bedding her, and she kept saying no, ignoring the invitation.

She snarled, thinking about Tink and her big mouth. The quartermaster didn't believe in privacy. The night before, she'd been snooping and found the bone dildo Emily purchased three days earlier in St. Barthélemy. The tall freak stole it and brought it out at dinner. She'd actually nonchalantly set it next to her plate, daring Emily to rise to the bait. There were days Emily hated Tink.

Emily responded by standing, taking her plate, and pouring it over Tink's head. She'd picked up the item, tucked it into her belt and left the cabin. Later, she'd asked Davis about how to put a lock on her cabin door.

"She'd pick it, luv. I'll help you devise a box she can't easily open for what you want to keep private. Will that do?" He'd been one of those who made it plain he'd join her in bed anytime she gave him the nod.

But she didn't want him in her bed. She didn't want anyone in her bed, despite the ideas her body tormented her with. Her lustful flesh only wanted Captain Alan Silvestri. Villain.

Her thoughts turned from the sex when she spotted a flowering shrub that might work for dying her paper. She'd been wandering for an hour and was ready for the break. She shook her head and wiped the sweat from her forehead, then examined the pink blossoms. It was a hot day with little wind.

❧

He watched from the tree line, hidden in the shadows. He squatted, thinking about the last visit with Mama Lu. A frustrating visit, since she offered him little. He'd turned a sizable cut of the galleon treasure over to her for research.

His spy reported on the Quill's whereabouts and routes, and Alan followed them, making certain the two ships never met. He heard about the quaint books Mrs. Pawes peddled. He actually possessed several of them and admired the intricate series of knots she used to bind the sections together. A large book would be handy for the ship's log. And Sam's wife appreciated the one he'd brought her, for the sketches she was fond of making.

Why was his favorite newcomer wandering away from her shipmates and collecting bits of leaves and flowers?

He considered her course and cut across the peninsula to intercept her. He feared she'd panic and dart away, or raise an alarm if he even approached her. After all, he was a stranger to her. He could have walked past her in a crowded city, and she'd not even know he was the man who spent that delightful night with her.

Setting the trap for the galleon, luring them in, and stealing away their cargo was diverting. Helpful, considering his nights returned to hot dreams and a constant replay of their one night in Tortuga.

Those visions made the nights more bearable. At least he knew the woman wasn't a phantom, sent to torment him. He used those memories, having no shyness in regard to relieving his hunger. His hands didn't compare, but at least using them allowed him to sleep. And the occasional cooperative whore eased his physical demands.

But a night with a pleasure woman never lasted long.

When his spy reported a stay on the Caicos, he knew what island Mick would head to next. It was time for a second visit to Mrs. Pawes and her alluring attributes. Pity it wouldn't be on his ship, but the great bath would be a sweet substitute. He looked forward to showing it to her. Yes, the cool waters and secluded haven would be the perfect place to sample her sweetness again. At this time of year, the large bath would be full, probably overflowing. It would be a divine place to swim, to bathe—to seduce her.

He waited less than an hour for her to approach his shelter.

The dark pink flower was perfect! She hoped it was vivid enough to transfer some of its color to the paper. She carefully collected a handful of petals, noting they turned her fingers pinkish.

"Ideal."

Dropping them into a paper envelope, she cautiously folded it to keep from completely crushing the blossoms. She'd stop her search for the plant dyes in another hour and work with them to color as many sheets of paper as possible.

"What *are* you doing?"

She dropped the envelope and spun, not believing her ears. Her hand went to the pistol at her belt, but she didn't pull it.

What the hell? The man from the mirror? The Hollywood pirate? But the voice was Alan's!

He held his hands open, slowly rose from a crouched position, and nodded at her. "Delighted to see your eyes have returned to full function."

"You?" She blinked. "How?"

"Well, I brought the ship. It's anchored on the opposite side of the island from the Quill, no worry that Mick will fly into some unreasonable action and endanger himself. I am assuming you know my identity. You have asked about me across the Caribbean. I'm quite flattered." He took a step toward her.

She took a step back. "No, don't. I didn't ask about you because I was interested. What do you want, Silvestri? What are you planning? Villain!" She drew her pistol, held it steady.

He was not going to use her.

Damn, she wished he'd use her.

No, that wasn't what she wished!

He took another step, and she straightened her pistol and cocked it. "Don't come any closer."

He tilted his head at her. "It's quite dangerous to fire on me, dear Mrs. Pawes. My curse tends to see pistols explode or malfunction. I'd rather you not need medical care. I have other plans for the afternoon."

"Yeah, that curse. I really believe that." She tried to keep her voice steady and her hands firm on the pistol. But he looked so good! She fought to keep from letting her eyes roam up and down his body. She hadn't seen him that night. She'd only felt him. Damn, he was a good-looking man.

His hair wasn't a plain gray—it was nearly white. A lovely, snowy shade that fell in wavy strands nearly to his elbows. His sleeveless shirt, the color of caramel sand, revealed muscled arms, dark and wiry. And his eyes—such a deep shade of blue. Gazing into them reminded her of the Mediterranean Sea. "Sapphires," she murmured, and only after hearing her voice did she realize she'd spoken aloud.

"Yes, you like sapphires?" He took another step forward.

She flinched, pulling the trigger. The pistol simple fizzled. He moved faster than she thought possible, grabbing the pistol and flinging it away seconds before it gave a loud pop and broke apart into several pieces. He reached for her and her recent training broke through the shock.

She kicked him, twisted, and managed one step away before he snagged her arm and hauled her close, her back to his chest.

"Kicking when you wear sandals isn't terribly effective." His voice rumbled near her ear.

"Yeah. Well, how about a heel?" She delivered a backward kick straight to his crotch.

He folded, and she wrenched free. Spinning, she drew a knife, threw it and took off running.

Chapter Nine

She kicked him! Fucking bitch kicked him! And it landed close enough to bend him double. But folding in half meant the knife missed him. If he moved fast, he might stop his curse from finding some way to get her into more trouble.

What a woman! He pulled himself erect with a grin and stretched, adjusting himself as he recovered. Snatching her knife free, he took off after her. She wasn't a quiet runner. The sound of snapping branches and rustling greenery left no doubt where she'd passed.

Her stride was no match for his.

What did she mean, sapphires? His mind played with possibilities while he followed her path. He bent to pick up one of her sandals, a strap ripped loose. Even better, one bare foot should slow her down. Ten feet further, he stopped, tilted his head, and listened.

She'd gone to ground.

"Mrs. Pawes, please do come to your senses. I have no intention of hurting you, and I have no nefarious plans toward Captain March." He scanned the greenery, searching.

"Mrs. Pawes…."

"I don't trust you." Her voice came from a thicket—dense shrubbery, where one great tree reached toward the canopy roof.

"What have I done to earn your distrust?" He stepped to one side, head tilted. He held up her sandal. "Yes, left me vulnerable to a heel kick, but you're down one shoe."

"I like bare feet."

"I like your bare feet also." He raised his eyes, her voice floated above him. He surmised she wasn't at earth level. She was speaking softly. It was difficult to pinpoint her location in the thick foliage. He circled the thicket. "Mrs. Pawes, I have dreamed of you."

"Fuck."

That one word made him laugh. A sudden shower of leaves fell around him, and he looked up in time to reach out and catch her.

"Let me go!" She struggled in his arms.

"No," he said. He seized her flailing arms and trapped both wrists in one hand. He took a step to the tree and pressed her against it, keeping her secured between his body and the trunk. He raised her wrists and let her legs drop, making sure she didn't have room to knee him.

She took a breath to scream and he kissed her. He'd wanted to do that since seeing her earlier. He pressed tightly to her long enough to feel the tension leave her body and to make one light foray with his tongue. Pulling back with care, he examined her. Eyes a bit out of focus, mouth open while she took one deep breath after another. He released one wrist and she lowered it to the level of his arm, her fingers brushing against his bicep.

"Let me go, please."

"If you swear to stay calm, and not run away. I am not here to hurt you. Give me your word, and I will release you." He gazed at her, waiting.

"I promise. No more running."

"No more throwing knives or kicking."

She looked away a moment, then slid her gaze back to him. "Can I curse?"

"Of course. You wouldn't be Mrs. Pawes if you didn't curse." He let her other wrist go and took a step away. "Now, here is your sandal. It's a simple repair. Where is the other?"

He'd noted both her feet were bare.

"I kicked it off to climb."

"Well, find it. Walking on the sand without shoes is easy; hiking through the inland will leave your feet bloody. Give me your word that you will stay here, and I will fetch your basket."

"You know where it is? You can find it?" She spun, arms gesticulating. "I have no idea where I came from."

"I know this island. I won't be ten minutes." He stopped, studying her for a moment. He changed tactics, attempting a humble plea. He needed her to stay and trust him. "If you stay, I have a pleasant surprise for you when I get back."

"Uh huh. Bet you do. Go on. I'll find my sandal and stick around. I want my stuff."

He left her slowly circling the tree, eyes on the ground as she searched for her missing footwear. The thick brambles made it a bit of a challenge. Good, she'd be busy.

It took less than ten minutes. The basket was heavier than he would have thought, but after examining it, he understood. She brought enough supplies to keep her provisioned for the night, if need be. The thought made him smile.

He found her perched on a mossy rock, examining her broken sandal. "You're right. I can fix this with one of my needles, back on the ship. Good thing because I don't have a second pair."

She appeared remarkably calm, considering her furious reaction of earlier. He'd like to think it was the kiss, but doubted that.

"Where we're going will tear your feet to shreds. Stand," he directed her. To his surprise, she rose without argument. "Odd, I expected more battle."

"I'll fight later. Right now you have my basket. And…I want to talk to you."

"Good." He tossed the basket to her and swept her up in his arms. "You can't walk until we fix that sandal. I can do that at the bath."

She'd frozen, no doubt expecting him to drop her. Clutching the basket to her chest, she slowly relaxed. Clearing her throat, she said, "You're quite strong."

"Yes, I work the ship. And you have lost weight."

"I have. Working the ship is proving to be more exercise than I've ever known."

"Too many of the portal walkers are thin. Good to know that not all of you are starving."

She glared at him, surprising him with her lightning shift in temper. "*Oh really?* What is that? Some backhanded way of saying I'm fat?" She kicked out in a display of anger.

He stopped walking and stared down at her. "Fat? You're not fat. Damn, you travelers are fixated on weight issues. You are perfect. And I like how your hair is growing out."

"Didn't like it short? Was it too masculine for your romantic sensibilities?"

He rolled his eyes. "There is no pleasing you. Now, don't move—it's tricky here." He took several careful steps down a steep slope. The sound of running water grew louder. They were close to his goal.

She'd grown quiet. He turned a corner, rounding a large mossy boulder, and she softly asked him, "What were you dreaming? I mean, you couldn't be experiencing anything like me. Why did you mention it? Just trying to distract me?" He quite enjoyed it when she babbled.

"I've been dreaming of you, dear Mrs. Pawes. Always of you." He turned and gently set her down on a grassy area to protect her feet. She stared out at the bath, speechless. He took advantage of her preoccupation, hauling his hamper of goodies from its hiding place. He spread a blanket and set out the small feast he'd brought.

She eased her basket down, still gazing at the placid water.

He found Emily without words a wonderful experience. Spreading his hand he explained, "This is the large bath. It's over twenty feet across. The waterfall to the right is fed from a spring at the center of the island. It is quite a fortuitous geological feature. The autumn storms have seen it overflow and continue down to the beach. This is the larger bath of Bath Isle." He took a seat. At his side was a line that trailed into the water. He reeled it in.

"There is a smaller, I assume?" She was still mesmerized by the lovely pool. He thought her appreciation charming. A smile grew on her face with each passing moment.

"Yes, I'm sure the Quill crew is enjoying the smaller. The string of smaller baths receive more sun, are warmer, and cascade one from the other. Mick always preferred the sunny pools." He heard a soft clank and reached for the bottle at the end of the line. Ah, nice and cool.

She turned when he uncorked the bottle.

He held it out to her.

Turning the label, she read it, snickering. "French champagne? Isn't that unusual to have here, now?"

"There is nothing unusual here. Come, sit. I have bread, cheese, and fruit."

"A picnic? You brought me here for lunch?" She went to her knees, lifted the bottle and took a sip. "Okay. What the fuck. Why not?"

He chuckled. "You do have a filthy mouth. Have you no other swear words that cross your lips?"

"You're a shitfaced son of a bitch." She thought a moment before continuing, "A cockeyed, ass-kissing poser."

"What is a poser? And quite impressive language."

"Get me drunk, and I'm extremely foul. A poser is someone who fakes a persona. The Hollywood pirate."

"Explain, please." He continued to unpack the food.

"Hollywood is a city where no one is what they seem. Where dramatic stories are told by actors who sell the role so completely, they lose track of who they actually are and begin to buy into the idea that they are all that. I first saw your picture in my mirror. You were posed against a railing. I thought your costume full of flash and glitter. And you were older than most of the pirates Hollywood sells to the public." She took another good swallow of the champagne, washing down the bread and cheese he'd handed to her.

He reached for the bottle and she surrendered it.

"I saw that picture, in your mirror and assumed you were hunting for me. It startled me."

"When?" she demanded. "I lost that picture! It fell out of

the mirror at the festival before I woke up here. Or went insane—whichever. You couldn't have seen it!"

"The mirror slipped from your pack the morning I left you in bed. I nearly woke you to ask why you carried it, but when I looked again, only my face stared back at me. I left you and went looking for answers. I feared you were a trap."

"How would that have worked? I set a trap for you, tricking the vampires into blinding me?" She snorted. "Great plan. Wow. I suck at being a private eye."

She tossed a last bit of bread into her mouth, hauled her basket around and removed several of the morning's gatherings from it. He watched her set two flat boards on the ground then open the paper envelope with pink flowers in it. She painstakingly arranged the petals on a single sheet of paper, selective in how she spaced them. He inched closer to watch. Next, she set another sheet atop it and used a smooth, rounded tool to continually press the petals between the paper.

"What do you hope to accomplish with this? Some pagan ritual? Gathering flower essence?"

"Nope. I'm hoping to get some color into the paper for the books I craft. I want some color for the covers, and the dyers won't share their secrets." She lifted the top piece of paper carefully. There was a bit of pinkish blush to both top and bottom sheets. She sighed. "Too light. I was hoping for darker."

He grinned. "Stay here. I know what will transfer better."

When he returned, she'd worked two other of her morning collection. Some dark leaves pleased her. A group of yellow flowers gave her some highlights. He held out a branch of deep purple flowers. "Try these."

"*Oh!*" She smiled. "Those might work!"

He knelt beside her as she went through the process again, and this time, the results were quite satisfactory. She repeated her actions, mixing some of the petals and greenery, until they were gone. "Nice! I'll have some stock to work with. I hope the colors don't fade too quickly."

"Which dyers were stingy?" he asked, an idea growing for a third rendezvous.

"On St. Marteen. Some guild rules." She shrugged. "They

bought several books, but won't trade for dye. Bastards."

She packed away her papers, wood, and tools. "Will you show me where the purple flowers are?"

"Of course. Later."

"Later?" Spreading her hands, she looked directly at him. "What do you want from me? I won't spy on Mick for you. I won't betray my shipmates."

"That's good, I don't need you to spy on Mick. I already have a good source on the Quill. But thank you for crediting me with such a nefarious purpose."

Her hands fluttered. She glared at him, brow furrowed. "A spy?"

"No, a source. To make certain our two ships do not anchor near each other."

"Yet, you are here." Her voice dropped in volume.

"Because I needed to see you, Emily. And three months was too long. The dreams become impossible to sleep with."

"No, I'm not ready to talk about trying to sleep—tell me why Mick is determined against you. I know he says you stole the Immortal from his father, but what is your side of this?"

"You are certain I have a story and am simply not a villain and thief?" He tilted his head at her, interested in her reply. Why wouldn't she believe Mick?

Mrs. Pawes turned her legs, one thrust out in front of her, the other tucked under the first, and she crossed her arms and studied him. "I find there are generally at least two sides to any story. Usually more than two. He won't talk about it. Other than to glare and stomp off. That tells me there are truths he isn't facing or won't acknowledge. I find myself doubting his justification for this vendetta and I think he doubts it also. Just a sense I have."

"Ah. Did I steal the ship from his father? No. His father gambled her away, and I took her back." He reached toward her. "Toss me your sandal; I'll repair it while we discuss my villainy." He reached into a small pouch at his belt, and removed a large needle and some twine to set about insuring her foot safety.

She sniffed. "He lost it to you. The man with the curse of

good luck? Wouldn't that be stealing?"

"No, he didn't lose it to me. He lost it to another, and I won it from that other. Mick's father gambled to excess. Sometimes he was quite fortunate. He first took possession of the Immortal from a wager. He and Mick did quite well in the colonies, then came to the Caribbean. Daniel wanted to take his luck back to England. Where it deserted him. And he discovered opium."

"Opium. Oh. Does Mick know about that?"

"No, no reason to further tarnish his memories." He wove the twine through already existing holes, binding the strap on tightly—waiting for her to ask more. She was being unusually quiet for a woman, in his experience. He glanced up at her to see her staring intently at him. "Yes?"

"You care for Mick."

It was a statement, not a question. He declined to comment. After a long moment, she continued the interrogation.

"If he lost the ship to a wager, why is Mick convinced you stole it?"

"Daniel's solicitors delivered a letter at his death, accusing me of trickery, deceit, a true litany of all manner of criminal behavior. Mick was grieving and believed it. He never asked me for 'my side', Mrs. Pawes."

"And you never attempted to correct his misguided vengeance?"

"No." He intended his tone of voice to curtail any further curiosity.

She unwound her arms, bent her extended leg and clasped her hands atop the lifted knee. "But your curse could be at the heart of Daniel's luck changing. Right?"

"My curse *could* be at the heart of anything and everything that touches anyone who gets within 100 miles of me. Or not." He blew out a breath and met her eyes. "Generally, I need to be present. I wasn't, when he lost the ship. I did consider that my influence might have been involved. And I left funds with a lawyer to keep Daniel out of debtors' prison. To return the ship to him while he was lost in Madam Opium's embrace would have been irresponsible."

"That was extremely conscientious of you. And I bet he resented the hell out it." She shook her head, eyes still on his face. "Begrudged it, decided it was an admission of blame, and grew more and more bitter. Very tangled. And Mick started out using your curse for his good fortune. I heard how he kept company with you for some time. He stayed close enough to benefit from your luck, but kept enough distance to not be hurt. I can see Mick doing that. Which means he likely blames himself along with you for his father's losses. He tempted your curse to strike back, take its measure of blood one way or the other. How miserable." She looked away for a moment. "I've thought a great deal about how good luck could be a curse. No one else seems to blame you for the curse. Save for Mick."

His breath stilled; his mind went blank. How did she do that? It took him years to reach the same conclusion. He nodded. "I'm impressed, quite astute of you. Are you satisfied with your observations? The explanation of *my* side?" He tried not to sound bitter, but her prodding brought up thoughts he'd rather not revisit.

She shrugged. "It's a hypothesis. This luck thing sounded so nice, but it isn't, is it?"

He dropped the subject completely and ignored her question. Setting the sandal down, he leaned back. "In my dream, the same one I've had every night this week, we are in my cabin."

Chapter Ten

She swallowed nervously while he related his dream. It was the same one she kept having, causing her to toss and turn every night and wake wet and trembling on the edge of orgasm.

"...the light is enough. I lift you to the tabletop and ask permission. You nod and tremble...."

She shivered, instinctively hunching in a hypothetical effort to protect her breast.

He lifted his hand, voice full of passionate wonder. "...your right breast. My favorite. The needle slides through easily, and you give a small cry. I can feel your body, taut and frightened, but also"—his eyes met hers—"curious and alert, aware. I ease the ring through and close it. Wipe the small amount of blood away. I take a step back to look and it is perfect! The soft, burnished gold contrasts with the blush of your nipple. We kiss, and you are wild with demand."

She shivered, feeling that bite in her right nipple, remembering the dream with an aching bit of vividness.

"Hours later, you reciprocate and I take your ring. Small, silver." He stopped.

She stood up and turned away from him. Almost without thought, she stripped her shirt away, letting it fall to the grass at her feet.

"So hot," she heard herself mutter. "Too hot. Damned hot."

A small part of her wondered what she was doing, but it was miniscule. The larger part knew, understood. Knew the immediate need to cool her body. Mixed into the chaos, a voice screamed at her to tear his clothes off, make him give her what she wanted, what she needed.

She opted for the water, instead. She undid the small corset and let it fall atop her shirt and the tie of her breeches. Without looking at him, she stepped over the rocky edge of the bath and into the water.

Better. It wasn't too warm, wasn't too cold, but just right for her fevered skin. She moved into the deeper water and bent, then began to stroke her way across the bath, ducking her head down, trying to drive away the clamor inside. She swam underneath, enjoying the quiet, the cool. She let it wash away the need to think.

Finally, the need to breathe brought her back to the world. She stood, only inches of her face above the water. The rim of her basket showed at the edge of the pond. He was gone?

A moment later, the water stirred behind her. She glanced down and there he was, swimming around her. The surface was like glass.

How interesting. You'd think it would be full of insects and little plants and the rich muck of this world.

Her brain shut off when he rose before her. The long tendrils of his hair obscured half his face. He stayed low in the water, eye to eye with her. Long, strong arms swept around her, pulled her close until they were pressed together, from chest to crotch. His cock was blessedly stiff, but he left it pressed to her mound, no attempt to burrow home. Yet.

She sucked in a fast breath, her arms, floating near the surface, seemed to move with a mind of their own, and one closed around his shoulders. The other brushed the hair from his face, to reveal the other eye.

"'Like a wine-dark sea,'" she murmured. "I never knew what that meant until I sailed on the Mediterranean."

He smiled. "Ah, Homer's words. But this sea, this pool,

does not inspire such thoughts."

Men could be so dense.

"Your eyes, Alan. If I could drink your eyes, I would stay forever drunk."

One side of his mouth rose. "I find the same upon your lips, Pawes."

"Emily," she whispered, as his lips drew close to hers.

"Emily." He exhaled and kissed her.

Her arms wrapped around his neck, pulling herself higher. The boiling fire at her pussy demanded she attend to it.

This is totally insane. This is totally nuts. This is totally—oh, shit.

He held her from climbing atop him. Instead, he walked to the shore, constantly kissing her. The man kissed like a summer breeze after a long winter's night. This man could give lessons on kissing to Prince Charming. To Prince Not So Charming and the entire royal family. His mouth was wet enough, his tongue the perfect gentleman, or the rogue. He knew when to breathe, when to use his teeth to nibble. He made her forget how desperate she was to feel more of him, elsewhere.

He set her on a mossy ledge, releasing her mouth. She protested when he parted her legs and, standing between them, lowered his head. He still stood in the pool.

She lost the ability to think. The curse words poured from her, while her hands gripped his head, yanked at his hair until he peeled her fingers loose. Her legs tightened around his neck, and he removed them, spreading her wider.

"I want to look. I had no chance to admire this beauty at the Raven. Your eyes were too aware of light." He blew a cool breath across her and slipped his tongue down to dally with her again.

She'd caught her breath when he began again. And she'd thought he could kiss lips sweetly!

cঌ

When she dropped her clothing and walked into the pool, he'd been mesmerized. She'd already stroked her way nearly to the other side before he dropped his breeches, stripped away his shirt and joined her in the water.

It did little to cool his body, but it did bring focus to his mind. The water caressed his skin, energized him for further pursuit. She was a seal—he was the shark. She charmed him when she spoke of his eyes. She disarmed him, deflecting him so that he found control over the perpetual fever. He wanted to be buried in her cunny, but he wanted to feast his eyes upon it first.

Every morning, he woke to the scent of apples in his cabin. It drove him mad. Three days ago, the crew shouted when they netted a large wooden crate found floating near the ship. When they tore it open, a bounty of green apples spilled forth. Mama Lu told him to look for signs. One hell of an omen.

Once she lay open before him, he filled his eyes with the bounty revealed to him and tasted. Her curse words were a symphony, reaffirming his every move. Twice, she trembled then shuddered with release. Only then did he stand, climb out of the pool and lay beside her.

She still gasped as he meddled with her breasts. "I do like them both, but the right one, she was first and will always be my favorite. Shall I look for a ring, likened to what we both dream of?"

"Uhhhh!"

He chuckled at her inability to speak. He pinched the nipple and she flinched, lifting her head to snarl at him.

"Don't tease, you love it," he said.

"Not always!" she protested.

He gestured toward the blanket and she nodded, muttering, "I am insane."

"As much as I appreciate your mystification, I don't find it flattering that you continue to assert you are insane."

"Yeah. Well. All right. I admit you may not be the massive villain you're portrayed as, but you're still the perceived enemy of my captain's lover. I. Shouldn't. Be. Here."

"Don't fight it, dear Emily." He knelt down, guiding her to settle before him. "I don't know or understand. I don't care. I want what I want. You. Here. Now."

"Oh, shit. Me, too." She whimpered when he again claimed

her breast, marveling at how completely it filled his hand. He loved how her nipple hardened so delightfully against his palm. She reclined back on the blanket and he rose above her.

"This time, I want to see your eyes. See me. Watch me, Emily."

She gasped when he entered her. He waited no longer. He released her breast, locked his eyes on hers and moved. Her eyes widened, lost focus, found it again as he paused to give her time to recover. They were like two rich and wondrous coins. He moved harder and she spewed vulgarities. Determined to hear more than curse words from her, he held himself in check, keeping to a speed and rhythm that would put a younger man to the test.

At last, she lost the profanity and cried out his name. And he filled her, shuddering at the blessed release.

The afternoon was one of sweet excess.

The light failed and Emily started. "I have to head back. They'll be looking for me. If they find me here with you, it would be bad."

"They won't look until morning. By now, they assume you've made camp." He grasped her head and urged it back to his crotch. "You're not done."

"Alan! What if...?"

He increased the pressure. "You try a man's patience, Mrs. Pawes. I tell you, I know the crew. They won't come out after you now—it will be dark soon. And there is no moon tonight. They won't worry about you. The island is perfectly safe. Finish!"

"I'm not sure I'm doing this right." She examined his erect cock, one hand holding the base.

He laughed. "There is a wrong way?"

"I don't have a lot of experience."

To his satisfaction, she made a face at him when he laughed again, but dropped the objections. Her mouth was small, but the talent of her lips and tongue made up for that.

They finished off the bread and cheese some hours later, and he built a small fire. And they talked. She asked about the ship, about how his crew survived his curse.

He shrugged. "The Immortal itself is immune to the flip side of my affliction. The crew interacts little with me, but is devoted to the ship. I asked Mama Lu about it once. She agreed that my luck saw me hold the ship; my luck saw the crew able to work it. For without them, the ship would be of little use to me."

"Makes as much sense as anything." She traced a scar at his right side, followed by another that curved at his bicep. She went from one to another. He didn't know what she surmised about his scars, until she stopped and stared into his eyes.

"Each one is a dead man, right?" She sounded extremely serious.

He nodded, oddly reluctant to admit that fact.

"What is easiest? To kill a man outright, with pistol or sword, or knife, or to know that any who attempt to kill you will end up dead?"

The question unnerved him. He looked away, actually pondering the question. He cleared his throat. "I should have brought more wine."

"Alan, please. I want to know."

Deep breath.

"Outright." He kept it simple, hoped she would accept it and drop the subject.

"If this…" she traced a gash at his thigh, "…was the result of a ship's gun, did the entire gun crew pay?"

He lied. "I don't know."

Her brow creased. "In general, isn't that how it works? You threw my pistol away before it blew itself to pieces. If a ship's gun causes you harm, it will malfunction—it's only logical."

"Curses like mine aren't logical."

She thought a moment. "Oh, I think it is. It has to be. A guarantee of luck has to be deeply logical, or it's nothing more than normal luck, which fails on occasion." Her hand rose to touch the crescent line at his cheek. "And this? The man who did this must have seen his death coming."

"No man died for that."

"A woman?"

"No woman died. No one died. Enough." He hauled her

onto his lap. "You talk too much."

"No, you talk too little. About something that must be the bitterest part of your life. The one thing people can trust with Captain Silvestri is that bad luck will follow the good…for everyone and everything thing but you. Except, that is the worst bit of fortune there is. What a joke." Her voice petered off and her breathing deepened. He realized she slept.

What a long day. He stroked her head with slowness, barely stirring the cap of her silver-streaked hair. Thank God the necessity of a reply was gone. He wasn't certain he could have hidden the sorrow her observation brought to the surface. Carefully, he lowered her to the blanket, draped the loose bit of the fabric over her bare body and quietly left her.

He walked on the beach for more than an hour.

ॐ

She woke with the rising sun pouring onto her face. Lifting her head, she acknowledged he'd done it again. Disappeared before she woke.

"What the hell, he turns into a turnip when the sun rises?" she groused, pulling herself upright and letting the blanket drop.

The sound of morning songbirds, shrill and strident, filled the air. She was thankful there were no monkeys. Fun to watch, but she'd found them a real nuisance up close. Born thieves.

Well there were no monkeys, only an aged pirate who stole other things. She shook her head, distracting herself with a search for her clothing.

"Bastard could have left me something to eat." She pulled her breeches up and tied them, slipped into her sandals and lifted her shirt. Out fell two green apples. She laughed and bent to pick them up. "Where in the hell did the intrepid Captain Silvestri find green apples?"

She inhaled deeply, relishing their scent. She'd told Alan the night before that her perfume was fast disappearing and soon she'd have none. But if he found a source of green apples, she wondered if a perfumer might distill the scent.

"Not one of those hobbies that caught on with me," she reminisced, taking a crispy bite. She sat bare-breasted and finished one apple completely. Glancing around the area, she bent and buried half the apple core. She'd bury the second half somewhere else.

Once totally dressed, she thought about what to do about the blanket. She couldn't leave it. The environmentalist in her wouldn't allow that. But she hadn't left the Quill with a blanket.

She unpacked her basket and carefully fit the blanket in, as a liner. She maneuvered the original items back in and found a small bag tied to the handle, hanging outside the basket itself. She freed it, opened it, and poured out the contents.

"Oh, shit!" A pool of gold, silver and pearls filled her palm. Gingerly she lifted the strand. A soft gold chain, bits of silver detail work and a handful of cream-colored pearls came into view. "My God. He said he'd taken a galleon. What the hell am I going to do with this?"

Wear it.

Yeah, right. No one would notice if she turned up with a small fortune hanging around her neck.

Found it?

Oh, yes. Some foolish bit of royalty lost it while taking a walk.

She sighed, held it up to her chest and regretted she'd left her Kraken mirror in her cabin. Well, she'd figure out something. She wasn't going to leave it. She slipped it away and tucked it deep into the basket.

Her last discovery lay under the water bottle. A note.

Dear Emily,

Next time will be in my cabin. Follow the beach as it curves northwest. When you reach a rock bluff, turn inland. Keep the rocks to your right and you'll come out near the Quill. If you keep a sharp eye out, you will see the purple flowers, growing in the damp areas of the rock face.

Find the silver ring, Pawes. I will find the gold.

Alan Silvestri

She loved how he assumed she knew where north was. She

ought to follow the advice of bosun Janey and get a compass of her own. The woman did like to chatter, but she was also a master of protocol and practicality. Since she liked wandering the islands they stopped at, she thought a compass would give her more freedom. The ship was a congenial place to live, but provided little privacy—save for the inside of her cabin, and with Tink's lock picking abilities, even that wasn't guaranteed.

She'd secured Alan's first gift to the inside of her bag, and so far it escaped discovery. Next time she went ashore at a profitable port, she'd come back with it pinned to the outside and said she bought it or traded for it. As they'd conversed the night before, Alan assured her it was nothing Mick would recognize.

The walk back proved pleasant. She did find a fresh clump of the purple flowers, but took only a few. Now that she knew where they liked to grow, she'd leave them for another visit.

Last night was incredible. The entire afternoon shocked and surprised her with delight. Alan could keep going day and night. She raised an eyebrow. Wondered if the little, blue, magic pill crossed into this world.

Or the men here are naturally more vigorous.

It wasn't unusual for the deckhands to entertain the female officers multiple times a day. She bit her lip. Even her ability to enjoy repeated assaults without feeling raw and sore afterward amazed her. She was stronger after the last few months. Lost weight, slept better—when she wasn't dreaming about Alan and that damned nipple ring.

She reached up to cup her right breast, then shifted the heavy basket to her right arm. She'd thought about it for years. Tried to talk Tom into it. His concern about infection, about it doing some damage, his total lack of enthusiasm for it, dampened her thoughts. Now, with Alan, the idea wouldn't leave her alone.

Did she change when she arrived here? Or did this new world magically bring back her old self?

She found no answers before she reached the Quill. Janey came running up, shouting loudly to the rest. She clasped her hand and even took the basket. "I told them you'd figure it out.

Davis was ready to send out a search party, but Jezz and Mick believed me. Hurry! The Bountiful drew anchor this morning with an offer to join them in taking another French flute. Don't you love how that sounds?"

Janey babbled happily about the ship anchored near the Quill and the chance to liberate the shipment of silks and satins their victim carried. Emily listened, saying little. Janey seldom left much room in her conversations for comment. But what she said always proved useful, so Emily didn't mind.

"After that shipment we lifted last month, they're being a bit more difficult. Between the Bountiful and the Quill, they won't put up much of a fight. Neither of us are up to taking a galleon, though. We leave those to the Immortal and their bigger guns. The Spanish are nastier, anyway."

They climbed into the cutter, and Davis took up the oars. He smiled at her, his eyes drifting down her body. That glance made her shiver. She ought to take him up on a night in her cabin. Emily's thoughts drifted as they rejoined the Quill. She begged some time to catch up on sleep, promising to be ready when they reached their prey.

God knew, she wasn't much help in the last raid, but perhaps she'd do better this time. She could look fierce, if nothing else.

Before she lay down, the ship slipped into the wind. She held up the mirror, admiring the necklace—it looked incredible. Carefully, she lifted the precious piece of jewelry off, let it slide into the bag, before tucking the package into her pillowcase. She'd find a better hiding place after her nap.

She slid into sleep, one hand cradling her right breast, aching strangely. Did it ache at thought of being pierced, or at missing his hand? She had no idea.

Chapter Eleven

*T*hree days later, the battle for the French flute began. Emily stayed close to Davis, per Captain Jezebel's orders. The Bountiful took on the port side; the Quill took on the starboard. The Petit Monsieur put up a good fight, but they were outmanned and outgunned. But after the Quill negotiated their surrender, pulling close enough to lay a plank down between the ships, the tide turned.

Emily searched the captain's cabin, and once finished, turned to leave. The fabric being loaded on the Quill dazzled her. The richness of the colors literally made her mouth water. The crew babbled with excitement, unable to wait before peeling back the covers on the bolts and spilling the silks, satins and velvets out into the air. The blues, gold, reds, purples, and browns. It stunned Emily. She wondered what they were going to do with this treasure.

The Bountiful took the oil, the molasses, and whatever gold they found, even the weapons from the sailors, the gunpowder and ship's stores.

Emily gave the cabin one last scan, liking the small compass sitting on the table. With a shrug and an acknowledgement of the total disintegration of her morals, she pocketed it before turning to the door. Captain Jezebel stood outside the cabin, hands at her hips, surveying the action.

Suddenly, a man leaped to Jezzie's side, a pistol in his hand.

Emily froze when he pressed the pistol into the captain's side and shouted his demands, "Stop or I will spill her guts to the deck! Get off my ship!"

Crap. What to do? She was the only one with a clear shot of the gunman's back. She paused, slowly extracting a knife from her sheath, and turned it to throw.

She peered beyond Jezzie. As Davis stared at her, his chin bobbed, nothing blatant. She'd never killed a man....

"Not a smart move. You think we come here without our own secret weapon?" Jezzie spoke softly to the man holding her hostage.

Emily waited, her mouth dry at the thought of taking a man in back. But he threatened Jezzie.... He wasn't real, right? If she were insane, then she wouldn't be killing anyone.

His back presented a good target as he pulled Jezebel tighter to his side, shouting a reply, "You have nothing that will save you! If you order your crew to leave my ship, I will let you go!"

"*March!*" Jezzie called out. The rest of the crew stood frozen, hands to weapons. Waiting.

March? Oh, yeah. Michael March is how Mick introduced himself to her. Seemed like years ago.

Emily realized she hadn't seen Mick after the fight. He'd been everywhere during the battle. He was a deadly shot, with pistol and big gun and his was the shot that took down the Petit's main mast. But once they'd begun loading the cargo, Mick slid away. Not too surprising—hauling was grunt work. Mick didn't do menial chores.

From her viewpoint, she couldn't see Mick arrive, but she heard his voice.

"Dear Jezzie, you must make sure all weapons are confiscated."

He sounded lazy and uninterested for the most part. Emily held her knife, ready to throw.

"How is he a secret weapon?" the French Captain taunted Jezzie.

Good question.

Maureen O. Betita

"You know the one man who survived striking Silvestri?" Jezebel asked.

"That is a fable!" He practically spit in her ear.

"He survived Silvestri's curse! Struck him and survived! The curse still waits," Jezzie shouted.

The crew of the Petit murmured among themselves, and then shouted at their captain to let the woman go!

"Shall I come and assist you?" Mick's voice carried, full of an odd sort of deadly merriment.

"Non!"

"Non!"

Emily heard the shouts of fear and found the anxiety quite confusing. Jezzie's back stiffened. The man holding the pistol trembled and screamed at the crew to not be so foolish! It was a myth, he said, a trick! His grip on the captain's arm tightened as he pulled her even closer, the pistol must be bruising Jezebel's side, buried so hard below her ribcage. Emily tried to decide on a course of action.

"Do it, Pawes!"

The knife flew at the sound of Davis bellowing at her. Emily didn't even think about it. The sharp blade, purchased a week ago while ashore, sank deep into that broad back. Jezzie twisted free when the man screamed and spun. Emily froze at the sharp retort of a pistol. He'd fired at her!

Lucky for her, his aim was thrown off by Davis tackling him. But she was still hit? She crumpled to the deck, clutching at her side.

Damn! That hurt! She lifted her hand to her eyes and blinked at the bright blood. She came here to die this way?

Davis rushed into the room. "Pawes!"

Emily took a breath. "Am I going to die?"

He peeled the shirt away from her side and examined her wounds. "No. But I bet it stings. The ball struck that chair, and only splinters hit you. You'll be fine. Why did you wait?"

"I've never killed a man before, Davis. You sure I won't die? Get sepsis from the wood?" Her brain spun with the movies she'd seen, the horror stories of life before antibiotics.

"We'll get the splinters out, don't worry." He lifted her and

97

headed for the Quill.

"Are all men here so strong?" she muttered, more to herself than to him. She lifted her bloody palm and winced at the bright, red wetness. "Oh. I don't like that." She fainted.

She woke less than an hour later, placed on her side on a table in the ship's galley. The ship's cook painstakingly extracted each splinter. The slow tug of a particularly long extraction greeted her as she came to. Davis stood by, wiping away the blood. Emily winced, reaching consciousness. "Ouch."

"Sorry, lass. I won't leave any—I've got a poultice ready." Cookie kept working.

Emily looked out into the galley, her mind spinning. It hurt like hell, but she distracted herself by trying to figure it out. Mick was a secret weapon? Mick struck Alan and survived? How did that make him a secret weapon? Her head spun again, and bile rose in her throat.

"Cookie? I don't want to mess up your table."

Davis instantly switched sides of the table and held out a pan, making sure she didn't splatter vomit about the galley. He mopped at her face. Finally, she finished.

Cookie patted her hip. "One more and I should be done. You let me know if you feel anything feverish or your skin swells in the next few days. Pay close attention, you hear me?"

"Anything?" Emily snickered, trying to find humor in the idea.

"Here, take a sip of this." Davis held out a cup.

"Not a good idea to give me anything." Emily tried to pull away. "I'll only throw it up."

"This will make you better. Mama Lu's formula. Cookie's going to use one of her remedies on your side." Davis explained.

"Mama Lu, the miracle worker." Emily sighed, but allowed Davis to help her swallow the drink.

She tried to take a deep breath, but it made her moan.

"You'll sleep now and wake up in a few hours feeling better." Davis smiled at her and stroked her forehead.

"What did Jezzie mean? About Mick?" Emily tried to stay

focused, but the mental clouds rising from the drink filled her head. Before he could answer, she slipped into sleep.

∾

Alan went straight back to Tortuga, to report on the newest dream and see if Mama Lu could give him any fresh answers. Emily's questions filled his head with dread. He'd refused to consider the issues she'd raised after things turned sour with Mick. That idiot used to ask him, prod him, and they'd talked late into the night about the fallacies of his curse.

But he'd never told Mick the entire origin of his curse. He'd shared pieces of the story, trying to dissuade the man from seeking out Glacious. Mick could be such an idiot. Only Mama Lu knew everything. He'd gone to her seeking release and found someone with an uncommon gift of empathy. Expecting only magic, he'd found a friend. The wise woman promised to keep searching, and they'd become close. Over time, he'd discovered she held her own grudge against the ice queen. She didn't go into details; he didn't pry.

Mama Lu listened to him explain the new dream. Emily hadn't admitted to their having the exact same dream, but she'd let enough clues drop that he felt certain they'd suffered the same lust filled nights. He'd smiled when asked why they didn't dream about the bath also. And with that "also" he'd known the piercing dream was shared.

Mama Lu stroked her nose with one finger. A corner of her mouth lifted, then the opposite eyebrow and she beamed across the table at him. "This be the answer I been wondering 'bout!"

"Answer to what?"

"Since yer last visit, I been having visions from the albino Kraken. He wants to crack Glacious' ice palace, take her down into the deep. This ain't only about paying you back. You say Pawes shot you? And survived? That's two. I think that will be enough. Now, you make that dream come true, Alan. You get her to your ship and pierce her nipple. Have her do yours…catch the blood from both and this is what you do…."

He listened, resigned to follow the spell. She finished and he raised some questions.

"What if I use the needles?" he asked. "Place them in a glass vial, together. She's going to shy away from my trying to catch a drop of her blood in a glass."

"Fine, that works as well. What about the sexual fluids?" She leered, one eyebrow raised nearly to touch her braided hair.

"Easy to keep her too distracted to wonder what I'm doing there. I can sneak that easily enough. I have an idea of how to get her on board. Not certain how to get hold of the mirror." He paused. "Lu, I don't want to hurt her. Or...or lose her."

Mama Lu studied his face. Her dark eyes filled with sympathy, something he'd seen many times in the last ten years. But he took it from her—he always did. He shared much with her. She knew when his heart ached. But it wasn't pity. He abhorred pity.

She sighed. "I can't guarantee anything, Alan. You know how Glacious can be. She's a jealous bitch, and if you can't hide how you feel from her, she'll make it her business to destroy Mrs. Pawes. You can try, with Mick and the mirror. That might be enough to draw the Kraken to her palace. Mick can take care of himself. That woman, she been here long enough to learn some defense, but not enough to stand against Glacious."

"I won't take her into the palace. I can lure Mick; he'll cotton to what is going on quickly enough. Pawes won't, and she'll get hurt. Or dead. I'll take the chance on the mirror. And Mick."

It must work that way. That dear woman couldn't face the ice cold glare of his ice queen. Emily boiled with heat, with fire and fury. Glacious would do anything to snuff out that fire. Especially if she realized how much it warmed him.

Mama Lu shook her head. "You do the spell perfect, Alan. And you pray Mick remembers more than the hatred he holds."

"Em...Mrs. Pawes said something to me. About how Mick's anger doesn't ring authentic to her. I trust her judgment, Lu. Mick is playing a role because it suits him."

"You sure the role wasn't pretending to be your friend?" Lu always asked the difficult questions.

Alan took a deep breath, held it, let it out slowly. "No. But I trust him. And her. I have to. I need this done!"

"That's fine. Now, I know where ta get the ring you can use to pierce her. You give me two weeks and come back. And bring me some of that darkest rum. When you gonna see this dream inta reality? And where?" Mama Lu thrust the cork back into her bottle and set it aside, signaling he'd be leaving soon.

"She wants something from the dyers on St. Marteen. I'll make it worth their while. Set that up while you get the ring. What of the ring for her half of the dream? The silver one I will wear?" He rose from the table, anxious to keep the momentum going.

"I get that, too. And I'll make sure the ring is where she can find it when she reaches St. Marteen. See it happens soon, Alan."

"The tailors of Nassau haven't heard from the Quill yet. They are bound there next. I'll make sure the dyers offer to teach Mrs. Pawes, and send message to Nassau with enough promise of sharing dye secrets to lure her off the Quill in four weeks, Lu." He turned toward the door.

"You barely have time. Ya turn sixty-five in nine weeks."

"I know my own birth date, Lu. I'll be back in two." He left her snug house and began walking down the winding path to the harbor. He had some bribes to make.

᠅

Emily woke with her side aching. She tried to stretch and a moan escaped her.

"It will feel better soon."

She turned her head to see Davis propped on a stool in a corner of her cabin. She peered at him. "You watching me?"

"Yup. You need to take another dose. One to make you sleep more."

She must have made a face, for he chuckled.

"The Captain wants to see you once you've eaten," he said.

"Oh. I'd like to see her, too." Emily managed to rise with Davis's help. She took the cup he offered and swallowed the contents without discussion. Touching the bandage at her side, she grimaced to realize her breeches were gone. And she was wearing a new shirt.

"Did you undress me?"

"Yes."

She snorted.

"I don't take advantage of wounded women." He sounded offended.

"Hell, I didn't think you did! I'm not used to having anyone undress me." She looked around, not wanting to think about the last man who'd undressed her. Or the one before that.

"Only certain men, I know." Leaning on him, she made it from her cabin to the galley. She did not address his comment.

None of his business.

Once she'd eaten, her next stop was the Captain's quarters. She'd been in there before, but this visit was different. Jezebel acted quite formal, nodding when Emily entered, leaning on Davis.

She refused to be treated like an invalid in front of the captain and shook him off.

"Captain." Emily waited.

"Crewperson Pawes…it has come to my attention that you didn't follow the direction of Mr. Davis. Why did you delay in striking that bastard?" Jezebel asked. Her eyes betrayed no curiosity, despite the question. Her face gave no clue to what she might be feeling, holding a formal stillness.

This was not what Emily expected. She started, her spine straightening despite the way the stance pulled on her wounds. "Captain, ma'am, I'm not used to killing people. Sure, I've fought on deck and done some damage, but to throw a knife into someone's back? I'm so sorry if it disturbs you, my lack of bloodthirstiness, but I couldn't do it easily."

"The captain of the Petite held a pistol on me!" Jezz met her eyes straight. "I don't believe it is unusual for me to expect you to act according to your instructor and do something! Davis is the experienced man and you should have followed his lead."

"I did do something. I listened as you tried to talk him out of hurting you. I was ready to throw if the situation continued. I followed *your* lead." Emily found herself getting pissed.

Maybe she'd expected a bit of gratitude!

Jezzie threw her arms into the air. "I didn't know you were there, or my strategy would have been different. Davis! Leave us."

Emily swallowed nervously while the Captain paced a moment. Three steps to one side, three steps to the other, head bowed, arms clasped at her back. The cabin wasn't terribly big.

"Sit." Jezzie directed her to a chair.

"Ma'am, if I'm to continue being scolded, I'll stand, thank you."

"*Sit!*"

With a nervous swallow, Emily took a chair. It hurt to sit, but she tried not to let that show.

Jezzie walked behind her, leaned over and set her hands on Emily's shoulders. "Firstly, thank you for saving my life."

"Uh, you're welcome." Emily glanced from the corners of her eyes, trying to see the Captain. "I truly didn't know what to do. I'm sorry if the delay cost you something."

"Yes, well. Apologize to Mick. He doesn't want it bandied about the Caribbean that he is the one talked about. Luckily, he'd wrapped a scarf around his lower face. They shouldn't be able to describe him." Jezzie squeezed her shoulders and sat down across from her.

"Okay. I will, but for what? I didn't understand the strategy you used. Why would they care if he survived Silvestri's curse?" Emily found she truly wanted to understand this, considering she'd tried to kill the same man, albeit accidentally, and escaped unhurt. "Why did it nearly work?"

"You couldn't see Mick or the crew from where you were. Let me see if I can explain." Jezzie poured a measure of rum and offered some to Emily.

Being served by the captain was unusual, but Emily accepted the drink. Not to would be rude and offending the woman who offered her shelter didn't seem prudent.

Clearing her throat, the captain continued, "First, this strategy worked with the cloth merchant's ship because they were French. And the French are more superstitious than other sailors on the Caribbean. You know of Silvestri's curse?"

"Yeah. Basically, his good luck is stolen from the good luck of others around him. Even causing them bad luck." Emily sniffed, desperate to maintain some semblance of not caring,

"Yes. Ten years ago, Silvestri was able to remain in any one location three months maximum before the curse struck. As long as no one came against him, that is. Then his time shrank to three weeks, now it's down to three days. The shorter the time, the more vicious the bad luck grows. No one escapes. Mick did. Ten years ago. He nearly killed Silvestri. It's known someone escaped and assumed that the bad luck hovers around that person. I know it doesn't, but the French have reason to fear Silvestri's trail of bad luck."

"Why did Mick try to kill him? He knew of the curse, knew he couldn't succeed." Emily sipped at the rum, fascinated by the story.

Jezzie laughed. "Mick strike you as always thinking before he acts? He had reason to seek vengeance against Silvestri. Evidently, the good Captain Silvestri left the Caribbean soon after and spent some time in France. In France, the bad luck that followed him proved legendary. He bragged about it and was quite reckless. It's surprising the government didn't pay some magical worker to kill him."

"Yeah. This magic stuff…honestly?" Emily tilted her head at Jezebel. "I mean, I've been here over three months and aside from the insanity of finding modern conveniences scattered here and there. I haven't seen anything I'd call magic. There is really magic here?"

"Really. I've been here thirty years and I've seen enough to believe. Those splinters you took?"

Emily lifted a hand to her side. "Yeah?"

"In the historically accurate Caribbean, you'd be in a fever, possibly die from infection. Not here, because Mama Lu knows more than herbs. She knows magic. She does magic. Don't fight it; it works." The Captain locked eyes with her until Emily nodded.

"So, Mama Lu in Tortuga. Jeremy Verde in Nassau. Tobias Tiny in Barbados. They all know magic. Tobias started the story of Silvestri's curse growing stronger and he's likely right.

When the Immortal took a galleon a few weeks back, some idiot on that ship fired a single shot. The galleon blew up while the Immortal sailed away. Once, the idiot responsible would have merely tripped over a railing and drowned. This time? The curse took the whole ship."

"Jesus." Emily shuddered.

"I have good reason to keep Mick far from Silvestri. Tobias said when the curse closes in on Silvestri, it will draw the few who escaped back to it and swallow them. And everyone with them. Silvestri is down to three days before his affliction goes active? No one knows how much longer the plague has before it will swallow Alan Silvestri and anyone near him."

Emily's heart sped up and a sickness filled her gut. She pushed the rum away. A drop of sweat ran down her back. Was his wicked magic going to take her down? He'd batted the pistol away—just as he did with Mick? Would Silvestri survive the curse closing in? Why did she care? Damn.

She didn't betray how all this affected her. She leaned forward, curious, but didn't wipe the sudden sweat from her face. "Is Mick the only one?"

"I don't know. No one knows for sure. Perhaps Silvestri knows. I don't like to use Mick like I did earlier today. I resent having to use him. But you didn't know. And I do understand the hesitation of taking a man in the back. But if you wish to remain on this ship, you have to toughen up. Davis saw the opportunity for you to end it, and you hesitated. Don't pause again, Mrs. Pawes. Do you understand?"

"Yes, Ma'am." Emily bowed her head, furiously thinking. "Is Mick concerned about the curse closing in on him?"

"Mick doesn't believe in the curse, fool that he is. Although the truth is that he plays at not believing the curse. This ship keeps him secure, but he doesn't accept that. I paid all three magic workers to create a safe place here. We stay away from the Immortal, and we remain at sea. The curse will finish and take Silvestri eventually. Now, if we are done...? You need to return to your cabin, take another dose of Mama Lu's remedy and sleep again." Jezebel waited for Emily to rise from the table.

Emily stopped at the door. "Should I apologize to Mick?"

"No, he'd rather forget my eluding to his escape."

Emily nodded. Once back in her cabin, her mind spun with what she'd learned. She got some answers, but they weren't helpful. If Mick was safe on this ship...was she as well? What made Mick the exception, if the curse truly caught everyone?

Magic? Really?

She lay down on her cot and tried to make sense of what she'd been told, adding in what Silvestri related to her. Thinking of the curse only brought her more questions and a growing fear that she was being used in some way to get to Mick. If not by Silvestri directly, then by his curse.

Fuck.

Chapter Twelve

*E*mily recovered faster than she would have thought possible. The cook and Davis took good care of her. Her knife instructor never chided her for not throwing her blade when he first nodded at her, and none of the other pirates knew she missed her opportunity to help save the Captain. Mick acted as though the entire episode never occurred. Emily suspected her lack of taking the initiative wasn't told to everyone.

When they docked at Nassau, she went ashore. Janey burbled alongside as they walked the road to the center of the market terribly excited. "The party is in three weeks! Should be plenty of time to prepare a proper outfit and what a perfect time to take that cloth merchant. You have your favorite pieces with you, right?"

The effervescent pirate didn't wait for her to respond, only nodded as Emily held up the bundle of cloth.

"Good! The Tortuga celebration ball is incredible—you'll love it!"

Emily listened with amusement, wondering if she'd have time to continue her search for the way back to her time. She found this odd bit of the Caribbean comfortable, but she felt compelled to get back to California. She didn't belong here. She was supposed to be touring the Pacific Northwest in her new, snug little Mini-Winnie, writing that travel book she'd dreamed of for decades.

But the party sounded like a good time. If she didn't find her way home, well she'd enjoy having a lovely skirt or shirt made of her fabric to help her remember the sweet times.

She wanted to reach into her bundle and stroke the fabric. Modern silk didn't have such a luxurious feel. She'd claimed several yards of a deep reddish-brown, streaked through with golden dying flaws. She remembered her mother calling them that. Those sometimes serendipitous flaws added a uniqueness that Emily loved. The cloth wasn't on a bolt, but nearly tied up in knots. Likely too imperfect for most to see the unique value. But Emily fell in love with the streaks of gold.

She hoped the tailor would have some suggestions on making the most of her find. The cloth reminded her of the brilliant fall colors lining Walden Pond when she toured New England states one autumn.

She was no spring chicken to dress in the light blues and purples several of the other crew members selected. Though Tink found a red that nearly held a pulse. It fit the woman, and Emily knew she'd pair it with something black and ominous.

Emily's fabric didn't consist of much over two yards, but she figured a black skirt and a blouse from her stuff would suit her fine.

Janey led the way to a shabby tailor's store and handled the negotiations with an angry older man. Mr. Pomps.

Mr. Pomp-ass, Emily thought.

Nevertheless, she let him take her measurements without objection. Janey claimed the man was a genius with the needle. Afterward, they enjoyed a delicious afternoon tea, and Janey finally slowed her narrative, leaving Emily a chance to get a few words in.

"You aren't still hurting, are you?" Janey asked. "I mean, you're especially quiet today, and though I know I chatter…." She paused. "I'm worried. What is it?"

Emily sipped at the strong tea, almost good enough to substitute for coffee. A sudden welling of tears surprised her. She wiped at her eyelids and looked up to see the normally cheerful Janey near tears herself. The Bosun smiled crookedly and wiped at the dampness threatening to spill from her eyes.

"Oh, I'm sorry. I haven't felt right since the battle," Emily said.

"Is it killing the captain of the Petit? Because you didn't. Davis did." Janey turned away. "I found firing a pistol and wielding a sword hard at first. But after we were attacked, I got better at taking the initiative in battle."

"Davis killed him? I didn't know that. I wasn't even certain he was dead." She shook her head, determined to put it out of her mind. "When did someone attack the Quill?"

"Oh, the whole episode happened a few months before you showed up. These idiots didn't know who we were. Apparently, they spied on us from shore and thought we'd be an easy catch. We found out later they'd bragged about taking another ship and selling the women to the pasha in Arabia. Most know not to attack us." Janey picked at the remains of the pastries.

"Because of Mick?" Emily lowered her voice. "Jezzie explained it to me."

"Yeah, sometimes it's because of Mick. But mostly it's due to the spellwork Jezzie paid for. Our name refers to a curse. The writer's curse. Any who attack us risk a writer's curse."

"Okay. What would a writer's curse do?" Emily tilted her head.

"Oh! Well, a writer can write anything, right? So, anyone who sets it off might find themselves written into a cyclone. Or given pox that rots an arm, or a leg. Or some twitch or new habit that would see them laughed at across the Caribbean. It's non-specific, but quite effective."

"Who does the writing?"

"No idea. But it works. After we drove the idiots who attacked us off, they ended up wrecked on the far side of Tortuga. Then, thinking they were somewhere else, they charged the vampire's castle. They're dead now." Janey grinned. "No one messes with us."

"Sounds a lot like Silvestri's curse."

"No, nothing so widespread. The men we caught didn't suffer more than humiliation and being forced to work below decks for several months. And we don't bring bad luck being somewhere." Janey shuddered. "Damn. No, nothing like it!"

Emily wondered.

When they returned to the ship a few hours later, Emily found a message waiting for her from the dyers on St. Marteen, offering a trade. They needed several large ledgers. If she put them together, they would show her some tricks of the trade. But they wanted her there in three days, and she would need to stay with them a week.

She took the letter to Captain Jezebel.

"It's a good deal. The Lazy Day is sailing for St. Marteen with the morning tide. You can take passage on her, and we'll pick you up in ten days. We can head for Tortuga once you're back on board, the timing will work out perfectly." She set the letter down. "You want to learn something about the dyer's trade, right?"

"Yeah, I do. It's only…I've never been on another ship. Anything I need to know?" She shrugged.

"Be polite and stay out of trouble. It's a two day trip. Keep your knives handy in case some of the crew test you. I doubt you'll need to do more than wear them. How is your side feeling?"

"Much better. I'm a bit stiff, but that's about it," Emily said. "Janey told me about the writer's curse. Where'd you find that?"

"There used to be a writer on board. He came up with the idea, and between Mama Lu, Tobias, and Jeremy, it took." Jezzie smiled crookedly. "Quite devious."

"What happened to the writer?"

"He finished his book and returned to his world. Crosses over now and again, between book tours." Jezzie turned away. "You best get over to the Day and make sure they can take you. A week? Pack enough to be comfortable. I doubt the dyers will be generous with much of anything. I'm surprised they agreed to this; they must need new ledgers bad," she mumbled, leaving the cabin, "Someone likely hijacked their supplier."

Emily wondered who the author was and if she'd ever read his books. Then she did what the Captain suggested. The next morning, she boarded the Lazy Day for an uneventful two day voyage to St. Marteen.

❧

His messenger reported the strategy worked like a charm. He sailed about St. Marteen, waiting for the next step in his plan. After a quick stop near Nassau, undetected by the Quill, whose crew was taking their ease in the congenial port, he turned to the dyer's city.

She'd been stuck in the dyer's compound for four days by the time he arrived. He was standing at the single entrance to their private enclave when Emily appeared. Her clothing sported a great many stains and her hair stood on end even more than normal. This said a lot, considering the length it gained in the months since her arrival. She carried a large bag slung over one shoulder. With a scowl and an obscene gesture as the door slammed behind her, she stomped down toward town.

He slipped down an alley, signaling the two hired men to do their part with a curt nod of his head.

She was furious. They'd promised her a week; she'd slaved for two days over their ledgers, but was barely shown the basics at the dye vat. They'd hauled her out of bed before dawn to watch them perform some arcane ritual she assumed they considered spiritual. She figured what they thought a ritual was nothing more than chemistry, but wisely didn't voice that opinion. Over and over, they'd interrupt while she stood, trying to decipher how they were putting the color recipes together and drag her away to show her nothing helpful.

She figured they thought they were being quite accommodating. *Ha.*

Finally, they'd let her get some hands-on experience grinding some dried flower petals to add to water but ignored her attempts to ask about how this might be transferred to her needs for paper dye. By the fourth day, she had her fill of being given the run around. All the helping her was a ruse. It must be. No one was this deliberately obtuse!

She'd asked for a chance to speak to the man in charge. When she was shown into his workroom, she'd thanked them for the hospitality, but also requested to purchase a small amount of dye for the covers of her books on now and then, as she wasn't learning enough to do it on her own. He'd nodded, held up a hand and directed his sycophants to throw her out.

Hell.

No matter how much she ranted and raved about the deal they'd agreed to, they didn't hesitate to toss her to the curb. In less than thirty minutes, the door slammed behind her and she was out. The day nearly spent, she stomped down the street, wondering where she was going to stay for the next two nights.

When they grabbed her, she didn't stand a chance. A gag was thrust into her mouth, her satchel snatched away. She scrambled to reach her knives, but stopped with alacrity when the sound of pistol cocked near her head registered.

There was nothing to be gained by continuing to struggle at that moment. She resolved to wait for a more opportune time to attempt escape. If it came.

Her hands were tied behind her back and her knives removed from her belt. Her captors said nothing, and she couldn't see much detail in the dim light. She was blind, and then a bag was pulled over her head and secured. She was picked up and dropped into a larger bag, then thrown over someone's shoulder.

Her fear threatened to overwhelm any rational thought, and she fought not to cry, searching for anger to bring focus over how scared she was.

She'd wait for her chance and run. No, they'd tied her ankles together just before the bigger bag enveloped her. Damn, they were thorough.

They didn't hurt her or even feel her up. Was she being held for ransom? Who would pay to get her back?

Janey's comment about the crew of that other ship being sold to the pasha screamed through her mind and she whimpered. No, she was over fifty years old, plump, and wrinkled. Her boobs sagged. No self-respecting pasha would be interested in her for a sex toy.

Why, then? And who?

Did the dyers intend to dispose of her? Maybe it was some strange religious thing, and since she was an unbeliever, they were required to take her off the premises before slitting her throat? This wild surmising wasn't helping.

They were nearing the water. She heard the distinctive sound of waves striking wood. St. Marteen possessed a wooden sea wall of sorts she remembered. They must be walking near the port! She struggled, hoping to draw attention.

Her captor slapped her ass. "None of that, or I'll knock you out. No one cares, woman."

Emily lost the one bit of hope she'd harbored, and tears streaked her upside down face. She was going to die. She didn't want her existence to end this way. Sure, she figured her life was on the downslope, but she wasn't ready to reach the bottom.

And she'd never seen Ireland. She'd always hoped to see Ireland before she died.

Would Alan miss her?

◌◈

He waited near the cabin door, while they laid her on his bed. He tossed them a bag of coins, and the two ruffians from the port left the ship without speaking. Drawing closer, he observed the shudders wracking her body. His brows creased. She would be angry.

He tilted his head at her soft whimper.

Damn it.

Easing her to a sitting position, he undid the tie at the top of the bag. Drawing it down her torso, he spoke. "I thought to find you spitting mad and furious, plotting escape and contemplating some dire revenge."

Her head tossed when he pulled the smaller bag off. She stared at him from wet eyes. No, that wasn't anger. That was terror.

He shook his head. "Blast it, woman. I did not intend to frighten you." Pulling a clean, white cloth from his pocket, he wiped her eyes and nose, trying to frame an adequate apology.

He removed the gag and gathered her into his arms, trying

to offer comfort to balance the mistake. He should have been civilized. Offered an invitation! Damn it! How to explain that he feared her voluntary boarding of his ship might bring her to the attention of his cursed benefactress. He didn't trust the crew and suspected they would report any attempt at a normal relationship to Glacious. His misguided attempt to protect Emily terrified her.

She tried to pull away, then ranted and railed at him, choking back the sobs that shook her body. Every foul name he'd ever heard, and some he hadn't, poured from her. He stroked her sticky hair and said nothing, holding her close. He even hauled her legs up onto his lap and rocked her.

She finally wound down enough to cry, her face buried on his chest. She stopped trying to catch her breath and let her body find the equilibrium it needed. She took several deep breaths in recovery.

He heard her trying to say something and backed away to make room. She sniffed. "Untie me, please."

"When I'm certain you aren't going to attack me again." He attempted some reconciliation. "My curse, you know."

"Uh, huh, I'm not stupid." She sobbed again and shook her head. "Damn it, I hate to cry. Anyway! I'm not stupid enough to attack you. I know better. Please, untie me."

He stroked her face. "Why do you hate to cry?" Fifty years of wooing and seducing women convinced him that most women found tears cleansing. Unless they were using them to manipulate. But Emily didn't hold the artifice to use them as manipulation.

He felt her draw away from his touch, but his other arm held her tightly. Her eyes met his. "I don't like losing control. And I must look a mess." Her head ducked. "All swollen and snotty.

"Nonsense, you look soft and feminine and...."

She looked up and gave a great sniff.

He wiped at her nose. "And a little snotty. Now, I truly thought you'd simply be angry. I planned on teasing you away from anger, perhaps channel it to other actions." He attempted to soothe her with a play at joking and winked. She just stared at him.

He sighed. "I did not mean to see you reduced to terror. I am sorry."

"Yeah, okay. But what are you doing here?" She relaxed against him. "Damn it. I'm glad to see you. I didn't know who or what was happening. Janey told me about being attacked by white slavers and though I know they wouldn't want me, being old, but my imagination took off."

He listened while she rattled on about being old and wrinkled, even called herself a worthless hag. Rolled his eyes toward the ceiling and fell back on the bed, taking her with him. She shrieked when he rolled over and pinned her to the bed.

"Uh! My arms!"

He raised himself, taking his weight off her body. "In a moment. Now, you are not old. You certainly carry some wrinkles. Everyone does. Your breasts are not droopy, and you are enormously desirable."

She snorted at him and he growled, darted down and covered her mouth with his. He took his time, savoring the feel of her fighting him, and finally growing soft and complacent. He raised his hand and squeezed her breast, hard.

Her body arched toward him. Satisfied, he raised them both back to a sitting position and bent to untie her ankles. "You are not a dried-up, useless hag. You seem fixated on youth, and that truly must stop."

She shoved him back with her feet. Not hard enough to be considered an attack by his curse, but hard enough to show some displeasure. He glanced up at her. "Don't push my curse, dear Emily."

"It must be handy, when you do dastardly things, to toss your curse at your victims. *'Oh, hurting me will only hurt you more!'*" She parroted him with derision, eyes open and eyebrows raised. "And does anyone ever say, *'so worth it'?*"

She kicked him in the face.

He fell back, feeling the stir of his curse when she struck him. He whirled and caught her when she overbalanced and fell from the bed. A moment slower and her head would have struck the deck. He clutched at her, heart beating fast.

She wiggled out of his grasp, pushed herself away. Propped against the drawers supporting his bed, she glared at him.

He smiled, never betraying the rush of terror she'd given him.

He took a breath, let it out slowly. "No, no one has ever said that. Until now."

She snickered.

"Emily, dear." He surveyed her sweaty and tattered visage. "You need a bath. I'll have one prepared." Climbing to his feet, he left her on the floor. "Stay down, safest place for you right now."

Turning away, he spoke with authority, his voice level and carrying no lilt. "Do not attempt to engage my crew. They are more loyal to the ship than to me. We have tonight and tomorrow before the Quill looks to retrieve you. Let's make the most of it."

"I'll need my hands to bathe!"

"You'll have mine." He chuckled at her silence and set about giving the orders necessary to see the ship leave port and a bath prepared for his guest. His spies reported she'd purchased the small silver ring Mama Lu made certain intercepted her path. He reached into his pocket and fondled the lovely gold one the magic woman gave him. They'd reach a calm bay by the dawn, and she'd be ready.

Chapter Thirteen

*O*nce the initial adrenaline spun down, Emily felt her body give up. He'd stirred her with that kiss, making her go limp. After her near fall, she tried to enjoy knowing where she'd ended up. Not aboard a slave ship, not heading for the Middle East, but sitting aboard Silvestri's ship. The uncertainty of being kidnapped disappeared. He wasn't going to keep her; he'd spoken of a time limit. He'd be back and she wondered what he planned this time. She'd never been courted before, and for lack of a better word, she recognized this bit of drama was his attempt to court her. Even if the goal of that courtship was nothing more than some damned good sex. She could live with that.

She stretched her legs and surveyed her sandals. Damn, the stitching was giving way again.

Tevas were sturdy, but nothing was meant to be worn every day for months on end. If she didn't get out of here soon, she would need to purchase some shoes. Some real pirate boots might impress the locals at the next pirate festival, once she returned to her California.

Would she ever attend those again? After being here?

Maybe.

She'd be able to laugh at the things that the enactors got wrong and marvel at the things that ended up dead on. If anything she observed here was truly right. Truly accurate.

A hot shower would be nice.

And a pizza.

Closing her eyes, she shifted to make her hands more comfortable. She thought about pizza, the tart bite of good tomato sauce, the crunch of sourdough crust and the burn of red pepper flakes. Her belly grumbled and her mouth watered. But it served to keep her distracted while the fussing continued in the front of the cabin. She'd seen the sailors enter, ignoring her as they carried in a large tub and filled it with bucket after bucket of water.

She drifted into a nap and woke to Alan lifting her to her feet.

"This shirt is hopelessly stained, don't you agree?" he asked.

His eyes glittered in the light of several newly lit lanterns. The flash of a knife struck her eyes and she heard the fabric of her shirt being torn away. She opened her mouth to object, but shut it. He was right. The dyers seemed to take particular delight in seeing her dingy white shirt splattered with off-colored dyes. It galled her to hear them mutter derisively about some batch of dye, then nonchalantly fling it in her direction. Once she'd caught one actually wiping his hands on the back of her shirt. It was useless to object, so she'd borne their derision without making a fuss. It was just a shirt and they were going to show her how to dye things! *Ha.*

"Ah, a new corset! But nicely light and flexible. I thought I felt something odd."

"Don't cut it off, please. It took a lot of searching to find a modern bra that fit me, so my not-droopy boobs wouldn't droop." She glanced down at the bra. "You unhook it at the back, Alan."

Fighting would waste time. She'd rather be in the bath she'd noticed when he'd lifted her. An old fashioned copper tub with clouds of steam rising from the water.

She couldn't wait.

He carefully examined the bra after he'd removed it.

She was glad she'd found one without straps. He might

have discarded her objections and cut them away otherwise, since he seemed determined to leave her hands tied.

Tossing it to one side, he remarked, "Quite ingenious."

"Well, the leather bustier got too hot." She stopped talking when he knelt and pulled the tie of her breeches open. They were too large for her. She figured she'd dropped nearly twenty pounds since arriving. Not for lack of food, but lack of junk food as well as all the exercise. She didn't mind the loss. Not at all.

He let them drop to pool at her feet and leaned back to rest on his ankles, eyes roaming up and down her body.

She sighed, her body reacting to the examination. Even his eyes warmed her to the point of boiling.

He was certainly spry for a man his age. He shot to his feet, shaking his head, and led her to the bath.

She balked at stepping into the clean water.

"Wait! Let me wipe some of the grime off my feet first!"

He paused. "That is what the bath is for." He spoke slowly with a studied emphasis, as though she were an idiot.

She grimaced at him. "Yes. And I'm going to be lying back in a tub of grimy water if I don't at least wipe them off first, barbarian."

"Fine, no need to be touchy. I'd never thought of it much. Always assumed the grime rested at the bottom of the tub." He congenially babbled on, hauling a worn towel off a nearby chair, dipping it into the water and washing her feet.

The gesture totally undid her. Her fingers flexed behind her back, wanting to bury them in his head of silvery hair and hold him with a tenderness she found surprising.

A man washing her feet was a new experience.

He took such care. Making sure she was balanced against a nearby vertical beam, lifting her feet one at a time, slowly wiping, rubbing. She watched, mesmerized. He completed freeing her feet of grime all the way to the flesh between her toes and lifted his eyes to meet hers. He smiled as his gaze dropped to gaze upon her pussy, less than a foot from his face.

She gasped when he surged to his feet, lifted her and, with a single step, gingerly deposited her into the steaming water.

"Jesus!" she gasped. "Hot!"

"Isn't that the idea?" He chuckled. He pulled the chair closer and proceeded to use a fresh cloth to lather up a rough bit of soap. He paused, stripped off his shirt, and then, proceeded to scrub her clean.

He was intent and she appreciated the attention. The dyers were frugal with water, and though she saw their steam baths, she wasn't allowed their use.

Shitheads.

"I wish you'd undo my hands, Alan."

"You'll splash me, and I'm wet enough." He drew back and winked at her. "For now."

"What if I give you my word?" she asked.

"The word of a pirate? Have you any idea how little that is worth?"

"I'm a pirate? Hey, I'm only staying with pirates...and fucking one...and...oh, well. I guess I'm a pirate. How the hell did that happen?"

His scrub cloth hit her side, and she flinched.

"What is that?" he asked, suddenly quite serious.

"Oh, a bit of pirating adventure," she explained. He moved to the other side of the tub and urged her up.

He jerked the knots loose from her wrists and moved her arm away from her side. She flexed her fingers, and gently moved her shoulders, easing the tightness. He'd left a lot of room between her hands, but it still wasn't a position she'd been comfortable in.

"Someone did a good job with this." His fingers were gently, probing the cuts and ragged edge of the one wound requiring a few stitches. "How did it happen?"

"We took a cloth merchant and things got a little dicey. I knifed someone in the back, but he got a shot off at me. The ball smashed into a chair instead of me and I got hit by the splinters."

He grunted. "You knifed someone in the back? I doubt that."

He helped her sit again and studied her face.

She smiled crookedly. "I threw my knife into his back,

honestly. He held Jezzie with a pistol, trying to drive us off."

"Is he dead?" His brilliant blue eyes appeared black in the scant light. She swallowed at the anger there.

"Uh. Yeah. Not me—one of the crew did it. He didn't even know I was there until my knife hit."

"I imagine he didn't..." His head bowed and a shudder ran through his frame. "I thought the Quill's captain more sensible than to pirate against a well-armed crew."

She raised her voice in protest. "They weren't well-armed! The captain hid a pistol. We bested them! We were already loading the cargo when this happened. A bunch of superstitious Frenchmen." She stopped. She was not going into detail about Mick's role or what Jezzie told her. She looked away. "We took some lovely cloth. I left a piece for a blouse at the tailor's in Nassau."

He listened to her go off on another topic, knowing she'd left out something significant. He'd find out later.

Seeing her wounds shook him. He might have lost her without warning, no chance to see her again or tell her anything. He knew Captain Jezebel took care with the ships they raided, researching their armament thoroughly. A French merchant ship should have been easy prey. And for cloth, of course. With the celebration on the horizon, everyone was excited and looking for new clothing. Jezebel would be able to sell what the crew didn't keep for a bloody fortune. Especially if she left it a little late. The scramble to outdo each other always brought out the flash and sparkle on Tortuga.

Saying nothing, he shifted his position and helped her wash her hair.

What would the world say, seeing the feared Captain Alan Silvestri washing a woman's hair? Or her feet earlier?

Hell, the world wasn't here. She was.

And he liked washing her hair. It filled his hands, thick and luxurious. He wondered what it would be like long, drifting over his body as she rode him.

Fuck. The bath was over. He dunked her under the water with little warning. He couldn't stand it any longer. She came up sputtering, and he tossed her another towel and paced back to the bed.

Tossing his clothing aside, he shoved the covers back and settled onto the clean sheets, watching her attempt to ignore him. He wasn't fooled.

❧

The cabin was warm enough. She lingered over drying herself, completely aware of his eyes following her every movement. Her body, already fired up by his hands in the bath, did not appreciate the time she took. But she knew once she fell into that bed, there'd be no talk.

Well, not talk of much sense.

And she wanted to ask about a few things first.

"How did you know I'd be here, Alan? Your Quill spy keeps you informed on every crewmember's plans?" She rubbed her hair dry. It was growing too long, but she wasn't certain about having anyone here cut it.

He didn't reply, and she spun away, heading for the door.

"We're already at sea, Mrs. Pawes. Not to mention my crew would find your present state of undress quite entertaining."

His droll voice signaled, perhaps, a willingness to talk?

She turned back to him. "How did you know I was here?"

"You don't think the dyers changed their minds for a few ledgers, do you?" He laughed.

Emily narrowed her eyes. "You set this up?"

"I am quite determined in my pursuit of you."

"Yeah, well. Next time you can pay them enough that they sincerely help me."

Should she have told him that? He rose, his long legs dangling to the floor, then he stood and walked with deliberation toward her. The look on his face made her take a step back.

"Alan, they showed me enough. They only...what?"

He put a hand on her face. "You are concerned for them?"

"I do not want to be responsible for you camping on their doorstep for a week. I've heard enough about how your curse works. And I take on enough pointless guilt. Alan, what are you going to do?"

He stroked her cheek with his thumb, eyes locked on hers.

He lifted her other hand and set it on his erect cock, letting the towel fall to the deck.

"I'm going to take you to bed and fuck you." He bent, seized her lips with his and pressed tightly, making clear his intentions. His cock leaped in her hand.

It proved difficult, but she pulled free, lingering just a moment to run a thumb over the weeping tip. His kiss ended and she stepped away. Her body nearly shrieked in disappointment.

"No, what are you going to do to the dyers?" She turned her back and bent to pick up the towel. He grabbed at her hips, pressing her against his cock.

He ground against her and her cunt wept with want.

"Alan," she whispered.

"No, I won't go after them. I'm disappointed in them. But I shouldn't be. Their trade is their religion. The religious are always idiots. They aren't going to benefit from this, Emily. Grant me the opportunity to make it clear to them. When I pay for something, I expect goods to be delivered."

"How...?" She lifted up and leaned against him. His hands rose to cup her breasts. She moaned, rapidly coming undone. "How do you do this to me? Why?"

"Because...I want to." He whispered those words. She wondered at the pause, if it meant anything. What would he have said?

Because she let him?

Because she was desperate?

Because...?

He squeezed her right breast, the nipple between demanding fingers. "This one. I have the ring."

She sagged.

He swept her into his arms and strode to the bed. Instead of setting her onto the sheets, he set her back on her feet. The deck was smoother than she'd expect wood to be. No danger of splinters. She stood, confused as he returned to the bed. Reclining quite deliciously before her, he patted the pad next to him. "Your choice, Mrs. Pawes."

She waited, raising a hand to cup the breast he'd nearly

bruised. His eyes burned her. She fought to catch her breath. "You have the ring?"

"A perfect gold loop."

Shit.

"I found a silver one. When I reached St. Marteen. A street vendor pushed it at me. Alan, I don't understand this magic. This level of coincidence." Her voice trembled, no matter how she fought to keep it even. She turned away from him, her eyes scanning the cabin. "Where is my bag? Did they take my bag?"

A sense of panic rose in her. Everything she needed to make the books was in her bag! And her knives! Did they keep her knives?

"Mrs. Pawes, I am rejected in favor of what? Your bag? It's at the other side of the table." This time he sounded wounded, even bored.

She scurried over to the shadows, hauled her bag up onto the table. "My knives?" She shot a glance at him. "Get over it, Alan. I'll be there in a minute." One by one, she set her supplies out. And near the middle, she found a small box. She pulled it out, set it down. "My knives! They took my knives?"

"No, I put them away. You'll have them when you leave the ship."

Oh.

She ran her free hand through her hair, returning to the bed. He lay back, staring at the ceiling. One hand rested at his cock, stroking it idly.

She set the box on his chest.

Clearing her throat, she tried to make it clear that no matter his intentions, she wasn't going to go along with everything he planned. "You scared the shit out of me. Hired thugs to kidnap me, nearly drowned me in a tub, and offered me no food."

She watched as he lifted the box, examined it, and slowly removed the silver ring she'd bought. She wasn't sure why she bought it, what she intended. She wasn't even considering the outrageous idea of piercing his nipple.

He said nothing in response as he examined the ring, set it back into the box, and tucked it away. Instead, he turned on his side to watch her. Again, he patted the mattress.

She should be pissy, but his confidence was oddly compelling. Without objecting, she joined him.

"When did you last bathe?" she asked him. It shouldn't matter, but it did.

Hell, if she was going to go along with everything he'd set up, she might as well have one or two small demands.

"This morning," he answered.

"I'm not sure about my...about piercing...uh...either," she stuttered, when he swept an arm around her, pulling her atop him. His cock nestled at her thatch. It grew hard to think.

In the midst of her body's roar of want, he answered her concern. "We'll talk about the piercings later. Once we've both satisfied other needs"

His large hands gripped the inside of her thighs, spreading her more thoroughly around him. She couldn't take her eyes away, breathlessly watching every move he made, every expression on his face. She'd never experienced a response within herself that was so sharp and alert. She wanted to watch him, see for herself the power she held at this moment. For once, she felt in control and was going to enjoy it, if only for a little while.

She swiveled her hips. He drew a sharp breath, but his eyes were locked like a laser at the juncture where cock met cunt but was not yet welcomed inside.

She squeezed her thighs and he licked his lips. It was fascinating to observe how intently he paid attention.

She made Silvestri pay attention? Was that it? Or was there more to it. She didn't know.

❧

Silvestri battled with himself not to roar, grip her hips and hold her as he drove upward, into her sweet heat. It hurled him toward insanity. Every move she made saw him fight with the urge to pillage. To take what he wanted would be normal, but he waited and wasn't sure why.

Her hot cunny called to him, and he found it fascinating. He couldn't look away, lost in her manipulation, playing with him. If she didn't move soon, he'd spill like a boy. She stopped, raised up on her knees and gradually slid downward, taking him in. He groaned; his hands shifted to the outside of her thighs, to her ass. And she lowered herself onto him, around him...onto his chest. And he held her, wanting to know this place for the rest of his life.

Hours later, she slept and he kept watch over her. How totally unplanned, these deep echoes of tenderness he found as he stroked the lines around her eyes. So softly, she didn't stir. This woman he would keep safe. He'd use her, yes. Sent by the Kraken to give him hope, he'd be a fool not to follow the clues. He bet she succeeded beyond any goal that great creature envisioned. Through her, he found a reason to fight. And he'd find freedom.

Chapter Fourteen

She woke the next morning to find he'd left the cabin. She moaned. Her battered body was going to ache. Stretching, she blinked in amazement at the lack of pain. In fact, she hadn't felt this good in decades. Raising one arm, she examined it. Still a bit flabby, still some wiggly skin at the upper part. But underneath all that, her other hand traced the new muscles. In the faint light she realized how dark her skin had grown.

In the months she'd been here, in this strange new world, she'd seen no sign of skin cancer. And she'd looked. She'd asked the others if they worried about it. Tink laughed at her. She did that often.

Lifting a leg from the covers, she eyed it with some pleasure. It took months to stop the morning groans. When she'd first started helping on the Quill, she hurt—constantly. She'd been fairly useless for a long time. Stubbornness saw her persevere.

Sure, she took up the hobby of book binding at the captain's suggestion. And part of the money she brought in went toward ships funds. She'd wanted to do more. And she learned. Helping with lines, mending sails, cleaning. All that fresh air, the sunshine, the work, it did what steady visits to the gym didn't.

"I'll never be skinny, but I'm thinner," she spoke to her

extended leg.

"Heaven forbid you grow skinny." Alan stepped away from a dark alcove.

She dropped her leg and sat up. "Where the hell did you come from?"

He adjusted his breeches. "A small privy. Not much more than a simple hole, but better than the alternative."

"Bathroom? I don't have to use a bed pan or...?" She stopped. The Quill did boast one rather impressive bathroom, but the rest were little more than old-fashioned outhouses. On a ship, that confused her to no end.

Janey explained that the inside privies were sanitary due to a chemical mix tossed into the holding area that broke it down to basics.

"We wash them out every week." She'd grinned, obviously proud.

"They have this on every ship?" Emily asked.

"Not every, but most. The French don't believe in it. They think it's some evil thing that will eat through their hulls. It might if they don't wash it out."

Well, Silvestri wasn't French, so she shouldn't be surprised.

He pulled a robe from a drawer and held it open, beckoning to her with a broad smile. She eyed the robe with pleasure. A lovely shade of blue, almost turquoise, and covered with intricate embroidery of birds and blossoms. The colors mesmerized her.

He lifted it higher and she gave in, slipping from the bed and straight to the robe. He slid it over her shoulders and stroked her arms, mimicking the way it caressed her skin.

"This is the softest thing I've ever felt." She touched the sleeves.

"Not the softest, but I admit, it's close," he answered.

With a snort, she stepped away. "This privy, I need shoes?"

"No, it's clean." He gestured toward the alcove. "I'll collect breakfast while you see to your necessities."

She nodded, heading for the...what did they call them on a ship? The head? He'd fed her last night, after an initial bout of fucking that left her gasping. And they'd drunk, but not to excess. She was thankful. Throwing up on the Quill wasn't pleasant, no matter what they were tossing into the privy, er head.

They had done much more than eat. The passion between them flat out amazed her every time.

They ate and chatted. He asked about where she'd come from. About the past, about her family. Nothing about the Quill. Nothing about Mick.

"Did you gain anything from your days with the dye guild?" He stroked her hand where it rested on the paper she'd unloaded from her bag.

Why did he make her nervous?

She pulled her hand back, feeling a need for some distance. "Yeah. Some basic formulas I can use for a few colors. A light blue and a burnt red, of sorts. Would you like to see?"

He nodded, and she pulled out two sheets of a thick paper. "They wouldn't let me actually do more, and I snuck the directions out. I don't have a good memory, so I'd excuse myself to use the bathroom to write it down. They didn't want me to write *anything* down." She pulled out a tiny booklet, not much bigger than her palm and grinned. "Thank God pencils seem to find their own little portals." She opened the book and the stub of a pencil fell out.

"Quite sneaky of you."

"I try."

He carefully unrolled the blue sheet. "This is nice. I imagine if the paper will absorb it, you could deepen the color?"

"Yeah, but I wasn't going to experiment with this. I only have so much." She'd cheered her success when the off-white sheet took the dye nicely. "I can use this to make two books."

"Show me how you do it." He sat back, watching while she pulled out several plain sheets of paper. She folded them carefully in half, used a smooth bit of wood to make a clean crease. She repeated the process. It was mindless, but oddly calming. She smiled while working, glancing up at him now and again. He didn't ask anything.

She formed a dozen folios, the single sheets folded in half, and tucked them together. "This is called a signature, the basic form of the book." Holding a straight edged bit of hard wood, she looked at Silvestri. "I need a sharp knife with a narrow point."

He grinned and handed her a small blade from his belt. "It is sharp."

"You may need to sharpen it again when I'm done. Paper tends to dull the edge." She lined the paper up carefully, set the wood down and trimmed off the uneven edges. Next, she opened the signature. She used the tip of the knife like a drill and placed three holes at the fold.

She cut the cover next, from the blue he'd admired. She made it a fraction larger than the signature. "This is a simple book. Nothing fancy like those stupid ledgers they made me put together. Hey!" She looked over at him. "If you bribed them to teach me, why the ledgers?"

"An excuse. And I can always use a ledger or two. I keep accurate books." Those blue eyes were hard to resist, studying her.

She snickered. "What do you need books for? Not that I'm saying you can't read or anything. Or write. You draw in them?"

He smiled at her, raised a single eyebrow. "I am a successful businessman."

"Yeah, I bet. Lucky curses might explain some of the idiots with fortunes in *my* time."

"I am not an idiot, and I am more than my curse."

His voice lowered, and she glanced away from the book. He wasn't watching her any more, but looking into a dark corner of the cabin. She sighed. She and her big mouth.

"Okay, I know that. I'm sorry. Alan, were you born with this curse?"

Might as well try to get some real information out of him while she worked.

"No. I wasn't. I was born the fifth son of an impoverished English lord. I was sent to sea to make my way. Big brother snagged a rich enough wife to buy me a commission as a powder boy, at twelve. Two years later, I escaped the navy and joined a pirate crew. I'm sure I disappointed my brother, but he was always a pig-faced son of a sow." He scowled.

"Oh, well. Don't hold anything back there, Alan."

Must be more to it. Family stories tended to be full of many dramas. She'd been an only child, with few dramas. But she'd observed them from friends and neighbors.

She took some fine twine from her bag, threaded it into the holes and began the intricate weaving that brought it together. "What next? You rose through the ranks to captain, raided the Spanish Main, rallied a fine and loyal crew, and rescued some fair maiden from a corrupt admiral...." She glanced up to see him staring at her. She shrugged. "Sorry, Hollywood pirates. Lots of drama and romance, high seas adventure...." Her voice faded. "Never mind."

"Sounds like some silly melodrama. No. But I did meet my fate at fifteen. That's when I was cursed." He stood up and bent to examine the book. "That is quite nice. I've seen your work in several ports. I hope you get a good price."

"I do." She tied the final knot and set the book on the table. "Here, you can keep track of the ships you take, or the women you fuck or...something useful."

He lifted the book and smiled at her. "Something useful. Thank you. And I have a gift for you."

She put her supplies away, wondering what he planned to give her. A sudden thought lifted her head. "I don't want anything from that galleon. It wouldn't feel right."

"That galleon? What have you heard about a galleon?" He was searching through a tall cupboard of sorts. She didn't like the tone of his voice.

"Uh...nothing? Never mind." She lifted her bag and tucked it back into the corner where it rested before. Threading her fingers together, she sighed and lowered her head to the table. "I'm no good at this." Closing her eyes, she swallowed the sudden attack of nerves.

"No good at what? Lying? That is true; you have no talent for it." A door slammed and she shrank. She really didn't want to see him angry. He may have sounded as though it didn't matter, but the slam of that cupboard door told another story.

She wasn't fooled.

"You heard about the galleon. I did not wish for their deaths, Emily."

She heard him approach and sit next to her on the bench.

"I know that. At least, I think I know that. But I actually don't know anything." She took a deep breath, raised her head and met his eyes. "I think I'm insane. I think I drank some bad stuff at that pirate fair and am suffering one phenomenal delusion. Or I fell, struck my head and am in a coma. Or maybe I finally suffered a nervous breakdown…."

He touched her head and she melted into the security of his arms. She wasn't scared when she was with him.

This must be what she trusted him with. She trusted him to keep her safe.

∽

He set the bottle down on the table and pulled her close. She'd trembled at the harsh words she'd used to describe her thoughts. Insanity, hallucination, breakdown—none sounded positive. He sighed. "If I am a delusion, than I am a most fortune delusion to be sailing these seas with you at my side. Here, I ordered this made for you."

She looked up and followed his gesture to the bottle.

"What is it?"

"You said your perfume was nearly gone. I commissioned this. I feel it's quite close." He grinned. She snatched the bottle, carefully undid the wax seal and almost reverently lifted the stopper to her nostrils. The tart scent of ripe green apples filled the room. This was a heavier scent than what she normally wore, but the best the perfumer could manage. He'd been pleased with it. It made him think of her, even if it wasn't an exact duplicate of the scent.

"Oh. Wow. This is much better!" She dabbed the stopper on her wrist followed by a brush at her neck. "This is exceptionally thoughtful of you. My little bottle is nearly empty. Thank you!" She inhaled again at her wrist. "It's more concentrated—I'll use less at a time."

The smile she turned on him saw his stomach drop. Sweet, open, and without worry or concern regarding his motives. He remembered a tiny niece who would look at him that way after some small gesture of affection. They'd always been small gestures; he'd little to spare.

What was the little girl's name?

He couldn't remember.

Emily tilted her head at him. "Where did you go?"

"What?" He shook his head, reached for her wrist and held it to his nose. He took a breath. "Ah. Mixes better with your skin than the perfumer's. I can show you how to reseal the bottle so it will transport without spilling."

"Oh, that's good." She leaned toward him. "I'm touched."

"I truly do not think you are mad, Mrs. Pawes." He understood, but didn't resist the chance to tease.

When she actually initiated a kiss, almost shyly, it took every bit of willpower not to pull her closer and smother her in his arms. Her tongue ventured a small exploration of his lips. So incredibly gentle, soft, he suddenly felt terribly weak.

He raised his arms and held her, but not with the fever of a starving man this time. The silk of the robe cooled his pulse. Her presence calmed him, and he knew he'd keep lying to her. To tell her was to invite interference and risk her life. To lie risked this fragile relationship, but at least she would not be in danger.

Rousing himself from a bout of melancholy, he chuckled, rising from the bench. "Now, we have another twenty-four hours. Time enough to experiment."

࿔

She eyed him with trepidation. The loss of his simple embrace surprised her with a tug at her heart. Not only her body this time. She missed him? He wasn't ten feet from her, and she missed him.

This was insane. She needed to get back to her world. She had a book to write, a grand tour to take. She planned on getting a cat for the little camper, to keep her company. Yes, a nice, fat rescue kitty, and together they'd go everywhere she ever dreamed of. Run away from the entire idea of growing old. She wouldn't be bothered by being alone, she liked being self-sufficient. It was nice not to miss people.

Her mind whirled.

He returned to the table and sat, resting a hip on the edge, put a boot on the bench next to her, and handed her a deck of cards.

"You want to play cards?" she ventured a guess. "What? Strip poker? Not fair, you're wearing more clothing than I...." Her eyes drifted to the cards, fanning them out. "Oh."

"I ran across them at a little shop in Tortuga and found them quite inspiring. I've flipped through them, but waited for a woman worthy of such goals. Now." He leaned closer. "I'll pick two, you pick two, and we'll pick one together."

She swallowed the sudden surge of interest. Kama Sutra cards. She's always wanted to try those. But now? She was fifty-three years old! She'd never been terribly limber.

Oh! That was a nice one!

She tilted her head, well, maybe. It was a lovely deck, with photographs instead of sketches.

He took the cards from her and shuffled them expertly, then spread them out face down in a fan on the table. "Pick two."

"You're quite sure of yourself, Captain Silvestri. What if I...we...can't?"

"Can't? Why can't we? We've already mastered several of the more basic positions." He slid a card from one side, lined it up without flipping it over. He waited for her, eyebrow raised in expectation.

Emily wanted to do this. What the hell. She did!

She drew a card and put it next to his. He drew. She drew. He held her hand, closed his eyes, clearly expecting her to follow course. She sighed and let him move their combined hands over the deck, then fall to select one.

He flipped the first one over.

Chapter Fifteen

The light changed, shining through the window on the portside. He diligently rubbed and massaged her right calf while she moaned.

"It was that damned Trapeze Position. Lucky I didn't break my neck." She moaned again at the deep pressure he used to dig into the tight muscle. "On my head? That was nuts."

"You should have trusted that I wasn't going to let go. I held your hands—you didn't have to grip so tight with your legs. And the blankets were there for padding." He felt his cock stir at the memory.

It was going so well. He perched on the edge of the bunk, Emily's warm body pressed against his chest until she bent slowly back, anchoring her legs around his hips. His grip locked on her hands as he gazed down at her tits, her back arched, locking her cunt firmly to his cock. So sublime, almost perfect, until her foot slipped, causing Emily to twist in panic and end up with a painful cramp.

"I quite enjoyed the first three positions," he commented.

"Yeah, you would. What did you do, fix the deck so the oral sex was up first?" She snickered.

He glanced down at her face where a bright smile met his eyes. Good, she'd enjoyed herself.

"You watched the cards being drawn. Impossible to fix."

"Uh huh. It's your damned luck."

"And the last, which saw you incapacitated?"

"Got you a view you're enjoying." She looked up her leg at him. He smiled down, at her spread open cunny. She was right, of course.

She let loose a sigh. "There is one left."

"Not until you get the splinter out of my ass." He shifted, trying to ease the pressure off the nagging sting. It proved a bit uncomfortable. He'd known that bit of wood needed sanding, damn it.

"You got a splinter? Your curse must be lazy." She eased her leg away from him. "Good now. Let me see the damage."

"My choice to endanger my posterior." He turned about. Her hands were gentle as she examined his ass. A few moments of that and he'd be ready for that last card.

"Oh, you big baby! It's nothing!" She tugged and the bit of wood came free.

"It was a nuisance, but I didn't bellow about it. Took care of your leg first," he replied. "Let's see what the last card presents."

She hadn't reached her feet yet when he turned it over. He smiled down at it, easy, intimate….

She shivered, standing next to him. "Getting a little cold in here."

"It's the sweat; this one will help. On the bed, where it's sunny still." He held the card out to her. She slumped as she took it. He wasn't fooled—she enjoyed this play as much as he did, maybe more. He eyed the light at the window while she read it. If he wanted to take advantage of the last bit of the sun's rays to do the piercing, he needed her to agree, soon.

Everything necessary waited in a small box, under the table.

"The Outstretched Clasping Position?" She examined the card. "Well, no acrobatics, looks relatively plain."

He knew better. With their height difference, this would prove a challenge. He set the card down and gestured to the bed. She rolled her eyes, and nonchalantly headed for the back. He waited until she was engaged in making herself comfortable to grab the box and see it near at hand.

She relaxed on the covers; spread her legs, arms held above her head. "No tying me up."

"Maybe next time." He winked and eased down atop her.

Soft and warm. Her scent rose to surround him. The tart bite of the perfume he'd given her mixed with the earthy musk of the afternoon.

She'd no idea how enticing he found a woman who took such a casual, almost distant, approach to fucking. Oh, prostitutes certainly were able to embrace a good swing in a hammock and remain uninvolved. But this woman enjoyed this play as *play*, not professional work. She played with a sweet abandon that hinted at a capacity for a great deal more. He surmised they held different definitions of the word *play*, along with the steps from play to practice to real passion. What they constantly did to one another approached uniquely sublime pleasure.

He knew the difference between sex, fucking and making love. He knew they were beyond the first, well advanced into the second, and quickly approaching the third. But he suspected she wouldn't agree.

He would bring her there.

She took a deep breath when he settled between her legs. He clasped hands with her, stretching her arms above her head. He grinned. The tip of his cock nestled barely at her curly nest. She frowned then tried to lift her hips to encompass him. He stayed still, gazing into her eyes.

He kissed her, slowly lingering over her lips, dancing teasingly with her tongue. He pulled away.

She arched her body and he slid a fraction into her.

"Alan!"

"I like looking into your eyes," he murmured.

"Fuck me, you bastard."

"I am not, in fact, a bastard."

"Son of a bitch!" She again stretched, trying to maneuver him into her.

He used his weight to keep her from succeeding.

"My mother, though unpleasant at times, was not a bitch."

Her moving tested his patience. He growled. "You need to look into my eyes, Emily."

"Fuck me, Alan!"

"What will you give me if I agree to your charming demand?"

"Give you?" She stilled, met his eyes with some suspicion. "What do you want? You already have me here, in your bed." She tilted her head at him, blew a strand of his long hair away from her face. "I won't spy for you."

He sighed. "I have no need of a spy, love. No, I want our dream, Emily. I want to see it come true." He lowered his gaze, glancing at her breasts, then back to her eyes.

She swallowed and turned her face to the side.

He tightened his grip on her fingers when she tried to slide one hand away. She took a deep breath.

"Alan…okay, I admit I like the *idea*. I'm not sure of the reality. I used to talk to Tom about it. I've always thought it would be an interesting thing to do."

"And your husband didn't agree?" He found that puzzling. What man wouldn't be titillated by adorning his woman with dainties?

"He worried it would become infected, hurt me, be noticed." Her voice communicated some sadness.

Ah, not a matter of finances.

"Ah, you weren't worried about those concerns. You were more daring. You *are* more daring, Emily. And it won't infect. I have a cream from Mama Lu." He bent to kiss her, this time pressing deeply into her mouth, tilting his hips so that he slid a fraction further into her. He turned his mouth to one side, whispered, "Say yes."

He teased her, withdrawing, slipping out, and returning.

She moaned. "But what if I pass out?"

He laughed, not unkindly, and locked eyes with her. "I will catch you."

Her body relaxed, signaling acceptance, and his heart soared at this show of trust. And she nodded. He tilted his head at her, and she whispered, "Yes."

He squeezed her hands and pushed deeply into her. He

kept hold of her hands, stretched her further while she parted her legs wider, wrapped them around his hips, and began her litany of curse words, keeping rhythm with his energetic thrusting.

❦

Less than an hour later, Emily glanced down at her right nipple in wonder. It wasn't difficult. It hurt a little bit, but his hands were gentle and quick. And the ring looked wonderful. She flicked at it with one finger. He'd slathered it with the cream from Mama Lu, and it instantly cooled, the bite of pain faded. Within ten minutes, it appeared totally healed up.

Magic. Captain Jezebel knew whereof she spoke.

It made her think seriously about the entire situation regarding Silvestri and his curse. She sat on the bed, watching him clean up from the piercing. What if it was more than talk, or a matter of coincidence and superstition?

A part of her, she realized, believed it wasn't real. Now, that part needed to reconsider.

She took a chance. "Alan. You genuinely are cursed?"

"Oh, yes. I am cursed." He turned to look at her. "You doubted?"

"Yeah. I did. All the magic stuff." She smiled crookedly, admiring his legs. Strong, tan. Bare feet. She enjoyed looking at him, and found herself squirming. Again.

He moved about the cabin with total confidence. Sure of his balance, knowing where everything was. He'd reach for items without looking for them, place things without concern of where they'd land.

She was such a klutz, even in places she'd known most of her life. He was much more graceful than she. He set a bowl carefully in a box and closed the lid, then turned and strode back to the bed. He sat down next to her and wrapped an arm around her shoulders. "Yes. I am cursed."

"How?"

For the first time, real concern entered her mind, not only curiosity. He turned his head to look into her eyes. "It's a pathetic story. At fifteen, a beautiful woman offered me everything I thought I wanted. I said yes. The trick was played on me—to have everything I wanted and never pay for it. Ha!"

She swallowed. "You pay. You pay every three days. Alone on this ship. Jezzie said it wasn't always three days. And that it will grow shorter."

"Hush. I am not alone. You are here." He laid a finger at her lips. She sighed and said nothing further. Silently, he rose, dressed, and turned to the door. He paused. "Emily, will you make me a book from the red paper to match the blue? I will be back with a meal after I check on the ship."

"Oh, yeah. Sure. Can I go outside?"

"No. My crew thinks I keep you here against your will. You move out to the deck and your safety is compromised. Stay."

She nodded, actually understanding and not wanting to enlighten his crew with her real status. He didn't trust them, not fully, and therefore, she certainly wasn't going to either.

Making the book would give her something to do, besides think about more sex—or how he must feel about his curse. He left the room and she pulled out her work bag. And argued with herself the entire time.

You care about him.

No, I don't. It's just that the sex is good.

It's more than sex.

You're lying to yourself again.

No, I'm not.

None of this is real. I'm going to wake up back in Vallejo.

You don't want to…

"Shut up!" She viciously sliced too deeply into the paper and scored the table.

Damn it.

cʌɔ

He was not ready to discuss the inevitable shrinking of his allotted time as a normal man. There should be no more acceleration of his curse until the anniversary of his birth. He had a few more weeks to bring it to an end.

After the meal, she handed him the new red book and apologized for damaging the table.

He waved away the apology and turned to another subject. "I assume the crew of the Quill has told you of the celebration in Tortuga?"

"Yeah. Everyone is talking about it. They're planning what to wear, visiting tailors, hauling out more jewelry and sparkle than I've ever seen! It ought to be a real treat to see them dolled up that way." She chuckled.

He tilted his head toward her. "And you? Some lovely gown? You will wear the pearls I gave you?"

"I guess. I'm having a shirt made, and figure I'll buy a skirt."

"Mrs. Pawes, that won't do. The entire island will sparkle and shine. You need something impressive." He knew the tailors of Nassau and could get back there and make sure she shone.

"Why? Impress who? I'm simply an old wom...."

He shot to his feet and strode away from her. Her insistence on seeing herself as useless and worn out grew tiresome! With a growl, he turned to stare at her.

She'd stopped talking and looked away from him. Slowly, she lifted one leg, followed by the other and rested them at the very edge of her chair. Her arms wrapped around her calves. She swallowed. "Alan, I am old. It's a fact. No one is going to be impressed by me. If I wore a fortune in precious stones, the sparkle would impress them. Not me."

"*Balderdash!* My God, woman! What is wrong with you? Don't tell me I am the only man who wants you? All those lusty lads on the Quill? None of them have followed you with their eyes, slid up next to you on deck, helped you with lines? Done your fetching?" He strode back to stand directly in front of her.

He recognized a fire in her eyes, even though a tear dripped down her cheek. She let go of her legs and stood up, pushing at his chest. "Don't tell me those young men see me as anything more than a mother! If they help me, it's because of that! They *do not* want to fuck *me!*"

She screamed that last word.

He snickered, turning away. "Yes, they do."

"If they do, it's because men want to fuck every woman. Any woman that is handy!"

"Oh, how stupid!" He gazed at the ceiling of the cabin.

"I am not stupid."

"Oh, yes, you are. You are stupid, blind, and a liar." He spoke to the fourth ceiling beam from the right.

"What?"

He heard her stalk up behind him before she poked him. "*I am not stupid!*"

"Yes, you are." He turned and loomed over her, gripping her shoulders before she stepped away. "They want you. They dream about you. Wonder what secrets your body holds. What it would feel like to lie atop you, gaze down into the depth of your deep, brown eyes."

Another tear ran from her right eye.

"Precisely the way I dream of you, when you are not with me." He spoke slowly, weighing each word with meaning and worth. Damn it. He did dream of her.

"But...but you aren't...you...," She stumbled over words. "I mean, you don't..." He strained to hear the word, but she said it. "...count. Oh, hell."

"I don't count? Because I'm not young? I've fucked hundreds of women, am more experienced than most of those young men will ever know, and I want you. Desire you. Find you impressive each time I see you. Save for at this moment. Your blindness on this issue is not impressive. I count, Mrs. Pawes. So. Do. You."

She silently wept. No sobbing, no sniffing, only tears, while she appeared to study his face, his eyes, his lips, his chin.... She lifted a hand and lightly touched his jawline. Her fingers lingered along the bone, stroking the scruff as if it were silk. It felt good. Intimate.

"I'm sorry. You count—I know you count."

"And?" He waited for her to say it.

"I'm trying to count. But I don't know how to." She inhaled quickly, close to breaking down.

"Why don't you know this?" he whispered. "Who beat you down? Who dared to leave you this uncertain of yourself?"

This husband of hers? He'd kill the man if he weren't already dead.

"No one, Alan. Only me. And life. Where—*when* I live isn't kind to women my age."

"You live here now. Believe me when I say you are desirable. I find you…irresistible." He covered her hand with his, eased it from his jawline to his lips. Pressed a kiss to her palm. He kept his eyes on her, looking for her to believe him. He needed her to believe him.

To trust him. To….

No. Not love. He wouldn't risk that. Not yet.

He dropped her hand and turned away.

"Alan? Did I do something wrong?"

Damn, he would undo her confidence! He took a deep breath. "No, no. Not you." He quickly turned to smile at her. "Come to bed with me. I will prove to you what I say is real."

He wiped the tears away. "I want to spread your legs, Emily."

She looked away quickly, almost blushed, snorted.

Something crossed her face, but it was impossible to interpret. Disappointment? Grief?

A shout from the deck called eight bells, midnight. The night was already too far gone! There was never enough time.

She turned and walked toward his bed, untying her robe to drop it across the covers. This strange woman from another time and place slid between the sheets, then turned to wait for him.

The blood roared to his head. To tell her! Explain! Plead with her! She lifted a hand, cradled her breast, and pinched the nipple. "Too bad you don't have another ring."

Words fled. At her side in a moment, his hands trembled and his clothes dropped to the deck.

When she welcomed him, held him close with a divine comfort while he sank into her, his soul trembled and a shiver ran up his back.

❧

He woke her hours later with a great shout that set her heart stuttering. She shot up, reaching for him. He shook, shivering as though encased in ice water.

"Alan?"

He turned a blind eye toward her voice; the last candle in the cabin shed enough light for her to see the sweat on his brow.

"Alan?" She wiped his face with a corner of the sheet.

He moaned.

And shivered again.

She pulled the covers from where they'd fallen at their waist, making certain he was covered, and cuddled close to him. She lightly shook him. He flinched then violently jerked.

"Captain Silvestri!"

What the hell was going on? Was he sick? Was it his heart? A sudden fever? What the fuck should she do? "Wake up!"

He started awake, turned his face and stared at her. "I felt them. I felt them all."

"What?" She touched his face. Was he delirious?

His eyes darted past her to the window at the stern, about a foot away. Before she said another word, he covered her body, arms wrapped around her, and buried her underneath him.

"Quiet!" He hissed.

She froze, feeling a chill when his sweat dripped onto her. Since when was sweat icy? Her mind wrestled with the idea. Did he spy something out the window? Or was it just a night terror? She'd never experienced a nightmare so vivid it broke into the waking world, but she'd read about them.

He trembled again then slowly relaxed. He moved off her, placing himself next to the window, his front to her back. He quieted her questions.

"I sometimes have hard dreams. Nothing more." He kept his arms around her, legs entwined with hers. The covers were tight around them. It seemed an oddly desperate bit of protection, or a clinging to keep her close?

He kissed the back of her head and murmured reassurances until the length of the day overcame her unease and the motion of the ship lulled her back to sleep.

The next day, the ship returned to St. Marteen. He diverted every query she raised and made certain she left the ship unobserved, straight to a boarding house.

"The Quill will return tomorrow. I will see you again, soon." He nearly bruised her lips with the strength of his farewell kiss.

While he walked away, she sighed. Tall, confident, and scared to death of something.

Three days later, she discovered her mirror gone from her pack.

Chapter Sixteen

*H*e ordered the ship leave St. Marteen after stepping back aboard. He savored the experience of the short visit with Monsieur Jason of the dyers guild, to make plain his unhappiness at the treatment of Mrs. Pawes. They'd do damage to themselves, waiting for his curse to strike them. It wouldn't—he already knew that. The situation fell too far from him personally.

The amusement found by worrying them would suffice.

The Immortal dropped anchor off the small baths the Quill's crew preferred, and he left them to entertain themselves. He carried a small pack to the other side of the peninsula, aiming for the large bath he'd enjoyed with Mrs. Pawes.

The shadows lengthened into true dusk while he cleansed himself, using the powder Mama Lu gave him. He waited for dark and pulled out the mirror. He'd wrapped it well, protecting the glass from accidentally breaking. According to Mama Lu, this mirror was a precious gift. He would make certain he returned it to Emily intact.

He traced the face of the Kraken, almost smiling at the black eyes, so evident in the bleached white of the rest. He ran fingers up and down the tentacles. He swore, they almost gripped him. He didn't know where this artifact came from, but it was powerful. He set it down and arranged spell items upon it. First, the needle he'd used to place Emily's nipple ring. The one she used upon him. A small scrap of fabric, he'd collected their combined sexual fluids with. He lifted that to his nose first and inhaled slightly.

Divine.

A hair from his head and a hair from hers. And lastly, the seal from the last letter he'd received from Mick, denouncing him. It held fury and anger. But it also acknowledged their long friendship. The letter he kept—the seal would suffice to make the connection.

A sliver of moon rose from the sea as he walked into the surf. The water chilled him slightly, but nothing like the nightmare the night Emily held him. He'd seen her, Glacious. A frost appeared on the glass and her eyes studied him. Studied them.

He shook the memory off, praying it had been nothing more than a lingering effect from the nightmare. He walked until the water hit him below his waist and stopped. He held the mirror flat, barely above the water, as Mama Lu told him. A ripple of water reached for it, which was certainly strange. Well, spells should be unusual. He lowered it minutely, and the next ripple kissed the mirror, stirred the powder Mama Lu told him to sprinkle atop the rest.

A ripple flowed away from him, counter to the sea's course. It disappeared toward the horizon, barely visible in the bare light of a crescent moon. And he waited. Mama Lu said to be patient.

"Ya gonna get a sign. Some message or vision 'bout what way ta go. Wait for it!"

He heard her melodic cadence even now, floating above the sea. The quiet of the night, the lack of any breeze, nothing stirred the trees at his back. No birds called. He looked up at the stars; they blazed down at him.

He sighed and turned his head back to the horizon.

He fought the instinct to scramble away from the great, bulky head of the albino Kraken, not three feet from him, bobbing above the waterline. He swallowed and mastered his fear, while his heart galloped loud enough for the world to hear.

Two tentacles, wider than his waist, drifted to his sides. A fingerling tip brushed the back of his left thigh. He'd never felt so exposed, so vulnerable, small, and insignificant in his entire life.

Gazing into those black eyes, he slowly relaxed. There was no threat there. Simply interest.

Another tentacle snaked up his back, draped across his shoulder like the arm of a casual friend. A suction cup the size of his palm paused at his pierced nipple, brushing the metal as if tasting it.

Wonder where Mama Lu got this ring? It seemed to interest the Kraken.

They eyed each other—two old warriors, in a moment out of time.

He broke the silence. "Old Monster, you know me."

A blown breath stirred his long hair. It hinted at a depth of ocean impossible to imagine. Cold, colder than Glacious. He shivered.

The head rose, until they were eye to eye.

"I'll lead you to her, if you will come. I know she hides from you. She steals from you," he whispered. They were two Old Monsters, conspiring in the night to take down an evil woman who haunted them both. "Help me protect the woman I care for from the ice queen, Old Monster, and I will give you whatever you desire. Anything."

He should have said he loved. He knew it, but the words stuck in his throat.

A small tentacle slipped from the water and swept the items from the glass. He peered down at the mirror. Glacious' ice palace rose from its surface. It spun and shattered, pieces floated atop the reflection, sank away.

He chuckled. Another sweep of that tentacle left something. He picked it up and held it to the scant light. A white disc on a slender chain. He studied it and finally the image came clear. An etched Kraken.

"For my woman?" He stopped, looking up. The Kraken

was gone.

He'd received the only answers he was going to get. He'd take the disc to Lu. Clearly, the Kraken would help with Glacious. What it would ask in return he didn't know. But he'd pay whatever was asked. He draped the chain over his head and returned to the shore.

He'd get the mirror back to Emily in Tortuga. Ten days remained until the party. Afterward, he would sail north to find his queen and bring about her destruction to return a free man or die trying.

❧

Emily returned to the ship with a sense of unease. She'd barely slept the one night she'd spent in the boarding house. Instead, she stood at the small window, staring out at the city. It wasn't a busy port, like Tortuga. Once night fell, it fairly closed its doors and rolled up its streets. She had nowhere to spend her restlessness.

She fretted. What did he mean? Those words he'd spoken, as he woke from the nightmare haunted her. *I felt them, I felt them all?*

What did he feel? And what had he seen, or thought he'd seen? What would make the man she'd come to know exhibit such fear? Was it personal fear or was she involved? Just too many questions and no answers. No wonder sleep proved evasive.

She breathed on the window, leaving a small vapor cloud. She traced his initials, AS. An impish grin crossed her face.

Wonder if his middle name begins with an 'S'?

It would leave her a legitimate insult, since he'd ruled out SOB and bastard. Quite clever of him, actually. She wiped out the initials and sat back on the bed.

What would scare him? With his curse, he couldn't be scared of enemies, of accidents, food poisoning, infections.... She played with the ring at her nipple. Fear of infection kept her from doing this more than fear about how it might look to others. She never truly cared about things like that. Well, not with physical things.

She labored at being polite. She did her best to be

thoughtful and aware of how others might be hurt by what she said or did. If her appearance offended someone? Fuck it. But it had bothered Tom.

Insecurities plague everyone, she figured. Again, what would make Silvestri insecure? A threat to the security his curse offered?

Though she didn't think he enjoyed his curse. Or consider it an agent of security. A beautiful woman offered him good luck, and being fifteen, he took it without a thought. She didn't know his exact age, but he'd carried the weight of that decision a long time.

And could claim no friends, no family, no one to talk with because of it. He didn't trust his crew, that much was certain. And that confused her. A captain should be able to rely on his crew for more than just practical matters. She supposed he believed in their ability to run the ship, to obey orders, but not with any sense of camaraderie.

The idea of living so long aboard a ship without a friend made her sad.

Her life was solitary, too. Even when Tom was alive, they lived a lonely sort of life. They went out to events like the pirate festival, renaissance fairs and other historical enactment celebrations. They went to science fiction conventions, attended concerts and craft fairs, then they went home. They never had company over, never went to the homes of others for dinners, or parties.

It wasn't strange to her. It was how they lived.

Here, in this odd delusion she presently inhabited, society was different. The crew of the Quill certainly did their best to afford privacy to each other, but not to the extent she was familiar with. They often left the shower with towels barely wrapped about themselves. Sometimes they sprawled about the deck, mostly nude, to dry after a good swim.

No one hid who they slept with or when.

Save for her. But she was sleeping with the enemy.

Which turned her thoughts to Mick. Did he actually hate Silvestri? She entertained some doubts. Climbing off the bed, she paced in the small confines of her room.

Were they enemies? Silvestri didn't act like an enemy. He went out of his way to avoid the Quill. Was it to protect Mick?

Who was she protecting by remaining quiet about her rendezvous with Silvestri?

A sharp pain rose between her eyes, heralding the advent of a headache. With a curse, she threw on some clothes and left the room. Deserted streets might be the cure she needed.

Hours later, she sat on the sea wall, staring out at the stars. They touched the horizon, the night was that dark. A world with no air pollution or electric lights to obscure the night sky.

Her headache faded, but her heart felt raw. She wiped at a tear trailing down her face.

She wasn't lying to the Quill about Silvestri. She simply wasn't talking about her meetings with him. She wasn't ashamed; she didn't want to hurt them.

Oh, hell.

She bowed her head and let the tears fall. She was terribly confused.

Did it count if you lied to a delusion?

The sun rose while she trudged back to her room, still without answers. When she rejoined the Quill, she answered questions about the dyers with some bitterness. Her ill humor registered with the rest.

Janey poked at her. "Because they were idiots, don't mean you have to be."

Emily almost snapped back at the vibrant woman, but held her tongue. She straightened her back and took a deep breath. "You're right. I'm sorry. I barely slept last night and it was disappointing, how nasty they were."

"They're mostly Frenchman—they were born nasty," Tink commented from the stairs, where she used an extremely wicked looking knife to carve on a bit of wood. "Surprised they even offered you anything. Most unlike them."

"They only wanted two ledgers. I doubt they even kept them. They probably sold them." Emily tried to answer the comment without a lie. Maybe Silvestri paid them. He might have!

"They wanted something more than ledgers. You do good

work, but ledgers can be purchased other places. You use your flower dye on the ones you made them?" Tink asked her, tilting her head at the wood in her hand.

Emily paused to think a minute. Did she?

"Yeah, I did. But they know the flowers—even showed me how they got a weak green from certain leaves. I doubt they cared about that."

Trying not to lie directly proved difficult.

"Well, you'll find out eventually why they agreed to it." Tink sheathed her knife and threw the wood to Emily. "What do you think?"

Emily held it up, squinting. Tink was an excellent wood carver, but her subjects sometimes were hard to figure out. She turned the slender bit of wood in her hand and suddenly realized what she held. She grinned.

"A prick knife? This is quite cool. I like how you actually caught the bulbous tip and yet made it sharp." She tossed it back to Tink. "If there were mail here, it would make a great letter opener.

Tink tossed it back to her. "For you. Seems to be the only prick you'll touch."

Emily froze, struck to the bone by Tink's comment. The blood rushed to her face, and she fought not to retort with the news that her lover saw her well acquainted with his prick, thank you very much!

Janey must have read her stillness as hurt and quickly jumped in. "You sample enough prick for twelve sailors, Tink. Pawes can be particular if she chooses. When she's ready, she'll find someone." She turned her back on the sharp-tongued quartermaster and linked her arm with Emily. "We're heading back to Nassau. The tailors should be done with our outfits. We can shop for accessories and leave for Tortuga after."

Emily allowed herself to be led off, gripping the prick knife tightly. Tink was a bitch.

Two days later they sailed through a small storm, delaying their arrival at Nassau. They would have to raise every sail to reach Tortuga in time to peruse the shops before the party.

Emily faced the tailor while he spread his hands in apology.

"Merci! I am sorry! My assistant made the mistake, Madam! Your blouse is done and it is quite lovely, I assure you. But it is already speeding its way to Tortuga. Take this."

He handed her a folded bit of paper. "The blouse will be at this location. My friend, Mr. Reibe, will see the mistake on the invoice and hold it, waiting to return it to me. This note will see him hand it over to you!"

Janey held up her finished dress, beaming at the lovely mix of green and gold the man put together for the skirt portion. "Don't worry, Pawes! You can pick it up in Tortuga and get a skirt at the same time. Mr. Reibe has a nice shop."

"Yes! Yes! He does! Madam, you'll be pleased, I assure you!" He bowed and backed away, turning to help another customer.

Emily swallowed her disappointment. She never had good luck with special orders. Looked like this bit of reality followed her into insanity.

They returned to the ship and raised sail for Tortuga.

He wouldn't be there, she knew. He wouldn't risk facing Mick's anger, real or not.

She unpacked her bag from St. Marteen, searching for the perfume bottle Silvestri gave her. He'd carefully shown her how to seal it back up the morning they'd returned to port. She pulled out the bag her mirror normally rested in, only to discover it was gone. A stiff bit of paper had been inserted in the bag to hold the shape.

"Those fuckers!" she hissed. "God damned dyers! I'll sic him on them! Must be that Monsieur Pannsil!" She'd been careful but he'd seen the mirror despite her care. She'd pulled it out to see on how badly a splash of dye marred her breeches. She shouldn't have check it while he stood there. Damn it! He'd asked about it, and she'd hidden it deep in her bag afterward.

He'd tried to buy it from her!

"That prig nosed bastard, son of a diseased camel!"

"You all right?" A soft knock came at her cabin door.

She took a deep breath to calm herself, took the step and half to the door and opened it.

Davis stood there, looking concerned.

"I'm fine. Only found something missing from my bag. Probably one of the dyers. I'll see if I can get it back next time we're on St. Marteen, but it pisses me off!" She stepped outside the cabin. "Join me in a drink?"

"Of course. You're not missing one of your knives, I hope?" He followed her to the galley. She reassured him that her knives were safe and secure. She managed to fend off questions about what was missing.

She didn't lie.

Chapter Seventeen

$\mathcal{H}$e waited for her at the dressmaker's shop. Mr. Reibe expressed pleasure at receiving the business, even at the last minute. He'd taken the blouse and used it to create something sublime. Silvestri paid well for the dress. The shoes he pulled out of his stash on the Immortal. He'd known long ago these were special, and once he'd touched Emily's feet, he knew why he'd hidden them away.

He'd seen the Quill sail in an hour ago. The Immortal set anchor several miles away. Ascertaining that Captain Jezebel's favorite shops were much further down the hill, he'd set up in the back of this shop to wait.

The Immortal left him the day before and he'd used his time well. After the party, he'd leave and seek out Glacious. But these two days would be spent watching Pawes smile.

When she strode into the shop, one of the workers signaled him of her arrival. He heard the prearranged argument start. Mr. Reibe shouted he had nothing of hers here! That bastard on St. Marteen most likely stole her fabric, or ruined it and tried to fob the mistake off on him. She tried to stay calm—her voice didn't rise to argue with him.

Alan exited from the back and moved to the front, entering while she grew angry. He liked seeing the color in her cheeks.

"Listen, you jerkwad! I need something to wear tomorrow.

I don't care who fucked up, you show me something or I'll send Mick from the Quill up here to perch on your porch and drive away every customer from here to next Tuesday!"

Interesting threat. Would Mick do that for her? The idea pricked him. No, Jezebel would have Mick's balls in a satin bag if he played around on her.

He cleared his throat, entering the shop. She didn't see him at first. Mr. Reibe looked over her shoulder at him, and she spun, still shouting, "Deal with me, you weasel." She saw him and stopped, obviously shocked. "Oh, it's you. No, wait, you can't be here! What are you doing here?" She blinked at him, the rhythm of her rant interrupted.

"I often shop here, Mrs. Pawes. Has Mr. Reibe done something to anger you?"

"Between him and the twit on St. Marteen, they've lost my blouse! Now what will I wear to the party?" She took a step closer to him. "You can't be here. The Quill is in port," she said, dropping her voice to a whisper.

"I know that. And I know how to stay out of the way. I heard your voice while walking by, Mrs. Pawes. I'm certain Mr. Reibe will find a garment for you before tomorrow night. Yes, Mr. Reibe?" He raised his eyebrows, and as arranged, the tailor took a step back and bowed, babbling apologies.

Silvestri took Emily's arm. "Come, we'll return tomorrow, and you will look spectacular, I'm sure."

She sighed and took his arm.

Once outside, she nervously examined the street, her eyes darting down the road, tilting her head as if she could see around corners. "Honestly, you can't know where he'll wander!"

"But I can. Mick is quite habitual with his haunts. Jezebel will visit Madam Monteverdi's shop, dragging him along. He'll act bored, but secretly enjoy watching her play with the scarves and hats. She'll haul from store to store, ending up at the Orange Tabby for a meal, then the Barmy Cock for drinks."

She tilted her head, fascinated with the details. The commentary wound down and she shook her head. "You know him terribly well. You know both of them. How?"

"Spies," he said. "Now, since I have you until tomorrow. I want to show you a special place. I'm sure they won't miss you on the Quill. Too excited about the party tomorrow. Come with me?"

Emily sighed. "Might as well. It's getting hard to lie to them. At least if I'm with you, I don't have to try. You are certain he can find something for me to wear by tomorrow? It seems like everyone is flooding the dress shops. I was surprised to see this one empty."

"Most of his work is special order, and the madness is in the back room right now." He would address why she was lying to the extent that it burdened her. Later. Once they were at his retreat.

∾

Why did finding herself following him into the hills above Tortuga bring her peace? She'd actually been relieved to see him. The conflicts between the person she once was and the person now living in her skin quieted with him nearby. When he led, she trailed behind with questions badgering her brain.

Good thing she'd left Janey in the store near the docks shopping for jingle-jangles, as the bosun termed them.

Emily paused and took a deep breath. "Alan? Will Mr. Reibe tell Janey who I left with? She was going to join me after doing some shopping near the docks."

He turned to study her, offering a hand as they approached a steep step. "No, every shopkeeper knows to keep my business quiet. He'll say you left, still searching for your blouse."

"Good. They never ask me where I am or who I stay with. I'm thankful, but I don't understand. Aren't they curious?"

She would be.

He shrugged. "I'm sure they are, but sailors treasure privacy. If they want it for themselves, they learn to be circumspect with others." He paused before continuing; his hand touched her cheek. "Captain Jezebel has sources, Mrs. Pawes. She knows you meet a lover. It depends on how observant her spies are, whether they have identified me."

"Oh, shit." She shivered. "If Jezebel knew wouldn't she

throw me off the ship? Or tell Mick? Warn me?"

"Captain Jezebel is an intelligent woman. She's been here over twenty-five years, and Mick means a great deal to her. She wouldn't risk him. She obviously considers you intelligent enough to make your own decisions."

"If she knows it's you, then she'd keep Mick away. I get that." Her uncertainty made it difficult to enjoy the scenery. They'd climbed quite a distance. She noticed how the streets emptied into valleys that trickled down like streams to the port below. She expected trees, but the slope they climbed ran up a rocky area.

"Is this the lie that concerns you?" he asked. "It doesn't matter to them, Emily. I am no danger to them. I am not their enemy."

"Mick." She spoke his name with some reluctance. "He was the first to befriend me. He found me when I woke up and didn't know where I was. Because of him, I ended up on the Quill. I owe him honesty, Alan."

"No, you owe him the same as Jezebel owes him when it comes to me. To keep him safe from his personal obsession. Finding me would only bring him in reach of my curse." He smiled slightly. "The single person you hurt with this lie, as you term it, is yourself. Let it go."

She met his eyes and read comfort there. He wanted her to trust that he knew what was best with all of this. She wanted to believe him, but it battled with old messages regarding lies. Lies were always the wrong path to take. She'd always prided herself on being truthful. To be honest, truthful to the point of lacking any real tact. But this was different. She thought it was different. With a sigh, she looked up the path. "How much farther?"

"Not far. There is food, shelter. My secret retreat, Mrs. Pawes."

"Seemed like a fairly public path." She tilted her head at him, a sudden suspicion grew. "You screwed with the tailor, didn't you? Manipulated this entire scenario. Is my blouse there? I need to get it back, or I'll be wearing breeches with it instead of a skirt." She turned to head back.

Sure, it was nice to know she was wanted, but his single-purposed mind kept interfering with things she'd set herself to do. Like find the portal and regain her sanity. Return to Vallejo.

His arm swept around her. "Yes. I made this happen. But it's part of my curse. Events fall to my advantage. Do you truly regret my interference? I am part of your destiny. Give me this night. One more night and from tomorrow forward, it is your move."

"Unless your curse dictates events, Captain Silvestri." She closed her eyes, suddenly feeling the full weight of her fifty-three years. Gods, how she wanted to lean back into his embrace and give up. Would one more night hurt?

He kissed the top of her head, then gazed into her eyes. "Come with me, and I will devour you—serve your body as a feast to mine. All I have done in the past, I will do once more. We will continue this voyage of sensual delight. You will grow hoarse, shouting obscenities into the night." His hand rose to cup her right breast; one thumb brushed the piercing.

She quivered and felt his touch sink through her, straight to the juncture of her legs. Heat pooled; her nipples ached as they hardened. Her lips opened, and she moaned at the pictures he'd painted in her head.

More than desire dictated her agreement to go with him. She wanted to sleep in his arms. To feel the mysteries she could not define. Sensations that were terrible with sweetness and warmth.

No, one more night would not hurt.

She nodded, eyes locked on his.

For a moment, she detected relief. His shoulders sank a fraction of an inch, his eyelids relaxed. He swept down, bending his head to capture her lips and press home his advantage. A hand rose to squeeze her breast even as his tongue pushed into her mouth to claim her attention. All rational thought disappeared. He lifted her into his arms, released her mouth, turned and continued up the hill.

If she was insane, she was going to enjoy it.

He'd been right; it wasn't far. Not ten minutes later, he set her down in front of a small building, set into a rocky crevice.

She looked around while he opened the door. Turning, she surveyed an incredible view. He'd chosen a site with an impressive vista. Directly downslope from their climb, at least two miles away, the city of Tortuga sprawled.

She wasn't a historian, but she seemed to recall that the historical island was small, round and nothing like where she stood. Haiti should be in view, but it wasn't. The bay where this city rested was broad, a near perfect crescent with horns close to meeting. She assumed that guaranteed a safer harbor, hard to attack.

Though with vampires about, she doubted attack was a problem.

To the right the island spread to another shore of the Caribbean. Maybe that was the beach where the Quill anchored the day Tink led her over the peninsula. Was it one of the crescent horns of the bay?

Looking that direction, another island barely showed in the distance.

"Where is that?" she asked Silvestri. He stood at her side, joining her in contemplating the view.

"Jamaica. An extremely clear day. Normally it wouldn't be visible."

"Where is Haiti? I've never looked at a map while on the Quill. I guess I should have."

"I'm not familiar with that name." He gestured past the city. "That way lays Hispaniola, a Spanish settlement."

"Maybe the French never colonized here."

"The French?" He chuckled. "No, the French have colonies, but small and sparsely populated. They tend to inhabit areas already civilized, like St. Marteen." He turned. "Now, come see my hideaway."

She followed him into the simple home.

❧

He waited for her to say something about how plain it was, to compare it to his cabin on the Immortal. But she said nothing, just wandered around the one room, lightly touching items.

She paused to read the titles on the books. Most were

volumes of fairy and folk tales. He'd collected them over fifty years of sailing. Was that a smile dancing across her face? She chuckled, stopping to extract one book. He knew that one.

"Where in the world did you find an illustrated *Joy of Sex?*" She shook her head. "Evidently a lot of interesting things fall through the cracks between my world and yours."

"Many more than you can imagine." He pulled a chair off a hook on the wall and sat. "Emily, there is more here than from only your time and world."

She froze, set the book back and slowly turned to face him. Groping for the bed, she sat, staring at him. "Other times?"

"I once met a man who hailed from the year 2250. He claimed to be a historian seeking accurate information regarding the formation of a Caribbean nation, which stretched from the Bahamas to the island of Barbados. He seemed quite surprised to find no political movement toward that end." He watched her digest the news.

Her hand shook slightly, brushing at her shaggy hair. He quite enjoyed how long it grew. But he imagined the length took some getting used to for her. He took a moment to imagine that thick luxurious mane down to her waist, shining in the sun. It would glow in the moonlight, the silver standing out from the dark, nut brown. If she stayed, he'd see that.

"How will I ever find my way home if there are so many possible portals?" She spoke so softly, he wasn't sure he heard her.

But his fantasy of her remaining at his side took the hit. He abruptly stood, knocking the chair back. He stalked to the bed, stood directly in front of her, and stripped off his shirt. He tossed it to one side and worked the buckle of his belt. He'd make her forget about any portal!

"What are you doing?" She scooted away from him. "We only got here, I'd like to clean off the sweat, get some food."

Interesting how she tried to deflect her desire, even while her eyes followed his every movement. She licked her lips when he cast off his belt.

"There is a spring outside. I'll feed you afterward." He jerked his boots off, leaning over to almost touch her, his bare chest inches from her face. With a final wiggle, he left his breeches on the floor, turned and walked out the door. He heard her snort, and then the patter of her ragged sandals on the wooden floor as she followed him.

Ten minutes later, they stood under the small waterfall, lost in kissing, touching, holding.

She'd laughed when first spying the small pool and waterfall. Her comment made little sense to him, but the water feature delighted her. And that was enough to make him smile.

"A real bit of cinematic license! A private shower provided by nature—it's so Disney!" She stripped quickly while he walked into the water.

It took him years to expand the pool to its present size. First, he'd removed the larger rocks, carried sand up from the beach, built a retaining wall, and directed the water to flow down the other side, away from his cabin. Smoothing the large rocks lining that side, sitting near the pond, rubbing one stone face upon the other until they carried no rough patches took the most time, but provided the most comfort. The stones faced the sun so they grew almost hot. He'd created a relaxing place to recline after the cool of the water, even planted a small bit of soft grass that ran nearly to the pool.

One of those folk tale books in his library showed a place like this. An enchanted pond where a beautiful woman kissed a frog and became royalty. He wasn't a frog. But Emily *was* the first woman he'd ever brought here. Her smiles and laughter made his heart soar with pride.

He pulled the hair back from her face; the better to layer kisses down one side and up the other. Her small hands clung tightly to his hips. The water swept away the sweat and with it his uncertainty of bringing her here. He admitted, her approval meant a great deal to him. His sanctuary.

The light filtered through the overhanging ferns and caressed her face.

"Emily Pawes."

"Hmmm?" She opened her eyes to meet his.

Time stood still. His heart took a leap of faith. Here in the sun, far from the chill of the lonely Caribbean he sailed, he found home in the deep wood warmth of her eyes, and he spilled his heart. "I love you, Emily Pawes."

Glacious couldn't hear, couldn't follow him to this place. Her domain was the sea and cold places. He might say those words, mean them, and her ice cold eyes wouldn't sharpen, set their sight on this warm woman in his arms....

Emily's eyes widened and her mouth gaped. With the sparkle from the waterfall spilling down her face, he couldn't tell...was that a tear? Her hands dropped from his hips, then she brought one to touch his face. "Oh, dear, Alan. Captain? But...what if you aren't real? What if none of this is real?"

"What if my being real isn't important?" He fought to keep his heart light. What counted is that he said the words to her. She would know, no matter what happened from here forward. She would know he'd said *I love you* and he'd meant it.

He went to his knees, pressed his lips to her belly and moved lower. She'd know how real he was, he swore she would.

❧

This place and this man—they were parts of a *Technicolor* dream that couldn't be real. She was Snow White or some twisted bit of a fairy tale. An obscure story Disney would never film. An old woman and an enchanted waterfall, a world full of daring pirates. This wasn't real.

Oh, God. What was he doing?

He lifted one of her legs, draped it over his shoulder, took his hands and spread her for his mouth, sliding fingers inside her. She shuddered, hands gripping his hair, aware of every stroke of his tongue, every nip of his teeth, each breath he took.

His hands, his fingers!

"Fuck! Fuck! God damned, fucking shit. Hell...hell...hell! Cock sucker! Fu-u-u-u-u-u-u-uck!"

Alan broke through every wall she'd ever built, clung to her when she fell to pieces and folded into the water. Sweeping her into his arms, he smiled, touched her lips and walked with her to a smooth rock, the size of a small table. He set her down, gingerly.

It was impossible to catch her breath, and she gasped, staring into the sky. The deep heat of the rock sank into her back. Slowly, she relaxed.

Why didn't he fuck her? He could have done anything.

He did. He told her he loved her. What did that mean? *He isn't real.* He was only a figment of her imagination. He...no, she made him up. Right? She turned her head toward where this figment stood.

Under the waterfall, he posed rinsing his hair in the water. Its silver cascade fell to his ass. His concave, old man, skinny ass. She snickered. "I made up a dream man with an old man's ass?"

Her body hummed, drew to attention when he turned slightly. His strong, sinewy arms, painted from the decades of Caribbean sun, made her think of sculpted tree limbs. His thighs.... She swallowed, felt her nipples tighten.

Without even thinking, she sat up, staring at him. He continued to turn toward her. He was erect, one hand dropped to his belly. He had a slight softness there. It made him more believable. A glistening trail of silver hair spiraled down to his prick. His fingers were spread. She took a breath and felt it sink to her toes.

She hadn't made him up. A sudden clarity flew about her mind, wiping it clear of the fear that she was mad. A small thread of logic tried to tangle her thoughts and she ignored it. If she was mad, this was the most glorious madness of all. Of life itself.

She slid off the rock, her feet anchored on the sandy bottom, but when she stood, her body overbalanced and almost stumbled.

"Emily?" He quickly closed the distance between her. "Are you...?"

He stopped when she closed her hand around his cock. She looked up into his sapphire eyes and only nodded. She set a hand at his chest and pushed him to lean back upon the rock she'd vacated. He didn't resist, merely allowed her to direct him. She let her free hand trail up his chest, following the silver trail. Slowly, she bent and kissed the pierced nipple, sucked it into her mouth and hummed.

He gasped, and the sense of power this gave her steadied her purpose. He'd touched her every way possible. He'd swept her away with passion and a personality that she held no defenses against. And no regrets.

Save one.

She didn't know how to do the same to him.

But she was going to try.

⌘

He accepted that she couldn't believe in his reality. No yet, although in his heart, he judged she wanted to. He'd met many people who walked through portals into the Kraken's Caribbean, and some did go mad. The terror of that possibility kept her from accepting this was more than a delusion. He'd be patient and she'd find her way to him.

Fifty years of walking his own world burdened by a curse schooled him in patience—and resignation.

The rushing water barely cooled his blood as he inhaled through barely open lips, tasting her again and again. He smiled at the memory of her curses. How odd that profanity took the place of other softer phrases, other thoughts and feelings. His heart knew she held more depth; that it anchored all the way into her bones, her blood and her breath. When he studied her eyes, they spoke softer words.

He turned to glance her way and froze. Her eyes studied him; her fingers absentmindedly touched her pierced nipple. He remembered the sharp cry she'd emitted when his needle pierced that wonderful, dark nipple, the same instant she'd melted around his cock. She'd been a woman totally immersed in passion and lust.

But he glimpsed something different this time. He tilted his head, a fierce longing…yes! She radiated with fierce longing. For him? Did he dare believe that?

Did he dare to trust? He allowed her to take charge and move his body to her bidding. To lay him upon the rock, to kiss and suckle at lips, neck, to forge a fire path down his torso. And he stayed passive, keeping his arms limp, though it killed him not to seize her. She flattened his hands, left no doubt in his mind that she wanted him to act as though bound. He trembled at the fantasy. No one ever dared tie him down.

She feathered kisses on his chest, nibbled her way down his chest. She bit his belly, chuckling low. Her hands spread his thighs like he was a woman, and at last she sank her lips about his prick.

He stood it for only a short while, fighting his body's demand to wrap around this woman and bury himself in her. At last the drive won. He raised his arms, lifted her from his prick and she allowed it. He could feel her desire as he maneuvered her up his body, the heat of her cunny leaving a liquid fuse. He parted her legs, sat up and they became one.

They kissed and he tasted his near capitulation to her on her tongue when they melted together. She took a deep breath and rocked upon his lap. In his last moment of clear thought, he locked eyes with her.

"Alan…Alan…Alan…" he heard her cry out.

It was enough proof.

Chapter Eighteen

*F*or the first time since her affair with Captain Silvestri began, she woke up with him still abed with her the next morning. His left arm draped over her, his warm hand cupping her breast. Not aggressively, rather relaxed and in total ease. Such a wonderful night. No talk of serious things. Very little talk.

They'd touched, stroked, and sat in companionable silence to watch the light fade from Tortuga. Few tiny flickers of light, from candle or lantern, reached the haven Silvestri built.

And no doubt he'd built it. She observed the pride he took, stroking the carving on the door, the polish on the table. How carefully he lifted the chairs to the hooks on the wall. He touched the headboard of the bed with lingering fingers. He eventually draped a light blanket over her shoulders as the night waxed and the stars shone intensely.

When the moon rose, she'd turned to him in surprise. "The moon is full?"

"Tomorrow night."

"Isn't that when the vampires waltz? How can they hold the party? Isn't it dangerous?"

"Tomorrow night is the blue moon. Second full moon of the month. They're only allowed one hunter's moon per month." He stroked her hair. "Have you ever worn it long?"

"Oh, sure. Nearly to my ass a few times." She'd leaned against his hand, wanting to purr, if she only knew how. She asked him later if the vampires would be at the party, and he'd assured her that yes, of course. But as participants, nothing more. He even promised to point out the swamp where the zombies wandered. It was well after midnight when they retired to the humble cabin.

It took her some time to fall asleep, even though her body craved it. Her mind spun with things he's spoken of earlier. Other times and other places? Her memory played back some of the things she'd seen when wandering Tortuga after her bath. She'd seen some strange stuff. A man in a top hat and tails. A woman in a silver cat suit, shawl tied around her hips. It wasn't just the blenders and microwaves that were out of place. She'd grown so used to seeing anachronisms that few of them registered as strange anymore. People, appliances, she'd even heard modern music sung at street corners and didn't think it strange.

The microwave on the ship. How did it find power? She'd never asked, just figured it was part of the vast delusion. Her memory produced a sudden vision of a man juggling in Nassau. *Rubik's Cubes.* He'd been juggling *Rubik's Cubes!* And the woman in the cat suit—holding a camera? Or maybe something totally different.

There'd been a lovely parasol in a window off High Street, with some sort of hydraulic tube attached to its handle. The proprietor could not say what it was for.

Suddenly, the story that Jezebel told her, how Tortuga was the site of washed up items from everywhere and every when became clear. She'd fallen to a black hole of lost items? Like where all the extra socks went when they disappeared from the dryer at home.

She finally fell asleep with visions of every lost item in the universe washing up on the beaches of the Caribbean like some vast landfill.

When morning came, her body was rested, but her brain still spun with all the possibilities. His breath was soft at the back of her neck. His cock stirred and she knew he was waking up.

The night before, he'd been near frantic in his pursuit of her pleasure. She'd been caught in the chase and run neck and neck with him. Like some mad contest, they'd pushed each other to a mindless state of satisfaction. Fun and furious, and she refused to consider any drawbacks. She knew he found her desirable now. There was no room in her mind for doubt after the night.

He pulled away from her, urging her onto her back. His hair covered her face when he bent to welcome the morning with a kiss.

The light slipped through partly opened shutters, illuminating his silver hair into a shining mass of brightness. She smiled, reached up and lightly pulled it away so she could meet his eyes. The sapphire appeared black for a moment. Then she wondered again at the depth of their color. She could dive into those eyes and just float away for the rest of her life. He met her gaze and examined her face. So intently, she wondered if he were memorizing it.

She understood the sentiment. She wanted to remember him always as well. Delusion or not.

She traced his crow's feet with her fingertips, loving how they drew attention to his eyes. She softly caressed the odd, crescent scar. He wouldn't tell her where it came from, making it a mystery. Wonder opened in her heart. This man loved her? He'd actually said those words to her.

If only she could say them back.

He winked, then murmured, "Doesn't matter."

"You reading minds now, Captain Silvestri?" Somehow the thought didn't surprise her.

"Not hard to see you toy with regret." He tilted his head at her. "Maybe even guilt. Whatever it is, it doesn't matter."

"It does too—"

He stopped her words with a kiss. One of his mind-numbing kisses, so soft that the thought of butterfly wings entered her mind. He continued to kiss her, and when his lips left her mouth, he replaced them with two fingers, silently asking her to drop her doubts.

She inhaled and smelled herself on his hand. And she kissed the pads, running her tongue along his nails, conveying trust and willingness to indulge whatever bit of decadence he wished to toy at.

He smiled, almost sadly, then moved his lips from her face, to her neck, to her breasts. He lingered on her breasts, using his tongue with pure magic. Her breasts were never been much of an erogenous zone. Until he woke them up.

She wrapped hands in his hair as he made love to each breast and nipple one at a time.

He touched softly, as if apologizing for the power of the night before as he continued down her body. He licked at scratches, rubbed bruises with a tenderness she didn't think many men were capable of. Each touch was in direct contrast the passion of hours ago. He made up for that desperate harshness with every move he made.

She didn't ask for it. Hadn't felt she needed the reassurance. He didn't hurt her and she'd never felt in danger. But a growing tenderness inside her signaled he'd been right.

He sank his mouth to her belly, and she could hear him speaking, but couldn't make out what he was saying. When his fingers dipped between her thighs, she didn't care anymore. His tongue and lips played her body like a symphony. Her brain shut down, stopped trying to understand or analyze. There was nothing in her experience to compare to this.

For an hour he savored her, coaxed words from her that she admitted in her heart as truth.

I want you. I want your touch. I want you. I need you. And finally *I love you.* That slipped from her as he slid her down an orgasm so intense and peaceful, she was no longer afraid of death, for just a moment. An hour of passionate progression about her body took her to nirvana. Every kiss, every touch, every gentle connection reinforced it. His cock anchored deep inside and she heard him murmur, *home.* She felt him release into her as she fought to keep from crying.

He sighed, took a breath, and kissed her. His arms wrapped around her, eased her up to sit atop his kneeling figure and he held her. For an eternity.

Her head rested on his chest, hearing his heart beat.

She'd just been made love to. She thought she'd been down that path before. Now she knew that was wrong. This was deeper than anything she'd ever come close to. With a sigh, she held him and accepted this new life and new love. Even this new world as her new home.

An hour later, he closed the door and they paused on the porch. Her head still spun, slowly adjusting to a new reality. She felt giddy.

He stopped before they began the descent to Tortuga. "Wait."

She turned to him. Damn, she loved a pirate. A cursed pirate. Somehow, the peace of that admission would stay here, on this mountain, where it was safe. He pulled a chain from his pocket. An extremely fine gold chain, and at the end, a pendant rested.

She reached to touch it. Smiled at the whimsical carving. "Must be the same artist who did my mirror. Oh! My mirror! I think one of the dyers stole it!"

"No, I have it. I don't know how it ended up left in my cabin, but I have it safe. I'll see it returned to you before the party is done. Meanwhile, take this. I saw it and knew it was for you."

Relieved to know her mirror was safe, she grinned. Turning, she drew back, eyes following the stark white carving descending to her chest.

"Do I return this Kraken when you get the mirror back to me?" she teased.

"No, dear Mrs. Pawes, this is yours. Promise me you will not remove it. I feel it may carry good luck. Not as mine, but good luck with no tricks."

She stroked the pendant and nodded. "An Old Monster, eh?"

He tilted his head at her. "Yes. Quite astute of you. Shall we head for the tailor's?"

Glad to know her mirror was secure and warmed by the simple gift, she merrily strode down the hill.

The day dawned with light mist. He directed her attention

to the north, where threads of vapor lingered despite the brightness of the day. "That is the swamp. The zombies seem quite content there. They gather ingredients for Mama Lu, and she takes care of them."

"Did she create them?" Emily asked casually, taking care to set one foot in front of the other. Her sandals were growing tattered.

"No one creates them. They are the nearly dead who choose to fade into the wilds instead of leaving with fanfare. The swamp takes them in, eases their last years. I understand zombies have a different evolution where you come from."

She paused, then turned to look up at him. She chuckled. "You could say that! They are the dead, raised by evil voodoo practitioners to be mindless slaves with a hunger for brains. In some fiction they are the result of a virus or pathogen that infects the living and the dead, turning them into mindless monsters. And they generally remain near the graveyards. Let me think, our swamps are said to be inhabited by lizard-like monsters. Or sometimes wandering mummies." She waved her hand. "All fictional, none real."

"There is little actual fiction here, Mrs. Pawes. Keep that in mind and you'll be safer than if you deny the reality of the Kraken's Caribbean constantly."

"That was said with such seriousness!" She waited for him to climb down next to her.

He kissed the side of her neck. "I am serious. It's best if you heed what others tell you regarding what you might see as nonsense and fairy tale."

"All right, Alan. I'll work at reining in my natural skepticism. You will keep us away from the Quill today? Or maybe I should go to the ship and check in?"

When she was with him—when they were alone together—uncertainty didn't enter into her thoughts. It wasn't that he made every decision. Though that was part of it. Tom had been so fair he'd often driven her mad by offering too many options, until making decisions was a burden. Alan simply led the way, and she wanted to follow him.

If they remained together, there would be more conflict, of

that she was certain. Right now, she was a visitor. But she'd want to lead, eventually.

The closer they got to the city, the more nervous she grew.

He took her hand. "I think it best if we remain on the outskirts. I will have your dress sent to the Tortuga Grotto, where the ball is being held. I have arranged a room for the day. You can rest, bath, and dress in comfort."

"You won't be there, right? At the ball?" Her heart tightened at this question. Because she wanted him there. Wanted to dance with him, wanted to see him dressed in finery. But she also didn't want him there. Didn't want to see Mick grow agitated and put himself in danger by attacking Alan. Didn't want to be revealed as a couple. Not yet. Not ready.

Alan shook his head. "Don't worry, Emily. I may linger out of sight long enough to see the glitter, but nothing more. I have a journey to make. You won't see me for some weeks, my dear."

"Oh." She took a deep breath, both relieved and disappointed. Turning, she looked into his face. "When you return, we must talk. Figure out a way...."

He set his fingers at her lips. "I know. We will talk, I promise you."

He kissed her again and quickly took her down a path that led toward the southern edge of the city.

Emily had done a fair amount of exploring the several times the Quill docked at Tortuga, but she didn't recognize a thing around her. The rock walls grew steep around them. One side of the path still presented buildings, store fronts and small shops though they grew sparse and a young forest took their place. But the rocky wall grew steeper and more formidable. She worried they were descending rather quickly.

Were they going underground?

They turned a corner and broad steps were before them, leading down toward a huge opening, where cascading ferns disguised how high the arch climbed. She gasped, "The Grotto?"

"Yes, the Great Tortuga Grotto. Home to the yearly

celebration, and said to house many portals. Obviously, not yours or you would know this place already. Do not be surprised at who or what you see at the ball tonight." He led the way down the steps, to a smaller side opening. He rang a bell, and they waited.

A lovely Asian woman rushed to greet them, bowing low to Captain Silvestri and taking Emily's hand shyly. "You come with me? We help you get ready."

"Go with her, Em. I will see your dress fetched and meet you in a few hours. You will enjoy the pampering."

"Alan?" She paused, took a deep breath and blew it out. "Can some word be sent to the Quill that I'm fine and will see them tonight?"

"I will take care of it. I look forward to seeing you polished."

She snickered. "If I have anything left to polish." She raised a hand. "Don't get on me about it. I look forward to seeing you bright and shiny, too. All right?"

He nodded. "Until this afternoon."

She let the woman drag her down the tunnel.

Three hours later, she'd been bathed, buffed, scrubbed, lubricated, dusted, polished, massaged, and scraped. She ran out of ways to describe it to herself. Oshi and Ishi, the first being the woman who'd brought her to the room, started it by leading her to a steam room.

Emily wasn't a prude, but it was a bit disconcerting to be stripped by two women, who then stripped themselves and insisted she allow them to take care of her. She was plucked and stroked. Her hair was washed six times, then dried and pulled back from her face with intricate combs. It amazed what they accomplished with so little length to work with.

Finally, she was given a robe and led to another room, where Silvestri sat waiting for her. A covered gown hung from a hook on a wall. He also wore a robe, but explained he'd barely begun to prepare, as he'd been running errands.

"First a good meal. It will be nearly midnight before they serve any food at the ball. And before you ask, yes, I sent message to the Quill. They've shifted the ship away from the pier. Other ships arrived and needed to unload items for the party, I imagine. There will be cutters available to get you aboard after the ball." He handed her a narrow box. "Your mirror."

"I thought you said it was on the Immortal. It hasn't come into port, has it?" A surge of worry tried to overpower the wonder of the day and her belly tightened at the thought of any confrontations.

"No. I'm sorry I didn't make that more clear. I found it in a room I'd taken. The Immortal is anchored miles away. Don't worry." He sat back when Oshi brought in a tray.

They shared an intimate lunch, deep in the rock carved rooms Emily gave up trying to understand why they were well lit, why the water was hot—all of the impossible aspects of what surrounded her. He'd said some portals opened to the future. Future technology might do this, she assumed.

He pushed away from the table and walked to a large padded bench, set against a wall. With total nonchalance, he dropped his robe and sat down. He leaned to one side, draping himself on the cushion. He gazed at her. "I want you now, before we dress. Come to me, Emily."

A sudden and unexpected self-consciousness rose in her. She'd been naked in front of her husband, but that was the years ago. As they aged, those times came less and less. But now, with Alan…. He lay before her, gloriously naked, posed to make her mouth water, and she wanted to be naked with him. But…she was old! Droopy boobs, stretch marks, and her belly sagged and her thighs dimpled and…she just couldn't move. This was stupid; she'd been naked with him, walked and talked and everything else. What made this different? Why did this feel so formal and even intimate? He sat back on the bench and tilted his head at her, totally relaxed with his nudity.

"Last time it was dark. I want to see you, Emily. All prettied up, polished and fine."

So easy for him to say. Sure, his body held some flaws. Wrinkles, scars, gnarly, ropy veins and even a bit of a belly. But he was a man with a ready cock, and that was all he needed to feel confident.

She needed more. She turned away, knowing she couldn't hide behind the robe forever. She wanted to be on that bench, with him. She needed to be with him. Slowly, she let the robe drop to her waist. Her back wasn't unattractive—maybe she could slide backward. Not face him.

But her ass! It drooped as flabby as her boobs. She sighed. The longing buried deep inside pushed her to just let go of the fear of rejection and just move. The last time she was in his bed, none of this mattered. Or in the water, at the island pond, she didn't feel naked there. He'd bathed her! Why now? Within the confines of this palace, her insecurities assailed her.

Let it go, let it go! She shouted at herself to release the baggage from a world she'd left behind. How many times would it take for her to hear he wanted her and that she wasn't old, wasn't useless and undesirable? Her head rang with the cacophony of the past. She wanted it gone!

Holding her breath in some vain attempt to keep her flesh tight, she dropped the robe to the floor.

Turning, she covered her face. She wouldn't watch his reaction. Moving slowly, she approached the proximately of the bench as he chuckled. Could she peek? Was he chuckling at her, at her boobs, her belly, her flaws? Now, in the stark light where nothing was hidden by shadow or water, she was totally revealed.

A warm hand touched her waist, drew her close until her knees touched the upholstery. His breath crossed the back of her hand. She shivered, ready to bolt, wanting to run. And at the same time, never wanting to be anywhere but with him. It was confusing. Why had this insecurity risen? Because he'd told her about his next voyage and she would miss him less if she could find fault with him? She must stop trying to protect herself and embrace this place and time. He'd return. He said he'd come back and they would talk of what was next.

He enticed her onto his lap and spent an inordinate amount of time kissing and touching her before urging her to open her legs and bring an end to the extensive foreplay. All her nerves disappeared once he held her—once she held him. He was an anchor of confidence. "I'd take you on the floor, but Oshi would skin me alive if I mess up your hair," he admitted. "I swore I would not touch your head."

Emily snickered, all discomfort gone. A relief to have it banished. She swore to get over past nonsense. He could have anyone, but he wanted her. She found proof of her desirability every time he met her eyes. She smiled. "I have no idea what they've done. They won't let me see a mirror. Oh, wait!"

She reached for the box he'd set on the table. He set a hand atop it. "Don't spoil their surprise. Trust me, you look wonderful."

He quieted her with a kiss, keeping his hands at her neck. When he revealed the dress, Emily stared. "Uh, that's not a blouse and skirt."

"No, of course not. But your fabric is here." He gestured at the bodice. "The rest compliments it, and you."

She carefully approached it, worried she might damage it. "It's thoroughly lovely, but I'll trip—it's too long."

He reached down and hiked up the front with several fabric ties. "No, you won't."

"Oh, that will work." She touched the bodice, laced with soft cord like a bustier. The skirt wasn't too full. She'd be able to handle this much fabric. The tailor managed to match the piece she'd fallen in love with. The skirt echoed the gold and red of the blouse. A deep red, almost burgundy belt crossed the waist. And a bag matching the sleeves was secured to the belt. A reddish petticoat peeked out from underneath the gold. The period slip was gold, but not quite. She examined it, trying to name it correctly. Like the shade of well-made Bavarian cream from a cream-filled donut.

Her mouth watered. She missed donuts.

She swallowed. The bodice was terribly low cut.

"I'm going to spill out."

"No, you won't. You ready to let them help you dress?"

"I'm going to need help? How will I get this off later if I need help now?" She snorted. Normally her clothing consisted of easy fasteners, like zippers. This dress had ribbons and ties and stays. "And damn, I have no shoes to do this justice!"

"Yes, you do." He pointed to a box off to one side.

She gave up trying to act surprised. She knelt and pulled the box over. Lifting the lid, she sighed in appreciation. The shoes were lovely. They matched the skirt perfectly. A pair of delicate short boots, with a stacked heel. Laces. She touched them. "Oh. Alan!"

He knelt and kissed the back of her neck.

"People will begin to arrive soon. Some are already gathering—the drinking starts quite early. I'll call Oshi in to help you while I see to myself."

"But you won't be coming down?" She looked up at him, one shoe held delicately in her hand.

"Don't worry!" He kissed her, careful not to disturb the small bits of paint the Asian women had used to decorate her, then left the room.

She was still kneeling when the two ladies hurried in to help.

Why did the crew knowing about Silvestri scare her? Most in Tortuga didn't look at Alan Silvestri with loathing or fear. She imagined they might if he tried to overstay his cursed allotment.

She might stay on here. She could work for the Barmy Cock—be here when he was able to make land. Would the ladies on the Quill ever forgive her? Would Mick?

The distraction lasted while they laced her up. The top didn't bind as she'd feared it would, and she would after all be able to get out of the dress by herself if necessary. It would take some twisting, but it was possible. The sleeves reached her wrist, snug fitting and edged with lace. The same delicate lace decorated the purse, with stays in it. She lifted it, once dressed and tried to figure out what it was for. It seemed unusual to brace a purse like this.

"Your mirror, my love." Alan spoke from the doorway. He wore a regal captain's coat in a burgundy so dark it looked black. A shirt of old gold matched her skirt, and his breeches were black. His boots gleamed.

She glanced over at him and smiled. "You are a rare treat for the eyes, Captain Silvestri."

"And you, a precious treasure." He pulled her mirror from the box and showed her how it tucked into the bag. "I don't want you to risk losing this again. The stays will protect it from harm while you carry it with you." He turned her to a curtain and drew it back to reveal a mirror.

She gasped.

This isn't me! This is someone else!

It reminded her much of a mix between the pirate and Goth world. Some steampunk? But in color—most of the steampunk costumes she'd seen consisted of mainly black, brown and some ecru. The skirt style she called a circle skirt, the blouse was relatively simple, save for the stays and bustier. It revealed a great deal of neck and shoulders. The girls did her hair up with delicate combs that sparkled with garnets. And he was right, the colors made her glow.

A corner of her mouth lifted. "You enchanted me, Alan. I don't know who I am anymore."

He stood behind her and draped a sparkling collar-style necklace down over her head. If drifted past her eyes and they widened in appreciation. Garnets—deep, wine-red garnets. It covered her neck and dipped past her collar bone. Garnets, citrines and even a handful of peridots. She lifted one hand to touch it. "Where did you get this?"

"Does it matter?" he asked, smoothing it down and holding up matching earrings. She slipped them on, feeling tears gathering at her eyelids. He wiped them away before they fell.

The white pendant fell behind the necklace, leaving the stark white monster to peer out from below the sparkle.

"You are Captain Silvestri's woman. I want you to always know that."

Her heart sang when she softly replied, "Emily's captain. I like that."

"Good! I shall escort you only far enough to be where I can see your crew observe your glory."

He hurried her along the tunnels. She heard the roar of a crowd and slowed. He allowed her hesitation. "We can stay in one of the side rooms for a while, until you become accustomed to the crowd. I know it is must larger than what you live with on the Quill. Shall I fetch you have a glass of wine to calm your nerves?"

"Rum punch," she managed to choke out.

He assisted her in finding a deeply shadowed nook to wait in. She could see the room but remain hidden until she was ready. She peered out at a room that Hollywood would have loved to film. A grotto made up of several chambers, joined to a massive dome, a ceiling covered with stalactites. There were pools along the edges, peeking through rocky openings. Light reflected onto walls, tables, and people. The room shone with colors, countered superbly with shadows, giving an impression of sparkle and shine everywhere. An orchestra tuned up out of her line of sight.

The acoustics here must be incredible.

Alan returned, holding an icy glass in one hand. She smiled in relief and drank a healthy swallow. He leaned close. "The Quill crew isn't here yet. Come with me; we can sneak in a waltz before they get here. I want to dance with you."

"Where do people dance? There's no room out there, and the floor isn't even." She took another deep swallow of the delicious punch.

He led her down another tunnel, and suddenly, they were in the room with the orchestra and a smattering of dancers. This floor there was smooth and polished. But the room held the same magic. Subdued lighting, sparkling bits of quartz, and hushed alcoves hinted of lover's meetings. She let the magic seep into her.

They stepped into the room and he lifted her glass away and handed it to a man standing nearby. He nodded to the orchestra, and they quickly ended the tune they were playing and a waltz began. A studied slow waltz.

She knew how to waltz. She had taken lessons, but never found the relaxation and confidence to enjoy the music and flow with it.

"I'm not terribly good at...."

He took her hand and gazed into her face. He wore no hat with this ensemble. His hair fell in waves to his elbows. The few bits of dark blond stood out from the fall of silver. She looked to her side in the formal manner she'd been taught by the dance master until Alan spoke. "Look at me, Emily. Please."

"Okay." Turning her head, she inhaled, and suddenly they were moving. She stumbled once, but his power and confidence soared into her and she let go. The shoes whispered to her. *Let us! Let us!* And she surrendered, not the strangest thing she'd experienced since arriving here. Let the shoes do the dancing.

He led, the shoes followed and she glided along.

They waltzed slowly, gradually building speed as they moved across the floor. There were other dancers, but once Emily and Silvestri spun and whirled the rest backed away, leaving the dance floor, and standing in a circle to admire them.

He watched her, those sapphire eyes sharp, yet warm at the same time. Blue was a cold color, right? Not his. She melted into his arms and those eyes. They whirled, spun, following the music to a sweet unity.

One, two, three. One, two, three. Her skirt swirled out in a graceful sweep. Her back arched, thrusting her pelvis close to his, and she flushed. One corner of his mouth lifted, one eyebrow. He took a decisive step forward, inserting his thigh neatly betwixt her legs. She obediently stepped back, albeit reluctant to do so. He released her hand, and she spun in a circle under his raised arm.

He pulled her back and continued to circle.

One, two, three. One, two, three.

Damn, what would it be like to tango with this man?

The music reached its crescendo, then slowed. Her heart calmed while the frantic circling eased with sweet deliberation. He held her closer, drawing their extended arms to tuck against his chest. The music faded away.

Her breath stilled, as she became totally lost in his arms. Without thought of where they were or who might be watching, they kissed. She wrapped her arms around him and sank into the passion binding them together. She clung to him, wanting him with a matched desperation and a calm knowingness, a deep chime of belonging rang inside her.

Very slowly, the kiss ended, as they pulled from each other, releasing the contact reluctantly. She sighed, turned her face and set her head upon his chest. She opened her eyes, focus gradually returning only to see that directly across the floor stood Captain Jezebel, with Mick at her side, and the crew spread out behind them.

Her heart froze.

Chapter Nineteen

She pushed Alan away, terrified at the exposure. How to get out of this? And Mick, fuck it! The look on his face did not bode well for either her or Silvestri. "Damn. Alan, you need to get out of here. Now."

"What?" he crooned at her. Until his glance lifted and he saw what she gazed at. His voice grew heavy, sounding of grief. "Oh, hell. My luck plays with us. You will be safe. Jezebel will see to it." He touched her face, turned and hurried away before she said another word.

"*Coward!*" Mick's voice carried over the new music. "*Face me!*"

Emily took several steps toward Mick, who was being held back by Jezebel. His gaze shifted to her. "You ungrateful, treacherous bitch."

"I'm sorry, Mick. It was never my intention to hurt you. I'll gather my belongings and leave the ship." She nodded at Jezebel. "Captain." She stepped around Mick and headed for the exit, hoping she could find her way out of the grotto. Tears gathered in her eyes, but she held them from falling. Standing straight, she walked like she owned the floor. She was not ashamed. Her back was straight, her chest thrust forward and she kept her eyes lifted. This is a good thing, she kept repeating to herself. No more lies, no more hiding. It is time to move forward. This was hard, but it wasn't impossible

Too bad the expression on Mick's face didn't echo her sentiments. She finally got someone to point her toward the main door to the outside stairs. She hit the fresh air and took a moment to just breathe.

"Pawes? Captain Jezebel directed me to stay with you."

She turned to see Davis at her side.

"You don't want to miss the party—I'm fine. Ready to leave anyway, tired of pretending...."

He took her arm. "Orders are orders, Pawes."

She closed her eyes and nodded. "Fine. He brought me here via some back street route, I'm not even sure how to get back to the port."

She appreciated his silence while he led her along a surprisingly short route to where the ships were anchored. He took the oars of a small boat, called a cutter, and helped her to the deck—even followed her to her cabin. She pulled out the largest basket she possessed and gathered items. Her book-binding supplies, the small things she'd bought in the various ports they'd visited. She even tucked Tink's obscene carving into the basket.

Next, she gathered up her few items of clothing. When she turned to leave, Davis stood in her way.

"Pawes, my orders included keeping you on the ship."

She studied him. He was her friend, but he also obeyed orders. He didn't seem to care for these orders, but he met her eyes and didn't apologize.

"On the ship? What am I—a prisoner? You can't keep me here!" She tried to push past him, but he was as impossible to break through as a brick wall.

"I'm afraid I can. I don't believe they mean to force you to stay if you don't want to, but Mick will want to question you. And Jezebel—she'll want answers, too." He touched her face. "Is it bad being here?"

She took a step back. "I love him. I know I can't be with him all the time, because of the curse. But I can be ready for when he can come ashore. I'll take whatever time I can get."

The words surprised even her. Had she told Alan she loved

him? She wasn't sure. Her heart accepted she loved him, but had the words actually crossed her lips? She hoped they had.

"Pawes, even I recognized you care for him. But you've managed to meet with him regularly and stay on the ship. Why must that change?" He smiled at her. "You always came back from being off-ship with contentment pouring from your skin. I'm happy for you."

"They aren't—Mick, I mean, or Jezebel."

"The Captain might surprise you, Pawes. And Mick will bend to her will, surrender his own agenda if she commands it."

She studied him, this man who taught her blades, who helped her with almost everything she attempted on the ship. He never lied to her. Setting the basket down, she tossed her bag on the bed.

"You're not going to let me leave. And if they stay for the entire party it's going to be hours and hours." She glanced down at the dress, a bit rumpled from getting to the ship. "I can get out of this by myself, but some help would make it easier. Will you untie the back for me? I'll change and maybe see what is available in the galley?" He'd always been an ally; she wasn't going to challenge him now. And perhaps Cookie left out some rum. She could use more alcohol.

She'd leave the ship tomorrow, find a room and see if Sam would let her work the bar, for tips if nothing else. It would be enough.

◈

Jezebel caught him in the room where Emily dressed. He bent down to gather the tattered sandals. He'd see them into the pack and back to the Quill. She'd need them….

"What have you been doing, Silvestri? And what in the hell were you doing here? Now? With her?"

He turned and smiled at the fierce Captain Jezebel. He remembered when she'd first come through a portal. All spit and vinegar, barely a woman yet. But she'd gone on to conquer Tortuga in record time. No one knew what to do with her. She dominated every man she took to bed and drew strong women to her with a magnetism that brooked no argument. She captained a ship of her own before two years passed.

"Jezebel, it's been too long since I've seen you. I hear the ship is doing well." His attempt at small talk fell flat. She glared at him. He turned and continued to pack up Emily's items.

"Don't try to avoid me. I've got Tink and Janey out there holding Mick back. You are not supposed to be here—that is the deal!"

"The deal. Yes. I am sorry. I didn't intend to be seen. I but craved one dance with her. My spies reported you lingering at the Barmy Cock. My sentries at the entrance failed to alert me of your arrival, obviously. The Immortal is over at Hockster Bay, and I'll be gone before the dawn."

She growled and blocked the door when he turned to go. He held out the bag. "Will you see this is returned to Mrs. Pawes?"

"Put it down. I'll see she gets it." The savvy captain met his eyes. "Shit. She intends to leave the ship. She'll find a room and wait for stolen moments with you, I'm certain. I won't stop her. You make sure she has good lodgings, she's been a good sailor."

"Keep her on the ship, Jezebel, please?" He pulled out a chair and offered it to her. She sat and he took another, across from her. "I'm looking to end this curse, Jez. But I might fail. Keep Mick close, and Pawes. She dodged the curse, too. Tried to shoot me at the baths. If I lose, it might take aim at them. Keep her for at least a month. You've bound that ship with enough spells; it should keep them both safe."

Jezebel eyed him a moment, sighed. "She isn't going to understand. She'll fight. But you've kept your word and stayed away from the Quill, so I'll do it. Mick is going to beat on her bad." Jezz crossed her arms leaned back.

He admired her outfit. Pure black, so dark it sucked light from the room. No color save for a bit of red trim at the sleeves and bodice. Yet she glowed at the center of it. Captain Jezebel, a formidable woman.

"Pawes can handle Mick. Keep that wolf close to her, he seems level-headed." Silvestri saw the bare twitch at the corner of her lips. Yes, he knew about her crew. He was well aware that Davis was from the forest werewolf pack. He knew more of her crew than she knew of his.

She tilted her head. "Why do you care about Mick, Alan? I know you two were friends, but it's more than that. The look you shot his way? That was pain. You two lovers?"

Silvestri grinned. "That would fit the box you have us in, wouldn't it, Jez?" He snorted and shook his head. "No, not lovers." He considered if it was time to reveal the truth to her. If he didn't come back, she'd be the only one to know. She would explain it to Mick.

He held up his arm and used it to cover his lower face. His hand did the same for the space above his eyes. He leaned close to the fierce pirate captain. "Look familiar?"

She froze, her eyes narrowed, then she blinked. He knew when she realized it. "He's blood!"

"Yes. That man he called father wasn't his father. Nor am I. I *am* his elder brother. Our father was a true libertine who seduced Mick's mother and got her pregnant. She never told her husband, but he knew, knew Mick wasn't his. Figured it out and threw it in my face when I tried to convince the idiot to leave the gambling halls. Mick suspected Daniel wasn't his father. Used to joke about it those months he spent risking my curse for his own greed. Neither of us thought we were brothers." He dropped his hands. "If I disappear, my solicitor will transfer most of my holdings to Mick. Explain why, Jezebel."

"Nothing for Mrs. Pawes?" Jezzie looked away. She never was one to easily address sentiment. "I saw that dance. That kiss. She is desperately in love. Exactly as you are with her."

It did his heart good to hear the later words. But he didn't reply to them. "What I have set aside for her will see her free to live here, a rich woman."

"And if you do return? Without a curse? Mick will have nothing to hold back for."

"He holds back for one reason now. He knows he's wrong. He doesn't understand it, but he knows he's wrong. His father played him a fool and started a vendetta where none exists. I have proof of my part in keeping that idiot from dying in prison. When Mick is ready to listen, I'll present it to him."

"He holds back because I make sure our ships do not cross!" She peered at him. "Don't fool yourself that he doesn't hate you."

"I believe he hates me. But he doesn't know why. And Mick is a pragmatic man. Leave it to me, Jezebel. Now, if you will excuse me, I have a letter to write. I will send it to you on the Quill. Please, give it to her only if I do not return."

Jezebel stood and held out her hand. They shook. She turned to the door and reached for the bag. She didn't turn as she spoke softly. "Why her? Why now?"

"An Old Monster intervened. And I run out of time to break this curse or be broken by it."

"The Kraken brought her here?"

"I believe so and Mama Lu confirms it. I have seen the Old Monster. Mama Lu is assisting me, to end this. I have a little over a week to see it done. I would explain more, but my luck is finally running out."

"How many times did you manage to meet with her?" Jezzie turned to look at him a she opened the door. "You toyed with her?"

"It began lightly. The way most great things do. The same as with you and Mick."

She walked hurriedly away. She wouldn't hear of loving Mick. Though the depth of her love glowed like the full moon in the night sky. That was Jezebel's way, it always had been.

He turned to the small desk, pulled out a sheet of paper and sat, considering the right choice of words to tell Emily goodbye.

Chapter Twenty

*E*mily fell asleep before the rest returned. Davis had assisted her in removing her dress, then stepped outside the cabin while she dressed in the cleanest of her sailor's duds. He'd accompanied her to the galley, where they found some fresh bread, butter and cold, roast chicken.

He didn't speak, and she was thankful for that. Hours passed. They shared a bottle of rum and the drink made her sleepy, finally left her ready to return to her cabin.

She woke to feel the ship moving. Jerking from the bed, she turned to the door, only to see Mick poised on a chair just inside her small cabin. He blocked the open door, one foot propped on the doorframe. His arms crossed, he glared at her, dark and foreboding.

"Damn it, Mick. I said I'd leave. Let me out of here before we leave port!"

He didn't move, even when she took a step toward him.

"Too late, false friend. You aren't going anywhere until Captain Jezebel and I are satisfied. Reconcile yourself to that fact."

"What? You can't keep me here!" Heart pounding, she took another small step closer to him. She reached out and tentatively pushed at his leg, blocking her way. He didn't budge. "Captain Michael, please. I've been a good sailor. I've followed orders. I...I saved Jezebel's life! Let me go!"

"No." He slowly stood, shoved the chair out the door. "Don't try to curry favor with me. Consider your story, Mrs. Pawes. We'll send for you at our convenience."

She jerked her head back just in time to miss being slapped by the door as Mick slammed it shut.

"You bastard! Let me out of here! It happened! Nothing planned! I love him! MICK!" Sagging against the door, she tried to open it, but found it barred from the outside. She hadn't known that was possible.

She pounded on it. "Davis? Davis! Let me out!" She sank to the deck, astounded at the turn of events.

"Yes, let her out, Davis. Some use your talented nose turned out to be. I wonder how many times she crawled from his bed to our ship without raising your hackles! I thought you wolves could scent a mouse from a mile away." Mick's derision carried through the door.

"I've never met the man, Captain Mick. I knew she took a lover, but that was her business. I work your sails, sir. I'm not your dog."

A bark of laughter answered that. She heard boots tread away.

"Davis?" She softly spoke to the crack in the door. "Davis?"

"I'm here, Pawes."

His bare feet were visible at the bottom of the door. "You spied on me?" she asked, her heart aching. He was her friend!

"No, I watched over you. I knew you met someone, but he made you happy. Your scent changed, from worried and nervous to calm and content. It still doesn't matter to me that it was Silvestri. I know he made you glow. Nothing else matters."

"My scent?" Her head whirled. "Mick called you a wolf?"

"I'm a werewolf. You didn't know? It's not a secret, Pawes."

Inside the cabin, Emily shook her head. "Doesn't matter. I suppose. Thank you for being my friend. Can you get me out of here? Please!"

"We're at sea, Pawes. They won't keep you aboard against

your will for long. Be patient and you'll be set ashore soon."

"I'm...scared. He is so angry," she whispered.

"Be brave."

She finally let herself cry. Again and again, she'd kept herself from a wet hysteria, but now she broke free. Curling up on the wooden floor, she sobbed. One hand held the pendant he'd given her as she worried he would try to rescue her. Worried he wouldn't.

She heard the crew come by, asking Davis about her. Janey tried to talk through the door, but Emily crawled back to her cot and stared into the dimness, too tired to formulate thoughts.

Hours passed before the door opened. Davis held out his hand, offering her company. "They want to see you. Privy first?"

"Yes." Her fifty-three years weighed her down as she rolled off the bed. She took his hand and leaned on him. He allowed her the time she needed to freshen up. Washing her face, she stared at her reflection in the small mirror. The glorious vision from last night was gone. She'd pulled the combs free the night before and tucked them carefully into her basket. Her hair no longer shone, it stuck up at odd angles, and the gray seemed more prominent than ever before. And it was dull, lifeless. Her eyes revealed signs of tears.

"Oh, Alan. How did this happen?" She softly spoke to her image. "Emily, what do you want? You want that man? Want to be there for him, however it works out? Well, get yourself out of here, woman. Come on! Snap out of it." Splashing water on her face again, she swept another handful back over her scalp, smoothing the messy strands into place.

Straightening her back, she left the privy, met Davis' eyes and walked before him to the Captain's cabin. She was ready to face the music.

❧

Silvestri reached his ship before dawn, climbed aboard, and ordered them to set a course north. Tucked into his pocket was the small vial of perfume he'd removed from her sailor's bag. It was empty, but the scent still lingered enough to bring her to mind when he unscrewed the top.

They avoided normal shipping lanes, heading due north, and Silvestri stayed at the wheel. When the wall of ice rose before him on the third night, he let the wheel run free, and the Immortal slipped through a secret passage, into the heart of the glacier. Where she waited.

❧

Jezebel gestured to a chair. "Sit and eat something, Pawes."

Emily nodded, figuring the captain needed to be civil.

The kidnapping bitch.

Mick glowered at her, leaning against a cabin wall and nursing a tankard. Sitting down, she emptied the plate in front of her. She didn't really taste anything, but eating bought her time to assess the mood in the room. Mick was still glowering at her, but Jezebel seemed almost uncomfortable. Maybe that would work to her advantage. If she could figure out how to use Jezz being off balance. When she was done, Mick moved forward, but Jezebel pointed to a chair next to her. "Sit, Mick. Let me question her."

It was time to be decisive. "Why question me? What does it matter? I understand I can't stay aboard the ship. Let me go and I'll never bother you again."

"Can't do that until I'm satisfied. And at the moment we're heading to Nassau." Jezebel tapped on the table. "I want to know everything. Every meeting, when, how long, where. What did he ask, and what did you tell him."

"You have to be kidding! It's none of your business!" Emily pushed back from the table. "Fine, I'll get off in Nassau and take passage back to Tortuga on my own."

"No, you won't. You'll answer, and then you'll serve as bait. He'll come for you and I'll have my chance." Mick grinned at her. "Spill it."

"Why should I?" Crossing her arms, she steeled herself to argue. "Why is it your business? Bait? You're a fool if you think you'll be able to defeat his curse, Mick. This vendetta is stupid."

"Stupid? You don't know all of it, Pawes." Mick made to stand up, glaring at her. Jezebel put her hand on his shoulder to stay the action.

"Not now, Mick. Emily, you'll answer my questions because he is dangerous—to us as well as to you. This is not a negotiation, Mrs. Pawes." Jezebel looked behind Emily and nodded. "Bring it here, to the table."

Emily twisted in her chair when Tink strode in. The tall woman carried the basket packed when Emily thought she'd just leave the ship, before she'd been shanghaied. Behind Tink were two other crew members, each hauling items belonging to Emily.

"What the fuck are you doing?" Emily prepared to push the chair back, set her hands on the table to get out the chair, but Davis moved behind her, setting strong hands at her shoulders.

"Nothing will be harmed, or stolen," he reassured her.

She stared in disbelief. One item at a time, Jezebel removed everything she'd packed. The items were examined carefully, flaps lifted, papers separated and scanned, books flipped through. Her book tools were set to one side, where she couldn't reach them. What did they think she'd do? Threaten them with a needle? Tink and the other women left the cabin before everything Emily owned was put on display. The jewelry Silvestri gave her remained on the table after the rest were packed away.

Mick tossed another bag on the table. "Such a thoughtful man," he said with a sneer. It was her small pack. When she saw her *Teva* sandals, her spirits lifted. He was a thoughtful man! No matter how Mick derided him.

In the end, the jewels were the only thing left on display. The dress she'd worn the night before was draped over a nearby chair, along with the three shirts he'd ordered to replace those the dyers had ruined, or he destroyed when his impatience saw what she wore damaged. The shoes she'd worn to dance were there. They'd even found the first pearl pin, which she'd left secured to the inside of her pack.

Jezebel studied the summation of Emily's life on the ship. She pointed to the pearl. "The first gift? It's humble-more of a symbolic gesture. The rest are much more grand—perhaps as his interest grew, so did his gifts."

Emily sighed. "Why? Why should I tell you?"

"Answer us. Were these bribes—to betray us?" Mick spouted off bitterly.

Emily brushed off Davis' hands and stood up. She walked over to where Mick sat and slapped him. He didn't react, but took it. Maybe he knew he's crossed a line, Emily didn't care. Turning to Jezebel, she nodded. "Yes, the first gift. I didn't know who he was. He'd pulled me away from watching the vampires waltz, but not fast enough. I was blind and scared. He…when my sight returned, he was gone. I only found out who he was when I prepared to return to the ship."

Surrendering to the inevitable, she told them about each item. She didn't elaborate, despite the demand from Jezebel for every detail. Now and again, Mick snickered but Emily ignored him.

"That dance…he is a good dancer." Jezebel touched the shoes. "I remember where I first saw these. He offered them to Mama Lu—she told him to keep them, to save them. They were special and belonged to someone else. He'd know who to give them to, she said."

"To Mama Lu? For a trade?" Emily asked. Was that why she'd danced so gracefully, why her feet hadn't stumbled, or tripped? Magical shoes? Who else would recognize they weren't ordinary shoes?

"Mama Lu is the only woman he knew as a friend, I imagine."

"You remember? You were there?" Mick asked.

"I often visit Mama Lu. My path crosses with Silvestri, Mick. Hell, I've known him longer than I've known you" Jezebel looked at Emily. "Anything else? Anything you have on you?"

"You gonna search me if I say no?" Emily smoothed the ties of the bustier she'd worn the night before, still draped on the chair. She'd looked so vibrant.

"Is there anything else?" Jezzie's voice was steady.

Emily reached into her shirt and withdrew the Kraken pendant. Mick leaned forward and put out his hand. Emily leaned away and snarled at him. No damned way was he going to touch this gift.

Jezebel took a step close and looked at the carvings of the pendant. "This matches your mirror."

Her mirror still lay on the table, tucked into the specially boned bag that matched the dress. Once Silvestri slid the mirror into the bag, she understood why the stays were part of the design. They provided protection to the trinket.

"Fascinating thing, that mirror. He ever touch it?" Mick lazily asked.

"Yes," Emily replied.

"He ever tell you...." Mick stood up, reached for the bag and pulled out the mirror. "Those days you searched for a portal, so intent on finding a way home. Did he ever tell you that you carried it with you all the time?"

"What? My mirror isn't a portal. It isn't big enough!" Emily snorted.

"Size has nothing to do with it." Jezebel took the mirror from Mick and held it close to the pendant. "Same artist." She turned to Mick. "You knew. Why didn't *you* tell her?"

He didn't answer, just looked away.

"Don't condemn Silvestri for keeping the same secret you did," Jezebel said. "You might have told her."

"She mixes good drinks." He stole a glance at Jezebel from the side. "You said you'd smile every morning if you woke to a Rum Sunset. And now you have."

"You kept her here because she's a good bartender? Because of a drink? At least he cares for her!" Jezebel, to Emily's surprise, seemed genuinely angry.

"He fucks her; he uses her." Mick stalked to the door. He thought to escape Jezebel's anger, Emily realized. She wasn't even part of this argument anymore.

Mick stopped at the door and turned to continue the battle with his captain. "Cares for her? Because he gave her baubles? They mean nothing! Remember, you told me that...."

Emily ignored their spat and took the mirror from Jez, who handed it over without resistance. She followed Mick, pushing him away from the door, and escape, deeper into the cabin.

Same artist? A portal? And he knew? If he'd told her, she would have left. She'd be back in California and her normal life. She probably would have never stabbed a man in the back, or been frightened of a kidnapping or...known Silvestri's touch. She tried to fathom it, her mirror was a portal. And Silvestri knew? Mick knew.

Davis packed her baubles back into her basket.

She dropped her sandals to the floor and slipped into them. "Did you know it was a portal?" Emily eyed the congenial werewolf, taking care with her mirror, her portal, as she moved closer to assist him.

"No. It's unusual for one to be this small. I don't know how Mick surmised. But he may be wrong, Pawes."

"You think Silvestri used me?" She sat again, uncertain.

"It doesn't matter what I believe. What do you consider the truth?"

"I don't know. He never asked me anything about the Quill, nor about Mick. He told me about this world. He helped me find my way. I'm a suspicious person, Davis. I assumed he wanted something from me. I don't know at this moment what I believe." She lifted the pendant at the end of the chain, glanced at it a moment, slipped it off from around her neck, and tucked it into her pocket.

"Can I leave now?" she asked the bickering couple.

When they ignored her, Davis picked up the basket and grabbed the bag. She took up the smaller pack and followed him past Jezebel and Mick, heads together. It looked like their argument was ending, no more shouting, but a lot of whispering. He stroked her arm and she laid a hand on his chest.

Outside, the sun was setting. It seemed hard to believe an entire day passed since leaving Tortuga. She wondered where Silvestri was at this moment, off on his mysterious voyage. She ignored everyone, went to stand at the rail and reached into her pocket. For a moment, she considered throwing the wonderful pendant away. Throwing everything he'd given her away was one way to handle her pain.

He knew she searched for a portal. Maybe he didn't know

the mirror was a portal? She kept her hand wrapped around the chain in her pocket and shook her head.

"You looked right together."

She turned to gaze at Tink, the last woman she'd expect to hear a kind sentiment from. Tink met her eyes, a crooked smile on her face. But it wasn't an unkind smile. It appeared thoughtful, almost envious. "You whirled and twirled, completely focused on each other. One would have thought no one else was in the grotto, just you two. Absolute perfection. Even the vampires commented on how perfectly you danced. They were enormously impressed with your waltzing. I talked with Keitran. He remembered you and regretted your escaping them. They do so enjoy a good dancer. I told him you'd never dance like that with them. They'd need to take him, too." She chuckled. "Made him laugh. Imagine a vampire with the devil's luck? Would the curse embrace the idea, knowing it would make him nearly immortal or see it as an attack? Boggles the mind!"

Emily took a deep breath, fighting not to cry, scream, or babble.

Tink lightly touched her arm, and they both turned to watch the sun set, saying nothing more.

❧

For two days, Emily ignored the rest of the crew. She felt old, and looking at any of them reminded her of exactly how many years she'd been around. She caught Mick eyeing her whenever she took to the deck. Davis brought her food to the cabin, but she barely ate.

The third day, they anchored at the Baths Island. Emily didn't even ask to go ashore. She knew there was no settlement, no way off and she didn't want to be marooned or risk reminding herself of how wonderful it was when Silvestri showed her the great pool. She examined her mirror again and again, and tried to will it to show her something. But it remained just the bit of bric a brac she'd won from the woman at the pirate festival.

Most of the crew remained ashore that night. Emily heard Mick return to the ship cursing and assumed he'd fought with

Jezebel again. It didn't matter, they'd work it out. Emily had grown used to watching them spit and circle each other. It was usually a prelude to their disappearing into the cabin for hours on end. Some people enjoyed the rush of a good battle. Who was she to judge?

Not like her and Silvestri. One thing about Alan, he wasn't argumentative.

She crawled onto her cot, wearing a tattered pair of breeches and a light shirt. She still hadn't taken the pendant from her pocket. So tired, confused by all she'd been told, she drifted into a troubled sleep.

When the finger of cold air crept through the thick hull to touch her, she shivered. A dream wove around her, of Alan, his soft voice and warm hands. But nothing was warm about this dream. The shivering grew worse, but she didn't wake. Finally, it stopped and her eyes opened.

But her eyes were blue, before slowly fading to brown.

෴

Mick couldn't believe how angry Jezebel was. Days later, and she still kept him at a distance. Usually, he found their fights energetic, and when they made up, the sex was incredible. She was wondrous when angry.

He burped, gazing toward the shore. The fires on the beach glowed where the rest enjoyed the night. The crew was subdued, concerned about the congenial new shipmate, but were following Jezzie's lead and feigning a lack of concern. Emily Pawes was keeping to her cabin. She hadn't mixed a drink since they'd left Tortuga. She should stick to what she did best, he fumed.

Lifting a hand, he brushed at the letter in his coat pocket. He hadn't shared it with Jezebel. A letter from Alan Silvestri, promising the Immortal to him if he came alone to the southern tip of Bath Island. He'd talked Jezzie into stopping there, but wasn't sure if he trusted the letter. Silvestri spoke of mutual respect and the truth. He knew the truth, already. Didn't he?

When her hand fell on his arm, he jerked away.

"Christ's blood, Pawes! What the hell are you doing,

sneaking around?"

She didn't answer, only pointed to the cutter tied to the starboard side of the ship.

He tilted his head at her, wondering what she was about. She touched his arm again, pulling him toward the rail. There was urgency to her demeanor.

"Ah, you know where he is, don't you? Know about the offer he made to me? What does it mean, Pawes? He's gonna turn the ship over to me? It's a trick, isn't it?"

She shrugged and climbed over the rail.

Mick patted his sash, where he kept a pistol ready for use. He was fine with using her to get close to that bastard, to make sure he didn't try anything. He grinned and followed her down the hull to the cutter.

She untied the small boat and lifted an oar. He turned, searching for the other. He didn't know what hit him.

Hours later, he woke up groaning, hands tied behind his back. He managed to sit up—it was still dark. But he couldn't see the ship or the island. He turned to see Pawes, one hand tight to the tiller, the other holding his pistol. That hand didn't waver, pointed the heavy pistol straight at him. He didn't think she could manage that for too long.

"Emily…this isn't necessary. Come on, woman. Put the pistol down." He glanced at the small mast where a sail had been rigged and strained for all its worth. He straightened his back, and an icy cold wind ripped his hat off. "Damn!"

That wind wasn't natural. He lowered himself in the cutter, shivering. A glance at Pawes, frozen to the tiller, caused that reaction to translate into something other than driven by icy air. She wasn't shaking with cold. She wasn't moving. The waning moon illuminated her face. No expression. Her hair blew forward, with the wind that carried them at such speed. She wore a light shirt, ragged breeches—damn, she must be cold!

He shook his head and worked at the knotted rope around his wrists.

Chapter Twenty-One

So cold. She'd died and gone to California Hell, where the sun wasn't warm, and the cold was deeper than an Alaskan crab boat on the Bering Sea. She kept trying to wake up and draw the blankets tighter....

A sudden jarring finally forced her eyes to clear and focus. But instead of the darkness of her cabin, she faced a wall of ice, coming at her fast and Mick staring at her. The small mast was too tall for the opening! She dove forward, Mick staring up at her with shock. He was going to get hurt!

The loud snap of the mast was the last thing she heard. Mick felt soft...and warm. Something struck her head and she was out. Again.

࿔

Mick cursed, trying to push Pawes off his back. He'd almost gotten the knot loose when she suddenly threw off the walking sleep, screamed at something behind him, and threw herself atop him.

He'd spent the night working on that knot. He tested her, moved to one side, and she aimed the pistol at him, another side, it followed. Yet her eyes didn't track him. It went on all night. Thank God she didn't pay attention to what was going on behind his back, with his nimble fingers.

The sun rose while the wind grew faster. The spray from

the bow soaked through the back of his coat. When the sail split, the little boat should have stopped. It didn't and he'd realized they were being driven by some devil current. Ice crystals sparkled on Pawes' hair. The spray had soaked through her shirt, her nipples stood out plain and they were stiff; he almost groaned. Another time, another place, he'd find them enticing, but he knew they were stiff with cold.

If she came out of this, she'd be in some serious pain. Then, to have her wake and just surge at him! What was the matter with the woman?

Finally, he was able to shove her body to one side, free his hands and assess the situation. The little boat still moved, though slower, and the wind disappeared. But the air surrounding them was frigid. Emily remained where he'd shoved her, limp and unconscious. He lifted her face and his hand came away bloody.

"Oh, hell!" The snapped mast must have smacked her in the back of the head. He carefully examined her skull, searching for the source of all the blood. She'd been cut, but it didn't seem too bad. She woke up, pushing his arms away. First thing she did was shiver.

He helped her up, keeping low in the boat, trying to conserve what little heat he could from the outside frigid air. She appeared dazed. "Mick? What the hell did you do to me?"

"Me? Wasn't me that kidnapped *you!* You snatched *me!*"

"What the fuck?" She raised her right hand and paled at the raw flesh at her palm. A massive shudder drove through her. She looked up at him and blinked. "Mick? Where are we?"

He studied their surroundings, almost absentmindedly urging her close to share warmth. He put an arm around her shoulders and pulled her nearer, tried to cover her legs with his coat. Hell, she was wearing sandals!

"I think we're inside a glacier."

"That's impossible." She gasped, drawing his attention to the port side. "Is that the Immortal?"

He twisted, and there bobbed the ship he'd always claimed, anchored and motionless. No one manned the rails. Taking up an oar, he tried to steer them toward her, but the current wouldn't let them loose. They slid past the ship without a sign from her decks. He cursed.

∾

Her brain didn't want to work. Instead, her thoughts just shot from one tangent to another, none of it making sense. What happened to her? She'd kidnapped Mick? And why the fuck was it so cold?

Her feet were like blocks of ice. Her hand pulsed with pain, but even that was fading, replaced by numbness. She huddled against Mick fighting for some clarity. She glanced at the tiller, then at her hand and nearly vomited. Her skin stuck out starkly on the frozen piece of wood. How did she do that to herself? Mick picked up a pistol from the floor of the cutter.

"I held that on you? Is that why you didn't just stop me? You're faster, stronger."

"Yup. Never said a word. Pawes...Emily...he wrote me. Invited me to come to the southern tip of Bath Island and he'd hand over the Immortal." He held her close and she appreciated the comfort.

"Give it to you? He told me, on Tortuga, that he would be gone for weeks, maybe months. You sure it was him?" Her teeth chattered.

"Right now, I don't know. There's the ship, but no sign of him."

"Where are we going?" She twisted to look over her shoulder. "Shit!" They were racing toward an ice shore, with no sign of slowing down to make an easy landfall. "Hang on!" She hauled him down with her.

The cutter hit the shore and ran right up about ten feet; ice and snow flew into the air. The tip of the cutter shattered, wood chips flew everywhere. Mick pushed her off again. "Your landing on me is getting old." He turned to survey the wreckage. "This boat is going nowhere."

"What do we do?" She tried to stand, but her feet wouldn't hold her. He caught her before she fell. "Mick, I'm freezing to death." She'd lost the feeling in her feet, her nose, her ears, her fingers were curled so tightly, they all but disappeared in her palms. And it wasn't helping! Her tits ached fiercely.

The Immortal was here. Did that mean Silvestri was around somewhere?

Mick stepped out of the ruin of the cutter. "I might be able to start a fire with the wood chips"

They were surrounded by a frigid fog. She heard the crunch of feet coming their way. "Mick!"

He set her down, leaning against his back. It was scant protection, but it was the best he could do. He pulled the pistol, facing toward the sounds. Emily peered from behind him, shivering. Four huge figures loomed out of the mist. Mick softly cursed.

"We...uh...come in peace?" he said. The bravado he normally spoke with was absent.

Emily tried to focus on them. Huge men, wrapped in layers of fur. One of them gestured to Mick.

"Come with us."

Luckily, Mick was smart enough not to resist. He tucked the pistol away and turned to Emily, who promptly fell on her face.

She heard him, sounding muffled and it was if he spoke from a distance.

"She can't walk, and she's nearly frozen...."

She heard deeper voices conferring and soon she was bundled up in a fur and in the arms of one of the giants. She drifted asleep. At some point, she woke again, when Mick was bundled into the fur with her. The cold must have gotten to him. The giants rigged a hammock and the two of them clung together for the rest of the journey.

❧

He'd little luck with Glacious. She delighted in keeping him guessing about the last year. Each birthday, he came to her ice palace and she ripped the memories of the year's victims of his curse from him. Seldom a pleasant occurrence, he left the palace determined to provide her with nothing to feed upon the next year. A resolution he never managed to keep.

Not from lack of trying.

This year, she insisted on entertaining him for days on end. He'd adapted to the cold and managed the wait, hoping Mick would show up. It was a trick, but one he hoped the man would fall for. If the appeal for a truthful meeting worked, Mick would show up, riding the current he'd bound around the cutter. Once Mick arrived, he'd have a short time to convince the man to work with him. Possibly no more than the time it took to walk from the shore to the palace, if Glacious sent him to fetch the visitor. It was a menial task she'd take delight in assigning him.

If Emily was right, it was possible to convince him. If he couldn't use sentiment, he'd offer to pay the man.

When Glacious summoned him from the hot spring, he dressed without enthusiasm. She knew the spring was the only thing keeping him from freezing to death. Undoubtedly, she'd attempt to entice him into eating again. Eating too often at Glacious' table was hazardous to the soul. He'd smuggled some light rations with him when he came ashore. The crew remained on board, in the hold, safe from meddling. Or more meddling. He knew they were held under some light enchantment. Otherwise, why stay with a cursed man?

He followed the messenger, a female creature of Glacious' magic. Formed from ice and snow, she wore almost no clothing. Nice to admire, but nothing pleasant to touch. He'd learned that long ago.

She opened the great door and stood to one side. He nodded politely and entered the great hall. At one end, Glacious stood, gazing out the crystal window toward the open bay where his ship bobbed. The palace was poised high above the icy harbor, a long climb up a steep, slick path.

She turned at his entrance and he stared, unable to look away. A beautiful woman, hair an icy blue that fell to her knees, eyes so black they put midnight to shame. And a figure that he'd once found incredibly desirable. Age tempered that desire. He admired her beauty still, but knew those looks held nothing but the cold at the heart of deepest ocean trench. Colder.

She smiled, and he shuddered.

This visit, she wore a gown of deep grey, arms bare and hair flowing free. Sometimes she braided it into intricate whirls and cascades. She never revealed her legs.

"My dear Captain, we have company! Isn't that delightful!" She gestured at the door, even now opening at her command. "Two ragged vagabonds caught by the currents. I'm so pleased. I do adore entertaining." She raised an eyebrow.

Two? Damn, had Jezebel come with him?

Her giants held a bundle of several furs between them. They set it down on the ice.

"Oh, unwrap them, Alan dear."

She stood nearby while he knelt and peeled back one layer, another. A familiar hand made him catch his breath. So small…that ring? He swallowed the balloon of fear growing in his throat and revealed the couple. Rage roared into blood. Emily, asleep in Mick's arms!

Fighting to hold back the urge to tear Mick's arms away and haul him from the woman he cared for, he reached across her and poked at Mick.

Mick's eyes jerked open, and he shot upward. Silvestri gripped his throat. "Not one word. Trust me."

The anger in Mick's eyes matched his, but when Emily moaned, the anger switched to concern for her.

Mick broke free and pointed to her. "She is desperately cold. Her hand is injured. You bastard!"

Silvestri kept his eyes on Mick, willing the man to understand the danger they were in. He hissed. "Mick! Kill me later…look around you, man!"

Mick sat back and studied the surroundings. And he got it. His body took on that lazy attentiveness he used to employ when they'd wandered into dangerous places. He took in the surroundings, the pure white of carved ice and snow, and the woman standing a few feet away, exactly as she'd been described to him years ago. When they were friends and talked deep into the night. Would he remember?

Alan took a breath, Mick's eyes slid to his, and a minor nod from Jezebel's lover reassured him.

Glacious moved closer, looked down on the Emily's pale form, trying to pull the furs back around her body. It frightened him, how fragile she appeared.

"Poor thing. She looks quite worn out—perhaps it would be kindest to let the cold take her."

The icy voice, pretending at a concern he knew she was incapable of feeling, fired Alan's blood. He slowly stood and bowed to her. "My Queen, that would be one course to take. Another would be to allow this poor sailor and Captain March time in the hot baths to recover. You often complain that no one visits. You'll have three to entertain, once she has recovered."

"Ah, good point, Alan. Very well, escort these two...wait! Captain March? Oh, my. You've spoken of him. Claimed familial ties as an excuse to block your curse from taking him down when he attacked you. I see little resemblance." She took a step around him and faced Mick, who rose at the words.

Mick stood perfectly still while she ran an icy finger down his face. Alan knew what that felt like, and admired his standing her touch without reacting. The line of confusion between his eyes smoothed out, and he actually winked at Glacious, lifted a hand and gently took hers in his, pressed a light kiss to her knuckles. "Ah, the Lady Glacious. Silvestri spoke of you, also. But his descriptions did little to address your true glory."

"You marked my knight and never paid for it, Captain March. A daring thing to even attempt. I look forward to conversing with you later." She turned and stared a moment at Alan, a cold, calculating expression on her face. Much different than the lovely simplicity she'd shown Mick.

Silvestri fought not to shiver. But she drew one long powerful tremble from him. With an arch smile, she blinked, turned to leave the great hall. "We dine in an hour."

Silvestri bent and eased Emily into his arms. "Follow me, Mick. Speak quietly—these chambers have ears."

Mick pulled a scarf from his pocket and rather awkwardly worked to bind Emily's raw palm while they strode from the hall.

"I remember your stories about her. I thought them fancies, I admit. My God, she's beautiful."

"Yes, and this palace is beautiful," Alan answered, loud enough to be heard. He lowered his voice. "Why is she with you?"

"It's more that I am with her. She tricked me into a cutter and knocked me unconscious, tied my hands. She wasn't awake, Silvestri. She woke up right before we entered this delightful place!" From a matching whisper, he let the last few words ring out.

Alan looked down at Emily, shivering in his arms. "Damn it. She did it. Somehow the icy bitch did it. I needed you here, but I didn't want Emily to come with you."

"I savvied that. You claimed me a family member?" Mick tucked her injured hand close to Silvestri's sleeve. "Nice trick!"

"No trick. You are my brother, Mick. It's the truth. I can't go into it right now. Help me keep Emily safe. And when the time is right, stand with me to bring the Kraken into this place." Silvestri turned to see Mick staring at him. "I swear on all I hold dear—on this woman, in my arms—I am speaking the truth."

"Yes, but about what." He raised a hand and waved it about. "Never mind. I understand we are in a perilous situation. The Kraken? How will we escape, Silvestri? I like my skin."

"The Immortal stands ready. Help me, I have a plan, straight from Mama Lu. After, take Emily and I to Tortuga, and the ship is yours. If I don't survive, swear to me you'll see her there. Either way, I am done with the ship."

They reached the hot springs, a cave of black rock in the midst of the ice. Mick took a deep breath. "Reeks of sulfur, but it looks hot. Thank God. She needs something warm to wear after she leaves the pool. And food. This meal, will it be enough to help Emily?"

"Eat little at her table, Mick. It will freeze you." He set Emily gently on a stone bench and pointed to a chest. "Provisions are there, from the Immortal. They are safe to eat. I'll have appropriate clothing sent. And boots. Dear God, her feet!" He tried to pry the tattered sandals off. One disintegrated in his hands.

He knew Mick was watching and calculating while he took care of Emily. The man always proved masterful at assessing situations and adjusting to them. He pulled open the chest and hauled out a small sack of apples, along with a wrapped package of cheese and pork. Breaking the pieces small, Mick coaxed Emily into eating while Silvestri stripped off her clothes. She ate, but showed no real awareness of her surroundings or who fed her.

It irked Alan to grant Mick such liberties with Emily's body, but it was the only practical thing to do. He turned to Mick, who was enjoying one of the apples. "Strip—you'll need to hold her in the water."

"She's your woman. You do it!" He looked toward the bubbling water with some disdain. Mick shared the sailor's normal dislike of bathing. Silvestri never did understand that.

"I have to get back to keep Glacious diverted. Make certain clothing is sent, prepare for the two of you to dine! I don't have time to see to Emily." Damn, he hated admitting that to Mick. "Don't be an idiot. It won't hurt you to get wet!" Alan snorted. "I would have thought Jezebel cured you of this dislike of bathing."

"That's Captain Jezebel to you." Mick set the apple core down with a sigh. "Fine. Her hand will start to bleed."

"I'll be sure to fetch a good wrap for it. The sulfur will sting, but it's healing. Hurry, man! She's ready!" He cradled Emily on his lap. "Where is the pendant I gave her? I asked her to never take it off. It might have kept her safe."

"Probably in her pocket. She's fingered something in there for days." Mick made quick work of his clothing, took one step down into the water and grimaced. "Give her here."

Reluctantly, Alan handed her over. Mick spoke softly into her ear, stepping deeper and deeper into the water. Alan looked away, taking up the ragged breeches and searching the pockets. He found the Kraken's pendant and considered what would be best. He lifted Micks' coat and slid it deep into one of his pockets.

Emily uttered a sharp cry and cursed.

He spoke, the pool to his back. "Make sure she puts the pendant on, Mick." He hurried away.

Chapter Twenty-Two

*F*ire! Her feet were dangling in hot lava! Have to get away from flames! Have to get away!

"Easy! You're all right, Pawes! Pawes! Stop fighting me!"

Slowly, his voice got through. The pain in her feet faded. Warm—she was warm again.

Her head fell back, and her eyes opened. Above was only white, but she could smell sulfur…and steam? She blinked and felt a shoulder under her head. She turned her face and recognized Mick, felt his bare chest at her back.

"What the fuck?" She tried to move away from him, but his arms held her still and wouldn't let her move away.

"Nope, wake up more first. I don't know how deep this spring is, and don't need you to drown. Relax. I'm going to ease your hand down into the water, and it's going to hurt like hell."

"What? Why?" Her head hurt, and suddenly her head was fine. Her hand! Shit! "Let me go!"

This time Mick released her. She stepped away, onto a slick rock under the water and slipped. She inhaled a mouthful of water before Mick hauled her out again. She came out facing him. "You're naked!"

"Yes, it's the most common way to bathe." He raised an eyebrow at her. "Your hand?"

"Hell." She raised it to her eyes and winced. "What did I do to my hand?" A faint memory rose of a cutter and cold wood.

"Froze it to a tiller, then yanked it away. Sorry, Pawes. We'll wrap it when you're warmed up. And your feet?"

She blinked, wrapped one arm up around her bare breasts and lowered herself further into the steamy water. "Okay, they sting, but getting better. Mick, how did I get to a hot spring?" She looked everywhere but at him. "Where *is* here?"

Mick sighed. "Silvestri brought me. At least I think that was the plan. You weren't supposed to accompany me. But Pawes…." He leaned forward, whispered, "We're in danger in this place. It's the birthplace of his curse. The bitch who tricked Silvestri fifty years ago has us too close for comfort. Alan has a plan. I can't go into it, but follow our lead, savvy?"

"Alan is here?" She looked around. "Wait. I was on the ship…a cutter? I dreamed, a freaky cold nightmare."

"Love, I think you were possessed. Now, you have to stay calm and you have to hold close every bit of anger, fear, anything! You give her any lever and she'll use it. Got it?" He reached out and touched her head, drawing her closer. "Nothing. Blank slate. Wait, and you follow our lead!"

She nodded and Mick let her go. She turned away from him, gazed out across the pond, and slowly let the heat work its way into her bones.

Silvestri used her? Or had this woman who cursed him used her? Mick was supposed to be here, but not her. Because of the bitch in question? She lowered her head and thought. Her heart ached, too confused to make sense of it. Mick said to wait. Fine, she could do that.

It wasn't long before she heard Mick leave the hot pool. He spoke to someone while she rubbed at her feet, her face, and finally her circulation returned to normal. They were surrounded by ice. How in the hell did a hot spring exist here? Her shoulders sagged. Mad, this was too insane to understand.

"Pawes, your clothing is here."

She turned reluctantly toward his voice to see that a woman stood next to him, a pile of fur items in her arms.

"I can't wear fur," she objected.

"Why not?" He gestured to her. "Don't be stupid. You have to wear something other than the rags you wore." He lifted up her shirt, nearly transparent in the bright white light of the ice world. "You'll freeze again."

"Fuck." She slowly climbed up the rocky steps, trying to keep some modesty, an arm across her breast, a hand to her pubes. She gave up after a moment, too hard to walk and be concerned about nudity. "Where do I dry?"

Mick, already dressed, gestured toward several hissing vents. "Hot air." He bent toward one and went to work on his long hair. She could see the sense of it. Wet hair here would be dangerous. She gingerly stepped to the vent across from him and quickly did what she could to wipe any remaining water from her body, let the air do the rest. The woman with the fur stood, waiting.

Emily bent over to work on her hair and the woman moved in, set a fur piece around one of her legs and wrapped it securely. After the initial shock of the intrusion, Emily accepted her assistance. The fur felt nice...and her legs were feeling the cold. Once both legs were covered, a sleeveless piece that worked like a Diana Furstenberg dress came next. It fell well past her thighs. Her arms were taken care of, lastly her feet with the fur traveling all the way up to her calves. She supposed to guarantee no ice reached her feet. It was warm, and that was all she presently cared about.

Mick snickered.

"What?" Emily glared at him.

"You look like a shapeless bear."

"Yeah, well, I bet I'm warmer than you are."

"That may be true, but my coat works well enough." He slid a hand into his pocket. A look of confusion crossed his face, but passed after a moment. Emily waited for him to share. Her helper finished and disappeared while Emily was looking for her shoes.

"Mick, where are my sandals?"

"Fell to pieces, Pawes. You were overdue a new pair of shoes."

"Oh, damn." She looked up when Mick held out his hand.

"What now?"

He dropped the Kraken pendant in her hand. "Put it on. I think it's going to help us."

She gazed at the carved necklace a moment, nodded and slid it over her head. He reached over and tucked it underneath the fur.

"Now, follow my lead. Dangerous ground, capice?" He raised his eyebrows at her and wouldn't release her gaze until she nodded.

"Now, our guide is up at the top of the stairs. Be polite." He gestured at her to lead.

She paused. "Why are you trusting him? I thought you hated him?"

"Something he said made sense, luv. Suddenly a great many things make sense. Explanations will wait. Oh, eat little from her table."

With a sigh, she climbed the steps, tired, but at least she was warm.

Chapter Twenty-Three

Silvestri walked away from the steam pools with a weight of worry settling on his shoulders. She'd done it—she'd brought Emily here. At least Mick knew where he was, what Glacious was. Hours of talking over bottles of rum educated him enough to take care. Emily didn't know. He needed to trust that Mick would tell her enough to keep her satisfied. And careful.

By the time the two joined the dinner table, the cold was growing inside him. It usually did when she prepared to pull the pain of the year before from him. He shuddered, trying not to anticipate that terrible glory. It never failed to heat him up to a near fever. An unholy sort of welcome that melted the ice away.

He almost loved her when she did it. And hated her moments later. For now, she toyed with him, pretending a simple sort of delight at the company. She'd known they were coming, but she didn't know what he planned. He hoped.

When the door at the end of the great hall opened, he fought not to turn. He wanted to know she was walking, that her hand was bound, that she was warm and comfortable. If he betrayed any of that concern, Glacious would use it against him. Against Emily. But would Emily understand?

It didn't matter; she must be kept safe. Hopefully, he could explain later. The words of Mama Lu played through his mind. *You'll know the right moment, the right thing ta do. Ya pay attention and accept opportunities. Follow instincts. The Old Monster gave you a vision. Follow it!*

The dreams came two days after the Kraken's touch. Visions of the palace crumbling, of bloody hands united and a great roar. He didn't understand any of it, but he watched and waited.

"Dear Captain March! I see our fragile sailor has regained herself. What do I call you, dear?" Glacious played at being gracious.

Mick answered, interrupting Alan's attempt to downplay Emily's position. Alan said she worked the sails on the ship Mick sailed. But Mick overrode him. "This is Mrs. Pawes. The talented bartender of my lady's ship, the Cursed Quill. She also crafts books of unique workmanship."

"A bartender on a ship? I thought you sailors drank rum and only rum." She laughed, and Alan again held back a grimace.

Emily spoke up, "Generally, that is what they drink, Ma'am. On board. But when they go ashore for relaxation, I mix what I can from the local brews." She did play the awkward sailor well, keeping her eyes downcast. A glance darted his way hidden under the unruly mop of her hair.

"Ma'am? I am the Lady Glacious, my dear."

"Pardon me, Ma'am. I didn't mean to offend. Uh, Lady Ma'am. Lady...I, uh, don't often spend time with quality, Ma'am." She shook her head. "Lady...Ma'am."

Alan almost laughed when Glacious reacted with shock to Emily's play at titles. He shot a glance at Mick, lips twitching also. A warmth grew in his heart. The possibility of having Mick as a friend again, and as a brother, gave him hope.

"You must pardon her, Lady Glacious. She is nothing but a simple woman, come to our ship with no home left to her. Captain Jezebel took her on and has made a sort of pet of her." Mick set his arm around Emily's shoulders and led her to a chair. "Sit and be quiet, all right, dear?"

"Okay, Captain March. I'm sorry, I don't mean to offend. I

mean...." Emily wrapped her arms around her chest and rocked slightly.

Excellent portrayal of a simple-minded woman. Alan relaxed slightly.

Glacious turned to him. "How do you know this stupid sailor?" The look on her face spoke volumes. She knew how well he knew Emily.

His belly twisted, heat growing above his groin.

"Oh, Captain Silvestri often enjoys the company of sailors from the Quill. I think it's his way of poking at Jezebel, who chose me over him some years ago," Mick commented, taking a seat next to Emily.

Glacious tilted her head. "Truly? I didn't know you pined for the captain of the Quill."

"It was a long time ago," he lied straight faced, and the burning eased.

She took a seat and he followed, relieved. Until he glanced across the table to see a tear trail down Emily's face.

Mick took up the conversation, obviously attempting to keep Glacious' attention away from Emily.

It worked for a short while.

She wouldn't react. She couldn't react, couldn't let this monstrous woman know what she was feeling. Was any of that true? Alan wanted Jezebel? Well, it made sense. Jezebel was a younger, nubile woman. Her bright red hair, her figure...of course, they fought over Jezebel.

No one ever did battle over Emily Pawes. She blinked back tears, suddenly convinced none of his passion was real. No, it was all about striking back at Mick and Jezzie. She'd been used. He fucked her and won her to get to Mick. He knew Mick would react to one of Jezebel's crew taking up with the enemy. Mick would be bound to take action, and she'd been the new one. The one susceptible to his charm. He'd been so cool about Mick. Now it made sense. Mick won Jezebel. Silvestri wanted vengeance! And now Mick was falling for the monster's charm. Her heart pounded erratically. Too much to figure out.

Emily fought exhaustion until a sort of lassitude blossomed

in her. She welcomed it; it was easier to bear than the hurt. Must be from being possessed. She snorted softly. The food before her was colorless, tasteless, and quite easy to pass on, despite the hollowness of her belly. Her hand ached, and after managing to take a bite or two of something crunchy, she set her hands in her lap. Her head hurt, but what was the sickness at her heart? It couldn't be hurt. No, she'd be angry—he'd used her. Glacious wanted to use her, too, just to egg the men on. Then she'd be tossed aside. Bait no longer needed. Mick was dismissing her. Anger would be better; it would keep her from breaking to pieces in front of all of them. Three schemers, they deserved each other!

She would avoid falling prey to any softer emotions or other explanation for her presence. Maybe she was having a heart attack. Maybe her mental breakdown was evolving into a real medical crisis, and soon she'd wake up long enough to see the doctors laboring over her. Such a tragedy.

A fragment of the talk around drew her head up. Brother? They were brothers? She focused on what Glacious was saying. She was an incredible-looking woman. Emily kept trying to decide if the hair was glacier blue or arctic blue.

Distraction. Yes, she needed other distractions to focus on. Not her heart. She could feel its steady beat where the fur was snug at her neck. She was okay. She knew the score. Fuck it. What did Glacious just say?

"I understand your claiming his portion of my gift, dear Captain Silvestri. He is your brother. And he marked you." She reached out to touch the curved scar at Alan's cheek.

Emily shuddered, the bitch considered the damage done by the curse to be a gift? Sick!

Ah, she'd wondered where that came from. It must be when Mick attacked him.

"But he should carry a reminder also." Her black eyes danced to Mick.

"Ah, dear lady, I do. Nothing romantic like Alan's. Only modesty keeps me from showing it to you." Mick grinned, and winked at Alan.

Too many jokes. Why was she here? Emily picked at the

bandage on her left hand. It unwound and she let it. The cold air felt good on the raw tissues. She could feel the Kraken's pendant at her chest, heavy and cold. Why was it cold? Even against her chest and buried in furs, it radiated chill. The rest of her was warm, almost too warm.

"Now, what did you bring me this year?" Glacious left her seat and walked to where Alan sat. Standing behind him, she set her hands at his shoulders, and bent over, the swell of her white breasts on display for Mick. "You're always careful, but I know my gift struck true. I felt it."

Emily watched her hands grip Alan's shoulders, and he groaned, while sweat beaded his face. He appeared to be in pain. A pain Glacious absorbed so that it shone forth from her. It was obscene, intimate, and impossible to look away from. Emily shuddered.

She's a vampire! An actual emotional vampire!

Glacious crooned, "An entire galleon, Alan. What a wonderful thing to bring me!" The icy blue woman flushed, head bowed.

Alan tried to jerk away from her grip on his shoulders and partial succeeded.

One hand still touching him, Glacious looked up straight into Emily's eyes. "And why did this one escape my gift? A sister? No, you're not that twisted. You know that isn't allowed."

She dropped Alan. He hauled himself erect, though the effort obviously cost him. The lines on his face truly betrayed his age. The vitality faded. He gasped, "*No!* I will pay for that! She didn't mean to fire that pistol! It was an accident, and she is an innocent!"

"You are gallant, dear Alan. Very well, this last time." Glacious gestured at him and he jerked violently and fell from the seat. Emily stood up and hurried to the head of the table to help him. Why she cared enough to go to him was beyond her. Instinct, probably. She paused as he climbed back to his seat before she got there. He held his right hand close, blood dripping from it.

His knuckles were pitted with bits of metal and black with

powder burns. Her pistol that exploded? His palm was gouged and bloody with mangled flesh. He met her eyes and hissed, "Get away!"

Emily stopped dead in her tracks.

Glacious ignored the drama, gliding to the other side of the table to confront Mick, also on his feet. "You seem a most practical and pragmatic man, Captain March. I am done with Alan—his luck has run out. Would you care to strike a bargain with me? Bear the gift of good luck while you sail the seven seas of the world?"

"Bad idea, Mick," Alan muttered. "I should know."

Emily turned her attention to Mick and watched in disbelief as Jezebel's man bowed to Glacious. Emily grimaced, appalled at the idea.

"Dear Lady, what a gracious offer. And terribly tempting...."

Emily couldn't stand it. Her loyalty toward Captain Jezebel reared up, overcoming her confusion regarding Alan. She reached out with her right hand, grabbed a handful of blue hair, and yanked, jerking Glacious away from Mick. The hair broke off in her hands. "Leave him be, you bitch! He is spoken for. He's Jezebel's." Shock traveled through her system. The strands she held sliced into her hand, wires of frozen ice. Screaming she backed into Alan, who kept her from falling.

Glacious turned to her. "Not so stupid are you! Simply ill-advised. No woman's claim supersedes mine."

Mick opened his mouth to reply when a shock traveled through the palace. A muffled cascade of booms could be heard.

Glacious swiftly turned her head toward the other end of her hall and threw up a hand. The wall of ice instantly grew transparent and showed a ship, firing at the glacier.

Mick grinned. "Jezebel! My dear captain!" He sounded both relieved and proud.

"The Quill?" Emily wept at the pain in her hands. The left palm now dripped blood from where she'd hit it on the side of the table trying to get away from Glacious. Both hands ached and bled red to stain the pure white world.

"Oh, too many stupid women today!" Glacious leaped to the tabletop and strode toward the transparent wall. It fell with a gesture when she walked to it, melting to a sudden rain of water. The chill outside rushed in. Emily cried out when the ice queen shouted out to the giants, "See that ship sunk!"

❧

Alan shivered as the icy wind dried the sweat of Glacious' earlier attention. He clung to Emily, trying to help her with the newly wounded hand. Mick hurried to them. "Now what? She's going to sink the Quill!"

Alan's vision blurred as he held Emily's hand, trying to fashion a bandage from a scarf. The fever from having his victim's pain pulled from his soul made it difficult to remember where he was and why. But a vision rose in his memory from his dream of the Kraken taking down Glacious. He kissed Emily's forehead. "Where is the pendant?"

"My neck." Emily tried to get to it, but only smeared blood on the white fur at her throat. "It's cold!"

Mick gently pushed her hands away and slipped the chain out, leaving the pendant at her chest where it pulsed and glowed.

"Mick, bloody your left hand and take her right. Emily? Hold on to us. We'll see you safe!" Alan took her left in his right, mingling blood.

Mick slid his left palm across the sharp edge of the table, hissing as he did. With blood flowing, he took up Emily's right hand. Alan turned, and they gazed across the open water to the transparent ice wall where the Quill fired her guns, dodging chunks of ice falling around them. The ship couldn't last long! The ice would eventually strike it and take them all down.

❧

The cold that traveled through Emily froze her solid, but this wasn't the cold of the glacier. This was the deep cold of the ocean, mixed with the warmer water of more temperate climes. Every ocean in the world pulsed through her. She suddenly stood up straight, hands locked to the men, power flowing through her. Alan felt it, and he was certain Mick also felt it.

Alan spoke first. "Come on, Old Monster! We cleared the

way! Follow your agents!"

Mick chuckled. "Old Monster, reclaim what is yours."

Emily felt the force rising from the sea floor. The entire ice structure shuddered from a massive collision. The three of them staggered.

Glacious spun, glared at them. "*No!*"

"*Yes!*" Emily shouted, hearing the words deep inside her head. A voice with a slight accent, like that of the old woman in Tortuga, whispered at her what to do, what to say. "Though the portal, straight to this frozen heart! Come, *Old Monster! Old Monster, come!*" The pendant at her chest exploded with impossible tentacles, sweeping out at Glacious. The queen of the ice palace screamed and ran, a Kraken slithering after her. Emily glanced down at the pendant. "Wow." It was just a pendant now. Her clear head fought with the physics of what just happened. Why didn't she fall back?

Then the water of the bay exploded with great tentacles of every color and size. Massive white suckers, the size of elephants, rose around the dining hall, enlarging cracks as they pushed through. They crashed through the ice and everything solid fractured. The physics of gravity became paramount.

The ice wall between the Quill and the enclosed bay disappeared, falling to pieces in the water. Emily roared with energy, no longer cold, tired, or confused. She was jubilant! Alan pulled the three of them out of the crumbling hall. They stumbled to the top of the long stairs. Ice melted everywhere, making the way treacherous.

Within ten steps, all three fell as the palace gave a great groan and tilted to one side. Emily lost her grip with Alan, but Mick swept behind and literally grasped her about the waist as the slide and tumble began. Alan fell to one side of the steps.

Emily knew with clarity why she'd come to this world and how, and the energy of the Kraken's single-minded purpose filled her with laughter as the ice palace was reclaimed by the sea. Explosions behind them signaled the sulfur baths sweeping away what held them captive. She shouted with glee as Mick controlled their slide and saw them come to a halt at the quickly melting shore.

Mick bellowed out to the Quill, *"Jezzie!"* Emily watched in a daze as he tried to gain the Quill's attention before the icy water swallowed the two of them.

The Immortal's crew worked swiftly to recover their captain. He'd ended up in the water, not far from their bow. They hauled him aboard. Only he turned and attempted to throw himself back into the water, hand stretched out as if to grab hers.

She raised her hand, suddenly sad. The bit of ice she and Mick stood on cracked, and the icy water rose up her fur-wrapped legs.

"Save them!" Alan shouted into the air.

A green tentacle swept around them. Mick grimaced, but bore it well as they were hauled through the water to the Quill and dropped onto the deck. He stood up and made to embrace Jezzie, who recoiled from him with horror. He wiped a gobbet of slime off his face. "Well, they are green and slimy when young. He brought the whole family!"

Emily staggered to the rail, hands no longer bloody. The Immortal hove to, while the Quill's crew followed Jezebel's orders and the ship turned to reclaim the open sea. The ice fell around them and instantly melted. The other ship disappeared in a sudden frozen fog.

A single, massive tentacle rose above the chaos. Wrapped tightly inside, the terrible beauty of Glacious, her screaming rose above the terrible crashing of ice until the albino limb carried her below the surface. Emily squinted, swore she saw smaller tentacles below the scrap of the grey dress. An errant wife? Daughter? She shook her head, certain her eyes played a trick on her.

The Quill broke through into the sea, as the last rays of the sun disappeared. There was no sign of the Immortal.

Emily fell to the deck, her energy gone. She turned to see Mick take Jezebel's hand. "I knew you'd find me, love."

"Go get cleaned up." Jezzie's voice was rough, but the relief on her face spoke volumes.

Emily wondered what her future held. It was obvious Mick would not leave the Quill. He'd never even entertained

Glacious' offer. The amount of subterfuge left Emily reeling. Suddenly, leaving was all Emily wanted to do.

Davis helped her stand and took her below to a sponge bath and to her cabin. He didn't ask anything and she didn't speak.

Hours later, deep in the night, she took up her mirror, poured a bit of rum on it and asked to return to Vallejo and the pirate festival.

∾

Mick tapped at her door come sunrise. When there was no answer, he slipped in to tell her the Immortal was sighted, listing slightly, but following their wake. But Emily was gone. Two letters sat on the bed. One was addressed to Jezebel and one to Captain Silvestri.

Chapter Twenty-Four

*T*he cold still surrounded her. She hauled herself up; one hand touched a hay bale at her back. She inhaled deeply. Exhaust, oil. A generator hummed somewhere. She picked up her pack and slung it over her shoulder.

"Miss? Excuse me, Ma'am. What are you doing here?"

A slender young man in the orange T-shirt, security in big bold letter across the front, glared at her.

Emily snickered, immensely tired. "Looking for the exit, asshole. You're security, escort me, idiot."

"Fuck you!" He stormed off, muttering, "Stupid old cow."

Emily leaned against the hay and laughed. Definitely back in her world! Morning she assumed.

She stumbled across the corner of a tent and nearly fell. A hand grabbed at her. "Hey, careful!"

"Listen, I must have fallen asleep last night, where is the exit? I'm trying to get out of here." She tried politeness this time.

"Sure, where did you park?" This guy was a gentleman. He set her hand on his costumed arm and led the way through the fog. It sounded like the festival was getting ready for the second day of fun and make believe. She'd had enough of that.

"I'm in the lot for the ferry building. Thanks!"

He left her at the opening in the fence, after pointing out

the right way to go. The fur was warm, but her feet were like ice. Nice of him not to comment on her arctic wear.

It took some maneuvering to get the key out of the bottom of her bag, but she finally slid it home and entered her camper. She didn't bother covering the windshield, simply stripped. No one was about, and no one wanted to look at her, anyway.

"Damn it, what a freaky dream. Yup, a bad hangover and some prankster with an excess of fur." She spoke to the empty camper, smelling strongly of chemicals, and her mouth tasted funny.

She shrugged and gazed at herself in the small mirror on the tiny shower door. Her eyes locked on her right nipple and the gold ring there. "Oh, well. I must have been rip-roaring drunk."

She turned on the water, gave a prayer of thanks for the new solar panel on the roof to keep the water hot, and tried to convince herself the entire fantasy was in her head.

She hung the Kraken pendant on a hook and slid the mirror into a drawer. She stopped at a Safeway for donuts and coffee, and headed for points north.

She followed the road away from the coast, longing for some mountain air. Over the next few weeks she visited remote locations in northern Nevada, gazed at the Grand Tetons, toured Yellowstone and stayed busy, always occupied. She spoke to no one about her Caribbean fantasy, as she termed it. And if she cried herself to sleep most nights, no one was there to see.

When summer eased into fall, she left the high country and aimed for Seattle and Vancouver. Seeing the Pacific before her, after the many months away, her heart finally shattered. She camped next to the water and cried for hours. She reclaimed the pendant and held it in her hand, stroking the fierce eyes and trying to figure out what hurt more: believing it was a dream or praying it was real. Did she walk away from a second chance at happiness?

That night, she fell asleep to the sound of the pounding waves and dreamed of him. That wasn't unusual. Most mornings she found herself waking up totally aroused with a sense of having dreamed of him. But this dream, he was looking for her.

It was dark, foggy and he didn't call out, he searched. Every night for a week, the dream came with more and more detail.

She turned her camper south and meandered down the Washington coast line. In her head, she carried on long conversations with herself.

I liked being the secret lover of a cursed pirate. Making books, and learning how to throw knives.

So did I. But it wasn't real.

Bullshit. Look at that nipple and say it again. Quit lying. You still have the mirror, go back.

It's insane. He never loved me, he loved Jezebel.

I doubt that and you never gave him a chance to explain. Probably only Mick talking nonsense.

This is insane. Even talking about it.

But it was fun. It was exciting and he was a fucking miracle.

What a mouth!

She giggled and thought about it. Thought about that mirror and whether it would still work. That night as she again dreamt of the pirate, she recognized something behind Silvestri. When she woke up, she pulled out her small computer and searched through old photographs. And she found it. The massive foot of the bridge that crossed the Willamette River.

"Oh my God, he's going to be at the Portland Pirate Festival? Is that what this means? Looking for me!" She quickly clicked over to the site detailing when the festival was occurring. Two days, less than two days to get to Portland.

It would be a hairy drive, but she could do it. And she could decide when she got there. If he was there.

☙

He folded her letter again. It left him little hope of reconciliation. Full of pain and a sense of betrayal. But if given a chance, he could explain. Mick would admit the lie he spun was all about trying to keep Glacious from taking aim at Emily. He lifted the tiny perfume bottle and undid it, inhaled softly.

She still lingered in the scent.

Mick and Jezebel had let him search her cabin. He'd found the bottle of perfume he'd given her and taken it. The jewels and shoes, the dress.... He took her book making supplies and set them up in his house above Tortuga.

He offered the ship to Mick, who shook his head. "No, I have a ship. I saw the proof of my not-father's gambling and what he set out to do. He made certain we became enemies. The ship is yours. You did right by the man who wasn't truly my father. Keep it. Now that the crew is fully awake, I expect being her captain will be much more of a challenge than it used to be." He and Mick talked for hours that night, mended fences, and admitted to some lingering resentment, on both their parts. They'd make a try at being brothers. Why not?

He'd no hunger for sailing anymore. He contracted the ship with the former first mate, Walter Hemmings. He kept a majority interest, moved permanently into the cabin he'd built above Tortuga, and went to work on expanding it.

He added a craft area where she could work on the books, then built her a table. He bought clothes for her and a closet to keep them in. He even set the dancing boots at the ready.

And he haunted Mama Lu until the woman found a way for him to go to her.

"It gonna be for a short time. Even with the Kraken's help, this crack between our worlds won't stay open long. And you'll be pulled back. Ya don't belong there."

"Will she be able to return with me?"

"I don't know. Depends on her. Other travelers have. She still got the mirror, the pendant...maybe. No guarantees, Captain." Lu told him when and where.

He didn't know what to expect. Enough travelers came through the portals that he planned on being tolerant and open-minded. The crew of the Quill gathered some coins and paper money from the era and warned him of the dangers he faced in Emily's time.

Streets. He knew to stay off of streets. Janey warned him of fast moving metallic vehicles that took little notice of pedestrians. Tink told him to not take any weapons. "The authorities will see you as an armed lunatic and take 'em away."

He slid a slender blade into his boot, anyway.

"It will be loud, most likely. And smell odd." Jezebel offered her two cents.

Mama Lu studied her scrying mirror the night of the new moon. She tilted her head. "Looks like you'll fit in, Silvestri. Some costume event. Now, ya have till three hours past midnight."

"Is her time likely to be different than mine?" he wondered.

"Nah, the portal take care a' that. It might make ya sick, so be steady. Now, you are sure?" she asked for a final time.

"Mama Lu, I need her."

She nodded. "I hope she feels it as keenly, my friend. Ya got the link to her?"

"Yes." He held up the perfume vial.

"Close your eyes and be ready."

The sound of the ocean filled his head when he closed his eyes. The sand beneath his ass was chilly, and he could hear the snap of a fire above the waves where the Quill's crew waited. They wanted her back, too.

He touched her letter again. Gripping the vial in his palm, which was still pitted from the pistol damage Glacious "gifted" him with at the end, he felt the world tilt. A bit of vertigo almost forced his eyes open, but Mama Lu warned him to keep them closed until he was settled.

The sudden warmth on his face signaled success. He opened his eyes to see a river before him. There were small boats, bristling with wires and lines, docked neatly at a marina of sorts. He shook his head when a red-sailed ketch passed before his eyes and a group of ragged looking sailors railed and cursed at it. The boom of cannon made him shoot to his feet.

There were cheers behind him. He calmed the instinct to rise for battle, and turned. A great crowd of spectators cheered when the land sailors fired on the ketch, then hauled out a small cannon and lit a fuse. There was another loud boom, but he noted no ball flew from the gun.

This was a play! He smiled slightly, observing the crowd behind him. Men, women, and children. Some dressed like pirates, others in simpler clothing. The roles he was partially familiar with. He read a banner behind them.

Welcome to the Portland Pirate Festival.

He'd arrived. Now, to find Mrs. Pawes.

He took a moment to scan the area. An expanse of green slope gradually climbed from the narrow river behind him. The river itself didn't appear to be part of the festival, other than the short bit of pirate fighting he'd witnessed. The red-sailed ketch drifted downstream, and the land-bound play actors slapped each other on the back, laughed and wandered away from their battleground.

He gazed upward at a truly impressive bridge. He'd never seen something span so far and so high. He could discern a soft roar from the bridge, but ignored it. He needed to find Mrs. Pawes, and he doubted she was on the bridge.

Setting his sights upslope, he followed the combatants as they wove through the grassy streets.

Merchants, he surmised. Very distracting merchants. Alan's height enabled him to view their wares and observe the haggling going on, the exchange of money and babble of commerce surrounded him.

Several women sauntered by, dressed quite provocatively in leather bodices and skirts much shorter than he generally viewed on the streets of Tortuga. But experience with travelers hardened his reactions. He barely glanced at them.

He assumed it was relatively early in the day. A soft fog drifted far above the revelry, the sun seldom breaking through with any real effect on the temperature. The sheer number of children astounded him.

Little pirates ran helter skelter up and down the streets, brandishing brightly colored swords, wearing eye patches and calico scarves tied about their heads. They screeched and shouted in excitement, chasing each other and shouting out challenges.

Children in Tortuga tended to be of a rougher sort, and this sort of play acting seldom took place. They worked, they grew up. They prospered. Tortuga didn't tolerate abuse of children, but he'd never seen any play with this sort of reckless abandon.

All the while, he scanned the crowds, searching for her. It was early; he had hours to go. His heart stayed calm. He knew fate guided him to this place and time. She would be here.

After seeing a man stroll by bearing a tankard of something golden and foamy, Alan found himself thirsty. "Pardon me, sir. Where might I find a place to purchase some ale of my own?"

"Oh. Up the slope, there's a group selling wine and different local brews." The congenial young man pointed to a red and black banner. "See? They're raising money for the homeless shelter. Good place to wet your whistle."

"I thank you." Alan bowed and strode to the booth in question. He fingered the money the Quill's crew gave him. Janey explained a bit of it to him. It certainly baffled him that paper was of more worth than coin! He stood in line, examining the menu posted on a board behind the serving girls. He took note of the cups most took their drink away in, and was prepared when one of similar fashion was handed to him.

It felt flimsy when he took it carefully in hand and turned away.

"Sir! Your change!" The buxom lass who'd flirted with him held out a pile of paper and several coins.

He did as he'd seen others do, took the paper and left the coins as a tip, smiling as he did.

She beamed back at him.

He'd chosen something called Columbia River Red Ale. It lacked the kick of a nice, stiff rum, but was tasty enough. The chill of it took some getting used to. He followed the path through more merchant booths, paused to watch a magic show, and another that involved several parrots trained to do tricks.

And he searched the crowds for Emily. Always on the lookout for her. He listened for her laugh, followed women he thought might be her, only to be disappointed as he realized they weren't.

Following a trail down a small gully and back up, he saw

several huge structures gyrating in an alarming fashion. The screams of children reached him, and he hurried forward. Only as he grew close did he realize it was more make believe. Knowing something about rubber, he figured they were huge rubber play structures. One played a pirate ship, with a slide the children were throwing themselves down, only to land in a pool full of brightly colored balls.

Another was a fair rendition of the Kraken, though the colors were completely wrong. The head loomed above the tentacles, which formed a frame for another pool full of balls. He smiled.

Children were much indulged in Emily's world.

He turned to return to the merchant area, thinking that since she'd never shown a keen interest in children, she was unlikely to be in this section of the festival. He took another path. Finishing his ale, he did as he'd seen others do, and tossed the container into a barrel.

"Hey, mister!" A tug at his coat hem had him looking down at a little girl. She had the loveliest light blue eyes, bright golden hair and wore a frilly little pink dress, though he noted a large brown stain marking the lace at the collar.

He knelt to reach her level. "Yes, miss? How might I be of assistance?" Closer up, he noted a flower painted on her cheek. The paint had smeared and one petal was nearly gone.

She shrugged and wiped at a tear on her cheek. "My daddy is lost! Can you see him? You're tall."

He sighed and introduced himself. "I'm Alan and you are?"

"I'm Stella. Princess Stella!" She held out her skirt and did a sweet curtsy for him. He noted her white shoes were dirty and her crown dipped to one side.

He straightened her crown. "Where did you last see your daddy, Princess Stella?"

"He was buying Mommy a hat." Her lower lip trembled. "I seen a man with parrots and followed him. Now he's lost!"

The sheer terror of her situation was obviously coming home. He needed to stop her from growing more scared.

"I remember where the hat vendors are. I'll take you there,

but would you mind riding on my shoulders? Maybe you'll see your daddy from up there. I won't let you fall, I promise."

She slowly nodded and he easily lifter her up to his right shoulder. She giggled a bit, but settled down, one little hand fiercely gripping his hair. He carefully turned toward the hat vendors, chattering with Stella as he went.

"What is your daddy wearing, Princess?"

"He's a pirate, like you! Though not as tall. But he's the meanest one here! Has a ship and a crew and everything!" She babbled on while he scanned the crowd. "You're a tall man. Where is your wife?"

"Not all men have a wife," he answered, a small smile growing at her assumption.

"But you're old; old pirates need a wife to cook for them."

She certainly carried conviction in her voice!

"I actually cook for myself. But I am looking for a woman. She's lost, like your daddy."

She sniffed and he realized he shouldn't have mentioned that. Now the little girl was worried again. "Maybe you can help me find her?" That might work to distract her.

"Are you gonna ask her to marry you? I won't help unless you make an honest woman out of her!" She nodded vigorously. "That's what my granny always says." Her little face scrunched with a frown and she stated, "Why buy the cow if the milk is free?"

He didn't know what the last bit meant. He bet she didn't either, but it was obviously important to her granny. She'd repeated it enough for little Stella to remember it word for word. But he was impressed with Stella. Why, the little Puritan! He chuckled. "If you insist, I promise to ask for her hand in marriage when I find her." He'd actually thought about it. Wondered if it was something Emily would want. She'd been married already. He'd never married. But the idea of her wearing his ring held a delightful appeal. Tortuga was mostly tame, but being his wife would afford her more protection than being his lover.

Tink told him the vampire king admired Emily's dancing. They weren't allowed to hunt married couples. Another good reason to marry. Not that Emily showed any attraction to living as a vampire.

"So, what does she look like?" Stella asked him.

"Well, she's short, with brown and silver hair, also short."

Stella sighed. "What's she wearing? Does she love pink, like me?"

"I've never seen her wear pink but I'm sure she'd look very nice in the color. But not as wonderful as you. Was your daddy wearing a hat?" Time to find this child's parents and return to searching for Emily.

"I don't remember. He wanted to buy a red hat for Mama." She took a deep breath. He feared she was preparing to cry again.

Her description wasn't helping him find her errant father. And it was uncertain whether the hat was purchased at all, once they'd discovered their daughter missing. He kept an out for a distressed looking couple, searching for someone small.

When he approached a booth with a banner of Lost and Found, he turned in.

"He's not here!" Stella exclaimed.

"I know, but he may have been here, looking for you!" Alan smiled at the man behind the table. "I have found this little girl, Princess Stella. And she has lost her parents. Perhaps they have come looking for her?"

The man let out a huge sigh. "Stella Montgomery! Your daddy was here looking for you! I know he hasn't gone far." The man reached behind the table, pulled out a ball on a stick and cleared his throat.

Alan jumped a bit when the sound was amplified tenfold.

"Will Mr. and Mrs. Montgomery please return to the lost and found? We have Stella waiting for you."

He repeated the announcement twice before a shout rang out. Alan turned to see a short, round man, wearing a sash, long pants and a scarf come running toward them.

"Daddy, I presume?" He lifted Stella from his shoulders. She was shrieking and nearly threw herself into the round man's arms. He swung her around in the air, laughing.

Stella chattered, "I saw parrots!"

"Yeah, I talked to the parrot man. He said you'd been there!" Stella tucked at his waist, the man turned to Alan. "You found her?"

"She found me, actually. I believe I was the tallest adult around, so she thought to use me as a crow's nest." Alan shook the man's hand, declined a reward and backed out of the booth, watching a woman come running up. She looked to be a bit of scold.

Stella waved at him, and he made an extravagant bow to her before fading into the crowds.

A good deed like that deserved a reward. He strolled back to the ale booth and bought himself another.

Only when the day grew chilly, showing signs of darkness approaching, did he begin to worry.

Several times during the day, he'd heard large musical groups on the elevated stage at the top of the slope. In a natural amphitheater, they would sing merry songs of pirates and sailors. He'd stopped to listen a few times. The day lengthened, and he surmised the group preparing to play must be quite popular. He noted how large the crowd grew, heading for the stage, laying out blankets and settling down to listen. He leaned against one of the great bridge pilings and surveyed the festival.

The amplifying tool was used again, to announce their name. *Captain Boggs and Salty!* The crowd shouted. He was bemused to see the children jump to their feet and race to the stage. But once he discerned lyrics, he understood. Songs for pirate children.

He smiled and turned away. And finally there she stood, shoulders bowed, turning away from the stage. His heart soared. Found! He'd found her! Now, to entice her to listen, to return, and to stay with him forever.

He stepped around the blankets, trying to hurry and keep her in his sights. She disappeared behind a group of standing adults and he moved faster.

She took a step away from that group, weaving her way through the watching crowds. When she reached the last of them, she came within reach. She shivered, and he draped his coat over her shoulders. "Found you. Thank God, I found you."

She whirled, threw herself into his arms and held on tightly.

He considered the joy Stella's daddy exhibited and copied it, lifting her into the air and twirling her about, laughing.

Chapter Twenty-Five

She drove through the night, a driving rainstorm hindering her. But the closer she came to Portland, the lighter her heart grew.

This is insane.

This is perfect.

Her mind spun with what she wanted to take with her. As she drove, she mentally packed a duffle bag. She'd bought a new pair of Tevas and a good pair of leather boots. They laced instead of pulling up, but she found that more practical. She'd take several pairs of socks, the kind that wicked moisture away. Oh, and face cream, every bit she owned.

She'd found, after returning to the real world, that she grew keen on how certain products were produced. She had purchased several slender books on soap, herbal creams, and dyes. Even how to make paper. They'd go with her. And her book of Whitman poetry. What would Alan like?

She included the book of macramé and the erotic poetry. The solar shower she'd bought to supplement her camper while she was out in the desert. A few towels! The great big bag of M&Ms—they wouldn't last long, but maybe someone else would pass through with more someday.

By the time she crossed the Columbia, she was humming and bouncing in her seat. Damn it, she wanted this!

She didn't give a rat's ass about the camper; the closest place she could find to park was a tow away zone. Fine, it would be towed. It was nearly dusk, and she knew she only had an hour, maybe a bit more, before the night concerts started, when they'd chase everyone off the grounds until the next day. She left the keys in the refrigerator, tossed everything she could think of in the duffle bag. She took a moment to hook up her electronic reader to the internet and filled it entirely with reference books, craft books, the classics, and a few favorites. She didn't know how long its battery would last, but she also packed a small, solar powered battery charger. She tossed that in also, forgetting that something must be powering the *iPods* she'd first seen when walking the Quill.

Damn, the sucker weighed a ton! She hoped they'd have somewhere she could check it in.

She tied her mirror to her belt, put the Kraken pendant on and took a moment to breathe. Glancing around the camper she considered her life here for a moment. Ordinary, little to look forward to. She'd miss pizza. And donuts. Ice cream—but she bet with some entrepreneurial spirit she could find some cooks on Tortuga willing to try new dishes. Maybe she'd be the Pizza Queen of Tortuga! She touched a small picture of Tom and herself playing pirate, from more than twenty years ago. And she tucked it into her bag.

With a laugh, she gladly turned her back on the rest of it.

After leaving her duffle at the check-in tent, she ran through the festival. In her dreams, he'd been standing at one of the great bridge stanchions, wearing a brown coat and scanning the crowd.

She circled the stanchions first, but he wasn't there. She quickly strolled up and down the rows of vendors, always looking. She wandered to the children's areas, though he'd never shown much interest in children. The greater fair was due to close down soon. She paused and bought herself a glass of wine, beginning to feel the fear of having missed him. Of his never having been real. His never being here or looking for her....

She chugged the wine, fighting not to cry. A band started

up on stage. A silly song of pirates and the peg-leg tango.

She cried and wandered. Fog was coming in, and she wasn't dressed for it, of course. Never brought a coat when she needed one.

She found a place to stand at the outskirts of the crowd, in front of the stage. Children dressed like pirates danced to the forefront, blankets were spread about the lawn and people huddled close, looking forward to an hour or more of innocent pirate music.

Emily sagged. He wasn't here.

A coat suddenly draped over her shoulders, and an arm swept around her. "Found you."

She whirled to throw her arms around him. He held her close, clinging to her. The crowd around them chuckled as he lifted her off the ground and spun her around.

Finally, he set her down. She looked up into his eyes. "I thought I'd never see you again."

"I thought you didn't want to see me again," he answered, brushing the tears from her face. "I have much to explain."

"I want to say it doesn't matter, but it does. But what matters most is this." She took a breath and swallowed. "Alan Silvestri, I love you. I want to be with you. I don't know anything else and I may be insane. But it's a wonderful sort of insanity."

"Emily, dear Emily. I love you and want to be with you! I am no longer cursed. The Immortal sails without me. Mama Lu gave me limited time, my love. Where can we go for privacy?"

"Well, I had a camper, but it's probably gone by now. Let's get my duffle, and we'll find someplace on the edge of things."

The music provided a pleasant background where they sat, down by the river. The children's band finished up, and a more mainstream band took its place. She leaned against her duffle, looking at him in the light from nearby streetlamps. He'd insisted she keep the coat on.

"I seldom feel the cold, love. After the days spent at the ice palace, I doubt cold will ever hold much power over me."

"And I find I get cold too easily." She took his hand, stroked it. "My cuts healed, but not this?"

"I took this on willingly the day you tried to shoot me. None of your wounds were done with deliberation. The Kraken likes you!" He grinned. From the corner of his eye, he saw a stark white tentacle rise from the river, then sink away as quickly.

"The Kraken. There was more than one, right? I'm a bit hazy on it. And why did it help?" She wanted to know everything, but Alan said they had until three a.m., giving her time to ask regular questions, and she wanted to approach the serious stuff slowly.

"I have no idea how many invaded the palace. Glacious offended the Old Monster centuries ago, when she established her ice palace. The deep cold of the ocean belongs to the Kraken. They acknowledge ice, but for her to make a home of it, to rise above it, so to speak…they have feuded forever. Probably related to each other. Families fights do linger." He turned his hand in hers and drew her closer.

She let her hand rest at his chest. "Why you? Why Mick? Or me?"

"Why were we able to help the Old Monster win?" He chuckled. "Glacious hid her palace, and though the Kraken searched high and low, they couldn't find it. I was summoned once a year. When I held her curse from Mick, it left her slightly weaker. My holding it challenged her. With you—twice I held you from her. When you shot me, and when you kicked me. Three cracks in her façade." He sighed as she lifted her hand and stroked his face. "Mick and I once pledged to help Kraken wherever we found them. Sailors would catch small ones and eat them, or simply kill them. We freed them. I believe we must have kept dozens from death over the years."

"But why me? Why did I end up there? With you?"

"My luck," he whispered, and kissed her fingertips. "Honestly, Emily. I don't know for certain. The Old Monster must have sent out that mirror, looking for someone to help. You found the mirror. And my life changed."

"Damn, no fuck." She shivered, pulled away slightly. "Alan, the things Mick said…."

"All lies. He'd accepted that we were brothers, but he still wanted to poke at me. And he knew to keep her attention from focusing on you. Return with me and hear it from his lips. I swear I never vied with him for Jezebel's favors." He recaptured her, closing the distance between them. "I did use you, desperate to escape from her curse. But I would not have sacrificed you, and I did not intend for you to even see her ice palace."

"She possessed me?" Her voice trembled and she scooted closer to him. He took advantage and swept her up against his chest, inhaled the scent of her hair and set his right hand at her hip.

"I believe she cast a spell on you. I planned on Mick coming to me. To join forces. She must have used the crew of the Immortal to spy and played a trick on me. Used me to catch you. I am sorry." He trembled as her lips touched his throat, a light kiss. Did he hear a soft *I know?*

"The crew is free of her cold influence now. She kept them content and uninvolved these many years. I suspected they were Glacious' agents, but I didn't know they were spelled."

"How long until you're drawn away?" She raised her head from the shelter of his chest.

"Mama Lu said three hours after midnight."

"Will I return with you?"

"She said that was up to you. You still have your mirror?"

"Yes, and I know how to use it now. I dreamed of you, here. And came. I spent months wandering and missing you. I don't care if I'm insane, Alan. I'd rather be deranged with you than sentenced to a sane, ordinary life here."

He chuckled. "What I experienced today was certainly not ordinary. I rescued a little princess named Stella who lost her parents. Stared at a fake Kraken full of children, witnessed a battle where cannon fired without ammunition, and heard some interesting music."

She laughed. "The play structures for the children! A much less fierce Kraken. Rescued a princess? Well, you did have an adventure!"

"Yes, and Princess Stella scolded me regarding my intentions toward you."

"What?" She sat up, staring at him. "She what?"

"I was instructed by her royal highness to make an honest woman out of you." He pushed himself upward, took her hand in his. "Emily Pawes, will you marry me?"

"Oh. Shit. Really?" She grinned. "An honest woman? If I marry a pirate, live in Tortuga, and sail with the Quill occasionally, will I be an honest woman because I wear your ring?"

"No. But you will honor me. Answer me, Mrs. Pawes."

"I sorta like the name Mrs. Pawes. I'll be Mrs. Silvestri?" She teased him, having no intention of saying no to his proposal. "Or Mrs. Captain Silvestri?"

"You can be anything you like." He frowned at her.

"You will get me a ring?" She smiled into his gloomy face.

"Only if you say yes," he answered dryly.

"Well, I don't know. There may be other captains who still have ships that might be interested in me."

He released her hands and sat back, glaring at her.

With a laugh, she sprang to her feet and dashed away. Calling over her shoulder, "Yes, you fool! Of course, yes!"

He leaped to follow her, caught her down by the water and kissed her soundly. A splash further downstream drew the attention of the remaining festival-goers. And a loud pop came from the children's play area. The Kraken didn't care for its doppelganger.

Emily and Alan ignored it, kissing.

They hid when security cleared the area some hours later and when three a.m. chimed from a local clock tower, and Captain Alan Silvestri felt the draw of home, that home included the woman in his arms. And her duffle bag of interesting anachronisms. Tortuga tucked itself around them, adjusting to the new toys.

Three days later, the camper was towed to the impound lot.

Maureen O. Betita

~ABOUT THE AUTHOR~

Maureen lives along the lovely Monterey Bay and finds great inspiration in being so near the Pacific Ocean. She shares her home with Stephen, her high school sweetheart, married for over 30 years; a cat named Isabeau and a dog named Bonnie. She travels miles and miles to attend pirate festivals, renaissance fairs, sci-fi/fantasy conventions and writing conferences.

Visit Maureen at: www.maureenobetita.com

~or~

http://believinginsecondchances.typepad.com

Immerse Yourself in Fantasy

with

Decadent Publishing

ᔥ

www.decadentpublishing.com

LaVergne, TN USA
11 March 2011
219716LV00002B/16/P